For the Women

whose voices were never heard

The Women of Great Island

Dianne Comiskey

Water has a way of seeking those vulnerable stretches of land that yield to the force of tide. It laps along—receding and advancing in lunar-measured rhythms, unmindful of its influence on the events of human life. Over time, water takes the course of least resistance, molding and sculpting the sand, the work of a great cosmic but seemingly random, hungry artist. Over time, water's handiwork creates a solitary mass of land isolated from the vast expanse of continental earth. It makes an island.

Part I

1690-1702

The Gathering & Settling In

"Wellfleet [Billingsgate] ...reserved an island across the harbor for its young men. In due time a brothel, a tavern, and a whale lookout were built there—just about everything a young fisherman needed." *---from* <u>*The Perfect Storm*</u> *by Sebastion Junger, 1997*

Chapter 1

1690

Dark Ray

The *Nausets*, my people, lived on this island ages before Samuel Hawes persuaded the town magistrates to build a whale station here. When I was growing up on these dunes, the blackfish were more plentiful than any Englishman could imagine, and they were still abundant when the Europeans took up harvesting them. My people knew the cyclic rhythm of the natural world. Our whole village lived on these shores during the months the blackfish filled these waters. I remember these times as wonderful winter sojourns. Although the women still had such tasks as meals to prepare, food to preserve, and hides to sew into clothing, there was an air of festivity when our people stayed on the island. Even the men, involved in the tiring fish work, joked and sported with each other. It was the time of year for storytelling. The tales that were told in the evenings around the great fires sustained our people during the summer months when the days were longer, and we returned to the mainland, where there was much planting and farming to be done, and no time left in the day for stories.

My ancestors honored the great cycle of life because it held the promise of the next season. This island conjured spirited feelings among us during the cold, frosty winters. The elders' stories told of the power of the island that pulled us back to it every winter. The elders would tell us young ones that some places on this earth hold magic. They attract beings to them like a lodestone. The blackfish had always been drawn to these waters as had the people to this land—first the *Nausets*, then the Europeans.

I felt this pull as a child and again later as a grown woman who had become used to living among the Europeans. The other women who followed me felt the pull too, as they found their way here when it seemed that only a fair wind directed them.

But long before those women whose lives intertwined with mine, the Europeans had arrived on these shores. When they did, the *Nausets* willingly taught them how to exist and prosper in what they called the new world. It wasn't new at all. However, when the English asked us who owned the land, we explained that no one owned it. The English took that to mean that they could claim it. We did not protest. Nor did we participate in that conflict to the south known as King Philip's War. We were peace-loving people who believed that there was enough abundance on this land and in these waters to nourish all beings.

So when the English began to live among us, we shared our methods of survival. Though our stories tell of the Corn Hill thieves who found the people's winter supply and took it for themselves, causing much illness and starvation among us, we taught the English to grow their own corn. We explained how to herd the blackfish into the harbor and wait for the tide to recede, leaving them stranded and dying. Then the butchering could begin. We taught the English these things, yes. And they imitated our ways well. Soon they decided to set up a permanent station on the island to sight what we called the blackfish but they named the grampus or pilot whale as it approached the harbor. By then, I was a woman, and my innocent days on the island were over.

We *Nausets* learned from the newcomers, too. We learned quickly of the greed that consumed them. As they claimed the land with their names when we said it wasn't ours, they claimed the fish too. As if there were not enough blackfish to go around, the town magistrates appointed individuals to monitor the whale distribution. That is when Samuel Hawes established a business on this island, and I found myself being pulled back to it for good.

Once Hawes built this tavern for the shore whalers, he wanted someone who knew the island to run his establishment. He wanted a basic, reliable woman. One who could keep the tavern rooms clean, one who could prepare food for the hungry and impatient men, one who understood how to serve them up and stay out of their way. One who would not distract them. He wanted no trouble with the town officials across the harbor once they bestowed the position on him after conferring about it for a full year. He also wanted no trouble with his wife who didn't approve of him hiring a woman—and a *Nauset* at that—to run the social side of the business. And part of that responsibility was to maintain civil conduct among the tavern dwellers and the fishermen. No. He wanted no handsome woman to interfere with the slack time when the whales were not in sight, to entice the men to the bedchamber for a tumble. Or two.

So, Samuel Hawes hired me, recently widowed, a *Nauset* woman whose husband had been a Frenchman and who knew how to handle people of all backgrounds. Having lived on the island as a child, I knew every sand dune and wooded valley. Now I was to live on it throughout the moon cycles—in the warm days as well as the cold. I was a good choice for this work, for as I grew, I became fascinated by the ways of the Europeans, and I began to consort with them—becoming increasingly comfortable around them though I didn't always agree with their values.

My allegiance to *Nauset* beliefs remained at the heart of all I did. I found the English to be self-righteous in their thinking, the Dutch to be very resourceful in their enterprises, the Portuguese to be great lovers of the sea but subject to profiteering, although I quickly learned they were all that way. Even the French, but the

French truly enjoyed their lovemaking, even prided themselves on being great lovers.

My husband had been one of them, and when he took me away from my people to live with him on the edge of Billingsgate, he taught me a great deal on the subject. It wasn't unusual in the early days of European visits to our shores for the French to have friendly relations with my people. They took a great liking to the *Nauset* girls, being much attracted by our physical appearance as the later visitors, the English, were not. My Frenchman and I married young and exceedingly enjoyed the pleasures of the senses. I would have stayed with him my whole life at our trading post in Billingsgate, if he hadn't died from consumption two winters before we were both twenty. I was left broken hearted and in need of taking care of myself. However, our trading post had been financed by French money, and so another took over the business and dismissed me. I could have returned to my own people, but by then, I was too used to European ways. Too independent. Too headstrong.

A kindly man, Hawes found me visiting my childhood friend, Solosana. She took me in when Sylvain died, and I was lost in grief. Hawes and Solosana were well acquainted. Her healing knowledge was much sought after by our English neighbors but only in private. Their church leaders didn't condone our beliefs. My friend had delivered his wife and child from a dangerous birth, and Hawes entered her home respectfully and sat with me.

"I know you have recently lost your husband. I am sorry."

I only shrugged, not ready to speak of my loss but wondering what interest he had in me.

"I also know you are used to making your own way among us, and you do it well. You have learned English, and you helped to bring the French trading post good commerce because of your inclination to communicate readily with different folk."

He paused, and I could feel him studying my face. I listened but didn't look directly at him. I didn't have to. His body smell, like so many other Europeans who didn't bathe, told me exactly how close he was standing to me.

"Will you consider running the tavern I have just built over at the new whaling station on Great Island? You are known to many, respected. I need someone I can depend upon as my other enterprises will rarely allow me to be a presence there."

I looked up at him. Now he had my full attention. I noticed he was carefully dressed despite his odor. I was intrigued, not so much by his offer although it was a sound one, but because as he spoke, I felt the island drawing me to it. The feeling started inside my body and radiated out with a warm, undulating rhythm much like the waves that lapped its shores. Seducing my senses. Offering to be my home. My haven. My solace.

"Yes. I thank you," I said, still under the spell of the pull. "I will work for you. Run the tavern as well as I ran the trading post. When may I begin?"

Hawes smiled, shook my hand to signal agreement as Europeans do, and then he explained how I would manage the tavern. Even though the whaling business would occur in the winter, the tavern would remain open all seasons for visiting sailors and local fishermen. I would be given a weekly allowance to purchase items for preparing food and drink. In addition, I would have enough money left over to maintain my own needs over the years—clothing and any other necessities I required. Hawes explained the extra money would be my wage, but I knew I would have no need of currency living on the island. Hawes even suggested that if the place became popular, I might want to hire some help, and then he promised my allowance would be raised if the place showed a profit.

When he left, Solosana took my hand and held it a long time. She was not one to leave the people and their ways. But in her gesture, I read her good wishes and within a day, left her warm home for my own.

Europeans and *Nausets* lived close to each other. The small villages across the region became home to many different people. Even some African folk who had escaped enslavement in Rhode Island and Providence Plantations found refuge among us. I was a friend to all and saw no harm in that. Hawes had been observant. My intelligence, business sense, and dependability were known all around Billingsgate, and I was respected among the English despite my *Nauset* background and French husband.

I was grateful for Hawes' offer, ready to return to the island and live my life there. It would be a good place to heal my loss and to start a new life. I wondered if I had made the decision to return, or if the island had done it for me. I remembered the elders' tales. I was under its spell and would live among the windswept dunes again. In this place, I hoped to blend my past and present to form the woman I would become. I had no sense at the time what life there would grant me, and if I had, wouldn't I still have gone?

So I worked for Hawes, but what he didn't know was this: I may have been larger than most men fancy, and I may have had dark hair and eyes as black as a moonless night framing an otherwise forgettable face. But when the candles are extinguished, what man cares what a woman looks like especially if she has a way of using her body that makes him forget he has been with any other woman before her? In the daylight, my countenance may be imposing as I serve up the chowder or draw the flip and place it before a customer. I may be more woman than a man needs. But the impression changes when we are laying together upstairs in the dark because I know how to move my body with a nimbleness that startles as it delights. My French husband taught me how to seem weightless when I am on top of my partner, making him feel that all the brawn is his as he gasps for more of my soft, supple body.

Hawes made me understand that activities at the tavern would be conducted in a Christian manner. I assured him they would, but when the workday was done, the toddy was consumed, and the wind was howling outside, those activities would run their natural course. Maybe Hawes was not as upstanding as I thought him. Perhaps he knew we would be discreet under my charge and not flaunt our animal nature in the face of Christianity. I never became a praying Indian like so many other *Nausets,* but I knew that religious morality of any persuasion has a way of being cast aside when carnal pleasure presents itself.

Another thing about me that Hawes didn't know, or again, perhaps he just chose to ignore. I am something of a healer like my friend Solosana. The English call a woman like me a witch, but I've been spared the gallows. I never believed I was in danger of arrest, and yet it was widely known that I could bestow and remove the evil eye—a curse that few openly discuss but blame for their misfortunes nevertheless. While I didn't need such a skill to run the tavern, it was useful when visitors from other regions who passed through thought they were going to take advantage of a woman tavern keeper. Once they started talking with some of the regulars, and the word got out that I was acquainted with the evil eye, they settled down and acted civilly. Since fishermen tend to be a superstitious lot, that fact alone put me right up there with their savior.

I have a *Nauset* name received at birth that I hold dearly to my heart, but I don't reveal it to outsiders. Once a *Nauset* undergoes a transformation in life, however, as I did being widowed and living chiefly among Europeans, she is expected to take a new name to mark her change. Over time, I became known to others as Dark Ray—for that smoky, tenuous ray of light only some can see in the darkness of a man's mind.

****

During the first year the tavern was open, I found myself with little time left over for mischief even if I wanted to cause any. With each new month, word spread of the tavern's existence, and in addition to the local fishermen, seamen from all parts of the earth stopped by looking for a pleasant resting place along their travels. There were times when customers spoke languages I'd never heard, but it was easy to figure out what they wanted with a little hand gesturing and common sense.

As a result of the growing business, I kept increasing the order of such items as flour, sugar, salt, and other necessary supplies. I would never admit to being a memorable cook, but I was proud of my flip and was continually brewing fresh batches of the spicy beverage. Then, of course, I was the only woman on the premises, and while I was not bashful, I was still only one. As the year progressed, the men started looking for more. Of everything.

" Ray," a new whaler bellowed at me across the dining room one night. "How about speaking to Samuel and getting us some women to occupy the time when we men are not working with the whales? It gets sorely wearisome out here in the off hours."

I turned to fill a tankard of ale, paused midway, and never one to keep my thoughts however blunt to myself, offered an alternative. "You want to relieve yourself? Help yourself to the sheep out back. Then we can have a great mutton roast afterwards. As I understand it, the livestock involved in your merrymaking must be killed according to your English law. We do want to do right by the law out here, good men."

"Ah, Ray, there is no need for sarcasm and talk of bestiality," put in another whaler who was sitting by the fire lighting his pipe. "We are human beings. We have needs, you know? What harm can there be in Hawes hiring a few women to help you out here? Companionship and assistance with the tavern work for you, and maybe the lasses will welcome a tumble from time to time."

I stood up straight, smoothed my apron, and wiped sweat from my forehead. "Odd, but you are beginning to make sense, Jeremiah. You men are wearing me out already, and we've only been open a year. At this rate, I'll meet an early grave. It's settled. I'll get word to Hawes with my next order of provisions."

I had more to say on the subject. I didn't stop there. "But, I'll tell you just once." I took the time to meet the eyes of every man in the room. They knew they were in for one of my lectures and silently braced themselves. "Like me, the women will decide what kind of activities they wish to engage in after their tavern work. Any one of you who forces a woman to do anything against her desire will answer to me. And you don't want to test me, do you?"

I made a point of bending over to place another log on the fire, my leather medicine pouch falling out of my dress bodice. Holding it deliberately in my hands, I stroked the contents through the soft leather with my thumb and forefinger, and again glared from face to face before I tucked the pouch back out of sight. Even the boldest of men looked away.

Fate, however, held more cards in the deck of life than mere men. Even before I had the chance to speak with Hawes, the women themselves found their own way to the tavern. They could have chosen other places of refuge. The shoreline abounded with friendly villages. Everywhere there were new faces mingling with the old inhabitants of the land. But the women came to the tavern, and I knew it was the unseen force of the island that pulled them to it. Like the blackfish, they set their course to home.

Chapter 2

1691

Light Ray

(Rachel)

What greater shame can a young woman endure than to be

cast aside by loved ones for committing a wrong against her

brethren? I suppose I should have been grateful that I was not

tortured and killed like so many others who have found themselves

under scrutiny in towns across the Bay. At the time, I was

miserable enough to believe that death would have been preferable

to the shame I bore. Everyone knew who I was. My family had

been prominent in Plimoth Colony since Englishmen first arrived to the New World. My ancestors had been ministers, deacons, physicians, business people—the founding fathers of Eastham and now Billingsgate. Our family members had been pillars of the church here in the New England. Our name is known throughout the Cape, Plimoth, even Boston. I am a Sloane, and I should have known better than to be tempted by the flesh. Like the other daughters in our congregation, I was taught that intimate relations were the rich reward of blessed matrimony and that these same relations were not to be sampled by those who were not wed. Young folk were expected to practice extreme self-denial in this matter. For a woman, gratification of the senses came with a husband and only with a husband.

That was my mistake, and out of it grew my greatest shame. I had not waited for a husband. I knew I was not the only young woman in the town who had heard the rules preached over and over from the mighty pulpit and who had consorted nevertheless with a man outside the conjugal bedchamber. I would venture to say that more often than not, folks entered the state of marriage having tested the waters of fornication beforehand.

However, my indiscretion soon became visible. I was small of stature, and when the pounds settled around my waist, my secret became evident to my father even before I noticed. And while I had used the popular methods of preventing unwanted pregnancies—laxatives, bloodletting, herbal suppositories—they had only worked for so long. One evening before we sat down to a light supper, my father's eyes surveyed my body.

"Rachel, you seem thicker than you were. Does that dress not fit you anymore?"

"Oh. Does it seem so to you, Father? Must be eating too much of my own good cooking," I giggled as I tied my apron nervously and found the ties wrapping tightly around my middle.

"You act surprised, Daughter. Do not you young girls speak of these things to each other? I would think you would want to maintain your comely demeanor until marriage and childbirth prevented such vanities."

I blushed. "Why, of course, Father," I stammered.

He explored my face for an explanation of my embarrassment. "I know this is a difficult conversation, my Dear. But, unfortunately, with your mother deceased all this time, I have been the one to impart womanly knowledge to you throughout your growing years. I know I have not been a very good substitute for a mother. Perhaps I should have married again as everyone counseled me. But you know the memory of that dear woman who gave you life is everywhere in this house, and I selfishly never wanted to remove it from our lives."

I tried to picture the image of the mother I had lost so long ago, but that image was faded, hardly discernible with the passage of time obscuring it. My father continued as I was engaged in this mental exercise. Once he started talking, it took a great effort to distract him. "I was not able to bring another in to take her place—for no one could. It seemed too cruel a thing to do to another one of God's creatures. I am afraid you were destined to be blessed with me as father and mother to you. I have tried to be both. Do not be ashamed. Please look at me when I talk to you."

He stopped and waited for me to meet his eyes.

"In the past we were able to speak openly of all subjects. Remember when you began your menses? I showed you how to prepare the cloths to catch the flow. Why do you hide your face from me? You accepted this kind of counsel when you were younger. Why do you turn from me now?"

Presently my father straightened in his chair by the fire. In a much sterner voice, he asked, "Rachel, what have you done?"

I remained still as death in the center of the room. It was only when he began to speak so directly to me that I acknowledged my condition. Until then, denial had blinded me. My father and I had been close ever since my mother's death when I was a child of three. He was right. We had no pretenses, speaking openly and honestly of every personal matter. I was convinced as I grew into a young woman that a girl child could not have been raised better. My father and I were everything to each other. Together we kept the Sabbath with our fellow citizens. We lived righteously in the community. We were Sloanes. Young men had started to court me, and my father knew them all, approving of my proper Christian behavior with them.

However, about a year ago, I fell in love with Deacon Sweet, a new member of the congregation, and there was no telling my father about this affair. It was the one secret I ever kept from him. The situation was complicated from the start. Matthew had come to Billingsgate already betrothed to another woman who was going to be leaving England shortly. They were to be married upon her arrival. This was common knowledge, but all the young girls were smitten by his dark, wavy hair and generous smile nonetheless. We joked among ourselves that there was no sin in looking. But my father unknowingly created a situation where looking became talking, talking became touching, touching became impossible to stop. Because the Deacon was living alone in the small cottage that the congregation had built for him, my father encouraged me to bring the new deacon a portion of the food I prepared for our afternoon meals.

It was not long before those visits to Matthew's cottage became the central joy of my day. At first, I was reserved as I had been raised. But then, the attraction replaced my prudent behavior, and I began to dread the arrival of Matthew's intended. Every day at the noon hour I visited him. No sooner had I placed the dish of food upon his table, would he be tearing at my clothes and pulling me onto the bedstead with him.

"Ah, here you are, my lovely sustenance. I hunger for you, not your food," he would say on many an occasion as he pushed the covered bowl aside on his table. "Come to me quickly. I am starving for you."

I had no prior knowledge of lovemaking. I had no sense of the passion that accompanied it. Matthew guided me through these early forays into the art of physical love. His expertise surprised me, although he assured me that I was his first as well. I wanted to believe him, and so I did. Our time was limited to those few moments after I delivered his meal, and to the few dark nights we stole out and met beyond the confines of the town.

Matthew could not visit my home under the pretext of courting me since he was spoken for already. When he did visit, it was to sit before the fire with my father to discuss scripture and church business. At those times, I was merely in his presence to serve him and my father. I was never invited to participate although I listened to their every word and yearned to share my thinking with these two men who I loved so much. However, while my father indulged every manner of conversation when we were alone, he adhered to social dictates in public, and I knew to remain silent.

At the next mid-day after one of these visits, Matthew would laugh when I arrived with his meal. "How submissive you were in your father's house last night, my lovely. I much prefer you as you are when we are alone. I prefer you passionate."

I could not keep such a delicious secret to myself. My best girlhood companions knew about my relationship with Matthew if my father did not. They were the ones who showed me how to avoid pregnancy. Yet, there I was, finally aware of my condition, and standing before my father.

"What are you asking me, Father?"

"You know what I am asking you. I had thought to tease you about a little weight around your middle. Now that I have observed your uncharacteristic shyness towards me, I begin to wonder if there is something you need to tell me. Perhaps I will simply ask. Rachel, are you with child?"

I did not answer. There was no need to respond. We both knew now that I was. I slumped in the chair opposite him and waited, stunned by my own stupidity.

My father sighed as he brought his right fist to his chest. "You have broken my heart, Rachel. Who is the father? That Stanton lad who walks you to Bible class?"

I remained silent, my eyes cast down at the hard, wooden floor, my hands twisting the folds of my skirt.

"No. I see the resolution on your face—you will not share the name of your transgressor." He paused and ran his fingers through his hair, not wanting to say what he knew he must. "You know that you will have to leave, do you not? And that is if the good townspeople take pity on our family's good name. Tarnished girls of a lower station would be imprisoned and scorned for life. I had hoped you would marry properly and raise many children of your own in this community. Now I too must renounce you publicly. Everyone will say that I was a fool not to have replaced your mother in this house. That you became wayward without the proper womanly guidance to teach you to protect your honor. I will bear your indiscretion to the end of my days. I will never forgive you." A pause and then, "I will never forgive myself." He covered his eyes with his hands. "Leave me. Go to your room. I cannot even bear to look upon you!"

When I could move my legs to stand, I left the room but like one who is in a trance, unaware that her body is functioning. The food I had prepared for the evening meal remained untouched on the table. We both cried throughout the evening, but we did not comfort each other. Our close relationship no longer provided solace. As I remained closeted in my room, I considered my course of action, and I resolved to avoid the public disgrace that awaited me and my father once the congregation became aware of my condition. While I did not look forward to the censure of the community, I could not bear my father's condemnation. I wondered how Matthew would accept my news once it became public knowledge. Would he be able to remain mute under such derision of the one he had taken to his bed day after day? In his limitless kindness, I feared he would confess and destroy his own future. I could not put him through that disgrace any more than I could bear to inflict it on my father.

Instead, once I heard my father retreat to his bedchamber that night, I left the house quietly with nothing but the clothes on my back and made my way to the dock where I hoped a boat would soon depart for Great Island. On bright nights, it was visible across the harbor, but I had never ventured there. No woman in my station would. A tavern was no place for a Sloane. Yet I knew that I could not travel far on my own. I had never done so. I had no choice but to remove myself from the congregation's gaze, and at the tavern I assumed I would be safe from that. The rumored goings on across the harbor led me to believe that my transgressions would not be scorned by the likes of the people there. As I walked quietly along the dark road that went to the dock, I tried to calm myself by thinking of Matthew. He would soon learn of my whereabouts and retrieve me under the cover of night. He would realize his betrothal to another was a lie, and he would denounce his station to be with me and the babe. Then together we three would leave and find another town where we could begin a life together. What a foolish young child I was.

****

(Dark Ray)

When I saw Rachel enter the tavern with the whalers, at first I thought the girl was one of the fishermen's daughters, she was so small and child-like. But as they settled into their familiar corners of the dining room, the young girl remained alone in the center of the open space, frightened, disoriented, not used to such surroundings. The pipe smoke seemed to have reddened her eyes unless she had been crying. She looked like someone I knew, but I kept her identity to myself.

"Who would you be?" I demanded instead.

"Whose daughter is this? Are you not aware," I called out to the men, "that this is no place for little girls? You may play out your bawdy tastes here, but I'll not abide with perverts!"

Although cowed by my loud voice and size, Rachel addressed me as the men watched. Not one of them was about to get involved. They knew who the girl was, too.

"But I am not a little girl. I will be fifteen next month. And I assure you. My father is not among these men."

"That old, are you? Listen up, good men, we have us an old woman of fifteen in our midst."

Even though she continued to appear frightened as she twisted the folds of her skirt into the balls of her hands, Rachel remained before me. More gently now, I pointed to a stool.

"Come over here. Sit. Tell me your name."

She advanced to the bar and sat beside me, but not before I looked her over and saw for myself the reason for her arrival.

"Rachel."

"Rachel? Good enough. I don't need the last name. What brings you here, anyway? Did you know I was looking for a new girl?"

"A new girl? Do you think I am a. . . a. . ."

" No, Little One. You don't strike me as a free-spirited woman who also knows how to work hard, but that's just what we need around here."

Rachel burst into tears, intensifying the redness that already rimmed her eyes.

"Now, now, compose yourself." I went behind the bar to pull a draft. "Here, take a sip of this flip. It will give you courage. You can call me Dark Ray."

Rachel wiped her tears and looked up at me to see that I was at last softening.

I leaned over to her and whispered. "Now, Rachel, tell me what I already know. But also tell me why you think being here is going to do you any good."

Despite the crowded room, the whalers ignored us and we were able to speak privately. Rachel drank the flip slowly as she began her story. By the end, the flip was gone as she declared that she was sure the father of the child would come for her. They would go off together where no one knew them—maybe up to Provincetown or maybe down to Rhode Island.

All the while I noticed the young woman's color. True, she had been through an ordeal, but the pallor of her face did not speak well for herself or for what she was carrying. For the time being, I listened. If I knew anything about circumstances such as this, Rachel would not be crossing back to Billingsgate any time soon. Nor would anyone be coming after her.

"Well, Little One. You have had quite a day. Why not find your way up to the bedchamber to the left of those stairs, and climb into bed? It's quiet and cozy up there. No one will harm you. These men will settle down soon. They have some whales to try out tomorrow. We can talk more then when they are out working, and my chores are done."

I left her and turned my attention to refilling the men's mugs.

Morning arrived, and at first light Rachel came down the stairs and looked bewildered as she surveyed her new surroundings—the rough hewn walls, the lack of genteel refinements, the variety of smells from tobacco to the whale stew simmering at the great fireplace—nothing she was accustomed to, I was sure. She sat quietly on a bar stool, again twisting her skirt with her hands. The men seemed to frighten her. Towering over her with a tankard of warm ale, I seemed to frighten her.

Nonetheless, she accepted the ale without meeting my eyes and sipped, lost in her thoughts. Rachel finally heard me offer her lodging for staying on and working at the tavern. At first, I might have been talking to the stool she sat upon, but after repeated efforts, she looked up at me and stared. Speechless.

"I am amazed that you hesitate at my offer, Rachel," I remarked as I scrubbed the bar. "Are you thinking you have a choice? You have lived like a woman. You can no longer act like a girl. And we both know you are no longer safe across the harbor."

I slapped down my sudsy rag. Rachel looked up astonished. "The righteous church folk of Billingsgate don't visit here, and the other citizens who do are discreet. They honor our code of secrecy. What happens here never travels back across the harbor."

Rachel opened her mouth to speak, but nothing came out. She seemed not used to such straightforward talk, but I sensed that she was smart enough to know that she couldn't go back to what was. She was forced to make this arrangement work for the time being.

Finally, she spoke in a whisper. "Yes, of course, you are right. I may be carrying a child, but I can help you until Matthew comes for me."

Now my eyes widened at her innocence, but I said nothing.

By the end of the day, Rachel accepted my offer with gratitude and immediately tried to impress me with her domestic skills. She threw herself into the work with a fury. For the next several days, she worked until dark shining the pewter, scrubbing the thick glass in the windows, washing the wide planks of the wooden floors on her knees. I had to grasp her shoulders to stop her so she could eat. The men kept a respectful distance from her. She didn't seem quite the type of woman they were hoping for.

Others knew who she was and decided not to meddle. Except for the fair distribution of the whaling efforts, the mainland rules didn't apply here, but they kept their distance nonetheless, and I was relieved that I didn't have to get rough with the men who are generally a good lot.

Only a week of relative contentment passed before word reached us that Deacon Sweet's long-awaited betrothed had arrived, and the couple had already married. Rachel overheard this news as she was sweeping out the dining room before the mid-day meal. The gray pallor had not quite left her face, despite my insistence that she drink nettle beer to strengthen her blood and sage ale to fortify her womb. I even made Rachel wear a leather pouch around her neck filled with unidentifiable powders and herbs that she hated because it smelled horrible to her. At the news that she never believed she would hear, Rachel's color faded to a chalky white. She reached for a stool but not before she cramped and fell to the floor.

"Joseph," I yelled to a fisherman who never made it out the door that day. "Carry her up to my bedstead. Hurry!"

Joseph scooped up Rachel and carried her up the stairs. Then he left quickly. By the time I bent down to examine her, the mass had slipped out unceremoniously in a dark pool of blood. As it did, I had to hide my shock, for even I was not prepared for what I saw. On the covers lay a creature so misshapen, it would never have been able to stand straight or walk without assistance had it survived to full term. Knowing this girl must be spared the sight of the monster she miscarried, I swiftly tossed the cover around the mass of distorted flesh. Then I removed it before Rachel could see it and carried it downstairs, placing the bundle in a corner of the kitchen. I returned to clean her, soak her feet in violet water and bind some leaves of the same plant to her forehead. Before long, the girl fell into what appeared to be a peaceful sleep. I wondered if the miscarriage came as bittersweet relief.

When I was sure Rachel was completely asleep, I left her and took the bundle with its bloody contents out to a hidden clearing away from the tavern and beyond the lookout towers and burned it. As I performed this grisly task, I felt pity for Rachel. Already she was proving to be a fine worker, and I must confess, a companion.

After she rested a day, Rachel's rosy color returned although her eyes remained vacant and lifeless over the grief of the deacon's betrayal and the loss of the babe. Although Rachel timidly inquired when she awakened for a brief time what I had done with her miscarried child, she didn't receive an answer, and she never again spoke of the incident. I thought her silence was a sign that she was still too bewildered by what she had experienced. I knew what the future held for Rachel and decided to speak frankly with her.

"Rachel, hear me out. Given your reason for leaving your home and what awaits you on that side of the water, it doesn't seem wise to return, does it? Your father will never forgive you. Your deacon will never acknowledge you—not with his new bride beside him. He may have wed her quickly to avoid suspicion. You alone will be shunned. Even the friends you had will be instructed to avoid you. What manner of life is that for you?"

Although I knew her enough by now to detect that Rachel was listening, she continued to look at the wall next to the bedstead. I guessed she was too ashamed to face me, but she knew I was right. She had no other choice.

My voice softened as I continued to address Rachel's back. "Here I need help. You need companionship and a way to support yourself. Think about it. We can never be sure of what life holds for us. We give what we can—we take what we can. You've been brought up to think there is some great master plan, but that's all deception. That's the way frightened people think. The fact that you followed your heart, listened to your body's needs, despite your father's good family name, tells me that you never would have thrived in that community over there. Surely, you understand that you never would have been happy. And then who knows what would have become of you?"

Finally, Rachel turned to face me. Her swollen eyes examined my expression as if she was reading an answer to her problems. I sat on the bedstead and placed my hand on Rachel's shoulder before I resumed.

"Maybe it's time to find out who you really are. That deacon had a sense of you, but even he took advantage, letting you believe that when his betrothed arrived, he would not marry her. I would not be surprised if she came with a substantial dowry. I have heard of these European arrangements. But I will not judge him further. Take some time. Think it over. If you can't live here, then I can arrange for you to be transported to *Noepe* where I have some distant relations. It will mean living with *Wampanoag* for a while, but they will take you in, and you will eventually find people of your kind if you so choose."

Rachel nodded weakly and promised to think about it. I left the room still troubled by the circumstances but unable to pursue the situation further. Although her young body healed quickly, Rachel continued to grieve. I was fearful that she was losing her desire to live. She refused to eat despite my warnings that by strengthening her body, she fortified her mind and spirit to survive her sorrow. But she would not listen. She was too lost in the empty space of grief.

Years later, Rachel told me she had never felt so alone in this great world. She looked out at it and saw a void, an amorphous abyss, she called it, where only she existed. Her dreams were no more comforting than her waking hours. All meshed together as one reality, a reality without solace, without love, touch, a reason to go on. She began to think that if she had remained at home and taken her punishment, she would have chosen the better path. She refused to believe the people she grew up with would have abandoned her in her time of need. Were they not good Christian folk after all? She believed their condemnation would only be fleeting. Then she remembered how another young woman suffered the degradation of imprisonment and later was sentenced to live out her days with her child on the outskirts of a town nearby. Rachel realized their condemnation would not be fleeting at all, and so she began to rally and to accept her lot.

That's what she told me much later, but those early days stretched on, and I began to wonder if I should intervene in some way—summon the girl's father, something. Before I could do so, Rachel slowly appeared on the main floor of the tavern. On the first day, she ventured out of the bedchamber and into the kitchen where she agreed to sip some broth. Her hair was matted and greasy. She smelled of dried blood, she smelled of sorrow and loneliness, but I ignored her filth and occupied Rachel's hours with making soap and tapers.

One evening a fortnight after the miscarriage, Rachel bathed completely for the first time since she arrived. She found an old but clean dress of mine, cut it and stitched it so it fit her small frame, brushed out her long blond hair, scrubbed her scalp, and then pinned her hair back on the top of her head. Gone was her English cap. Fine blond wisps of curly hair surrounded her radiant face. She descended the steps haltingly, unsure of anything from now on but the reaction she received from the inhabitants of the dining room. Her face registered surprise when several men whistled. One took up a fiddle and played, and another took Rachel by her small delicate hand and twirled her around the room.

Her first steps were tentative, and I wondered if she could endure the attention of the men. She explained later that night when we were in bed that she had never danced before, nor been that close to a completely strange man. She admitted her mind was lost in the cacophony—she was torn between the need to collapse in a torrent of tears at her sorrow and shame or the desire to give herself over to this kindly man who was saving her from drowning in her own self-pity.

I had witnessed that the dancer sensed her awkwardness and guided her, placing an arm around her waist and gently urging her hips to direct one leg this way, one leg that way. His other hand held hers firmly, and the building confidence his touch brought to her turbulent thoughts introduced her to the healing wonder of dance. Her once blushing face was now flushed from this new movement.

She told me that night she believed she could dance forever, ignoring all other bodily needs as long as the music kept playing. But the music did stop for the moment, while the fiddler reached for his mug of flip, and Rachel became momentarily confused, her eyes cast to the floor. The friendly fisherman continued to hold Rachel's hand as he loudly announced to the group, "Looks like we have another Ray in our midst, a ray of sunshine. I say we call her Light Ray with no offense to our esteemed tavern keeper—this one is such a spritely little thing, and she has already brought such illumination to this room. Elisha, play us another tune, will you? This lady wants to dance." And on that night, Rachel, our Light Ray, became the tavern's dancer.

****

(Rachel)

And I did. I danced that whole night, and I danced every other night thereafter when I had the time and a willing partner. Once I discovered dance, I removed my tired old cap and never wore it again. I could not have guessed that my life would take this strange but remarkable turn. When I lost the child, I asked Dark Ray what had become of it because I had thought to bury it with some show of religious observance, so engrained was that kind of thinking in my being. But something in Dark Ray's eyes told me not to inquire further, and though I was bereft. No. Out of my mind for days over the matter, I resolved to survive my lot and make a life for myself as it seemed I had been far too trusting of a man who abandoned me at his first opportunity. It took me a while to climb out of my self-pity, and when I could see the world around me clearly, I saw Dark Ray in the center. A woman to emulate. Perhaps a mother, after all.

Chapter 3

1692

A Papist Boy

(Mariana)

Tiny blue flowers grow in profusion in the wind-protected sandy hollows on this island. I do not know their name, but I look forward to their blooming in the late days of summer. Because they are small in size, they are best seen at eye level if one is lying on the sand and can examine their pure blueness, can see the darker hue in the middle of the delicate petals. That is how I first found them when I arrived. They were little blue greetings welcoming me to my new home. Hail Mary, full of grace.

It took me several weeks to arrive at Great Island. I had to get far from Salem after what happened to my mother there. Once she and the others were taken, I had no one else I could trust. I was a young girl accustomed to shadowing her mother, and when she was gone, I felt lost. The English women kept their silence, lowered their heads, and went about their duties with the fear of punishment if they drew attention to themselves. I could not go to them. They never showed any interest in my well-being. And besides, they were a dreary sort—disconnected from the natural world, instruments of the village fathers.

My mother nurtured me with a different view of a woman's role in society. Although she was raised Catholic, she was dedicated to the Virgin, a devotion that might seem extreme to some priests, so my mother avoided the Church. A strong connection to nature mingled with adoration for the Mother rather than her Son guided my mother's life. Wherever she lived, she found others like herself and worshipped with them. When our household work was complete, we would sneak out to the woods for prayer, meditation, dancing—which were the ways I learned to worship the natural world and the spirit within.

In Salem, we lived in a community of Puritans so bent on squelching papist and pagan inclinations wherever they sprang up, we had to be careful of being found out. But I soon discovered that worship of the Goddess was everywhere, even in a Puritan village. She survived persecution and time and now was called Mary because it was widely held that the mother of Jesus was a manifestation of the Ancient One who has had so many names in so many lands throughout the ages. When the air became heavy with the scent of roses, her worshippers knew she was nearby, watching them, directing them to do her will. Hail, Mary.

While my mother and I were loyal to the Holy One, the Sacred Mother of all, we had to be careful not to draw attention to our secret activities. My mother told me of the persecution that plagued Europe and seemed now determined to destroy worshippers in Massachusetts Bay Colony. She knew as well that the best way to avoid suspicion was to live among people whose religious persuasion was accepted in the community. That way, we could imitate our neighbors' particular codes of piety in public, but in private, we were free to follow our own rituals. It might sound sinful to some, but when one wants to survive, she will do whatever it takes.

Many years before, my fisherman father and his wife had come to the New World from Sao Miguel in the Azores and hoped to start a new life. Shortly after my birth, however, my father who I was destined never to know drowned in a fishing accident. My mother had no resources of her own and so was forced to remain in Massachusetts Bay and work as a housekeeper in an English home. She kept to her chores, inviting no suspicion from her employer. Being Portuguese drew enough attention since the English saw us as little more than servants. As I grew up, I became an added bonus to the family my mother served, as I too could be made to sweep, scour the pewter, do any of the household duties someone of my size was capable. Living among the English, I was able to learn their language, and that skill was to help me more in the days to follow than I ever would have imagined.

As my mother and I became acquainted with the other servants in Salem, we discovered there were other worshippers of Mary hidden among the Puritans. We became a close band of women who vowed to keep each other's identity a secret. Our anonymity did not last long, however. Young Puritan girls had developed the habit of meeting with Tituba, Reverend Parris's housekeeper, in the woods at night. This was one way the young rebellious girls escaped the strict rules regarding their behavior. While those activities did not include my mother's group of women, their practices were not so different from the rituals of the followers of Mary although we did not use animal blood the way Tituba is said to have instructed the Puritan girls. Instead, we preferred our menstrual flow that we allowed to drip unchecked out of our naked bodies onto the rocks we gathered to create the circle in which we prayed, chanted, and danced. Once the circle had been defined with blood markings, we entered it and began to worship. Although I was not old enough yet to participate in the marking, I looked forward to the day when I could contribute to this part of the ritual.

It was on one such night that our fate became linked to Tituba and her disciples. It had been a clear late summer night bathed in the white glow of the full moon—always the best time to worship the Goddess. My mother's group of worshippers had just completed the rituals. As we dressed, we heard screaming in the distance and male voices shouting that there seemed to be others still farther in the forest. Their torches began to appear alarmingly close to the Mary circle. Knowing danger and captivity were seconds away, the women scattered. Running together would mean certain capture for all. Fleeing in separate directions gave some a chance to escape and perhaps free those not as fortunate at a later time. I was not with my mother when they captured her. Sometimes I think she purposely allowed herself to be taken to divert the danger from me. When I have this thought, I cry anew as if the capture had just occurred. My mother sacrificed herself for me. How would I ever re-pay her unselfishness and love?

I escaped capture that night by hiding in a barn until daybreak. The uncertainty of my circumstances terrified me. And the thought of my mother being chained like an animal in the filthy prison caused me to whimper throughout the night even as I fell in and out of a restless sleep. I was aware of the fate of the captured. Chained, starved, and neglected, the unfortunate prisoners would await unfair trials, followed by public ridicule and in the end, hanging or stoning in the full view of the righteous congregation. I knew these things well. My mother warned me constantly to avoid suspicion because someone was always watching.

The next day was heartbreakingly beautiful. The warm sun beat down on the village, unmindful of what cruel treatment awaited the prisoners. When I thought it safe, I stole from the barn but kept hidden behind barrels stacked near the prison door and there tried to figure out how I was going to free my mother. But I was too late. Noises from within warned me of the approaching people behind the locked door. After the sound of the key in the lock, the heavy wooden door swung open, and I saw my mother and the other captured women being pushed out of the prison. They were stripped to the waist and herded onto a hay cart to be paraded and mocked by the village persecutors. Despite her shame and confusion, my mother scanned the growing number of people in search of me. She looked as extraordinarily beautiful as the morning, her long dark hair falling loosely over her shoulders, her strong naked breasts exposed through the cascade of hair. And then as she turned from my direction, I saw her back, oozing with the blood that rose to her skin's surface as a result of the whipping she had endured in the prison the night before. My mother turned again, searching for me, and that is when she saw my face in the

gathering crowd. In my horror at seeing my mother so abused, I

had left my hiding place, forgetting my own danger.

"*Correr*, Mariana, *correr agora!*" My mother shouted in

Portuguese as the cart lurched forward down the main street.

Run and leave her to her sure death? How could I run? I

looked around, and while my mother's voice had been muted by

the wailing of the captured women and the angry shouts of the

townspeople, some turned to gaze in my direction, and I knew I

was in danger. A child ultimately listens to her mother, and so I

did what I was told. There was no other decision to make if I

wanted to live. And the instinct was in me to survive despite the

horror I felt leaving my mother among the accusers. Hail, Mary.

Pray for us sinners. I ran.

Even at the age of ten, I had skills that would serve me

well. I was nimble and small. I knew how to hide. On my first

day on the road, I crept into a goodwife's kitchen while she was

tending to some chickens in the front yard and stole a knife to cut

off my long hair. I also took from the woman's clothesline a pair

of breeches that looked small enough to fit me. I did not like having to resort to thievery, but a girl on the open road would look suspicious. If I could pass as a boy, I would have a better chance of remaining safe.

For the first few days, I was too stunned and frightened to make a sound plan, so I hid in a neglected old shed outside of town. There I cried unceasingly for my mother and prayed to Mary with as much intensity. I believed that Mary must have heard my constant prayers because one day I woke up and remembered the elder women's talk of havens that existed among our kind, those who lived not at the heart but just outside acceptable English society. There was an island across the Bay from Plimoth with a tavern run by a powerful Indian woman who took in females to help run the establishment. Perhaps she would allow me to live there and earn my keep until I could plan where to go next.

I walked most of the way by day and slept in whatever shelter I could find at night—barns, abandoned dwellings, under lofty pines on dry nights. I knew how to navigate the woods as well as the coastline. My mother had taught me not only how to understand directions based on the placement of the sun but how to scavenge for food. I lived meagerly on picked berries, snared rabbit, clams that I dug out of the low tide muck with my hands and that stolen knife. I survived because it was summer. I survived because I believed that Mary needed me and protected me now that I was motherless. At times I felt Mary's blue cloak envelop me when I found myself in uncertain situations. I felt guided. I smelled roses. Blessed art Thou, among women.

When I arrived at Plimoth, I went to the wharf and waited for signs. And sure enough, I watched as a boat was presently being filled with cargo to be taken to Great Island. As they worked, the men joked with each other about their desire to get to their destination as soon as possible. They talked about their plans for a randy night of entertainment. I was standing quietly against the side of a tavern, but I could hear them plainly enough and wondered now that I was so close, what kind of place I was seeking for refuge. Once they had finished loading the boat, I watched as the captain and crew entered the local tavern for their mid-day meal. While they were gone, I stowed myself under some blankets aboard the craft and waited. I was terrified, but I was also very hungry and wished in my excitement that I had found something to eat before hiding. Yet I was too frightened to leave my hiding place to search the boat, not knowing the crew's habits or the speed of their return.

My intuition served me well. The men came back before too long and set course across the Bay. The ride was smooth because we were blessed that afternoon with a westerly breeze, and it might even have been soothing enough to put me to sleep, but I could not settle down to do so. My nose was itchy from the rough blankets I was under, and the heat was close to unbearable. My ragged clothes were soaked through with sweat. Yet what continued to plague me most were the images of the torture my mother must have endured. Despite what I faced, her end had surely come and gone, and I knew I would never see her again in this life. So I prayed to Mary to remove the unbearable thoughts from my mind, I cried, and my tears mingled with my sweat and burned my eyes. I felt loneliness and despair throughout my being. And I felt guilt. Why had I not stayed and tried to save my mother? There must have been some way to free her. I will carry this burden throughout my life. Did I make a selfish decision to save myself? Did my escape allow her to die in peace? I will never know. Pray for us sinners.

Once the boat docked in the island's harbor, I strained to listen for an opportunity to leave my unpleasant quarters. I realized how used I had become to living outdoors. This short confinement made me ache to breathe fresh air. The opportunity did not arrive until after dark. By then, I was desperately hungry and feared my growling stomach was loud enough to cause my capture. The last of the men went ashore for refreshment and entertainment. Finally there was quiet. Once I removed myself from my hiding place and went on deck, I could see the lights of the tavern in the distance. I could also hear singing and the playing of a fiddle. At one point, there was a loud whooping and laughing. I guessed the boatmen were not disappointed, and I decided to wait for morning before I sought the aid of the tavern keep.

Staying clear of the building, I walked around the edge of the great sand bank, and as I walked, the raucous din from the tavern began to recede. I was miserably dirty, hungry, and tired, but I could only attend to one of these conditions, so I slept. Right under the great canopy of stars in the open air—there was no other shelter that I could see on this grassy dune of an island, and I fell asleep almost immediately in the sand. Later I would learn that there were also lookout stations built to watch for schools of whales as they entered the harbor, but I would not have traded my bed of sand for any other place that night.

When I awoke, the sun was coming up, and my clothes were wet again but this time from morning dew. I rolled to my right side to shield my eyes from the rising sun and saw the little blue flowers gazing back at me in the sparse grass. Blue. Blue as the new morning sky. Blue as Mary's gown. I knew I would be safe. I had found a new home. The smell of roses was everywhere. Holy Mary.

With that sweet, heady aroma to give me courage, I stood up and brushed the dewy sand from my rumpled clothes. Running my fingers through my short hair, I wondered with fear, now that I was finally at my destination, what would await me at the tavern. I had lost track of the days and did not know if I had turned eleven yet, but I felt wise for my age. The weeks I had lived alone had sharpened my senses and stealth. I was tanned and tough and sinewy, but I prayed the kind woman who ran this outpost would welcome me—see that I was strong as a boy, adept at many chores. I straightened up in an attempt to stir up the confidence I needed to venture down the winding path to the tavern. In the distance, I saw several men walking away from the building and heading down to the harbor shore to the boat that transported me. The rowdy singing and shouting of the previous night were silenced by the gathering breezes of the new day. This would be a good time to acquaint myself with the woman.

****

(Dark Ray)

The front door was opened, allowing the sea breeze to cleanse the stale air of sweat, pipe smoke, spilled ale and food from the night before. As I entered the main room from around the fireplace, I saw a young boy step in cautiously, a wary rabbit, his large dark eyes surveying all they saw. I stopped and looked directly at him.

"Well, look at you. Have you been living with wolves, you filthy one? How on earth did you get here? You're too dirty to have taken a swim over." I scratched my ear and cocked my head to one side. "Am I going to be visited by young children who do not belong here every year? Do people think I am running a shelter for homeless waifs? Who are you?" When he didn't offer any information, my voice grew louder. "Speak up! I am losing my patience. Quickly, or I will feed you to the crows!"

Startled, the child took a step back and bumped into Rachel as she entered the room, having just returned from the spring. "Stay put, little man, before you spill more of the water I just fetched!"

The filthy thing moved to the right and fell onto the settle by the door. His child's eyes followed Rachel as she placed the wooden buckets by the fireplace and then straightened up, her hands resting on her narrow waist. I suppose she seemed less of a threat than I.

"Where did this one come from, Ray? What a sweet little boy however smelly!"

Rachel's steps were like little dance movements as she approached the waif, lifted him up by the shoulders, twirled him around for inspection, and sat him back on the settle.

"I was just trying to find that out. Are you going to explain yourself, Lad?"

The child stood up when I addressed him and sucked in his breath. Acting like a caged animal, his eyes darted to the doorway to measure how close to it he was as if he might have to make a run for his life. Then he faced Rachel and me and in his gaze, I read that he saw we were so unlike one another, he might have giggled if he were not so frightened. But then, he spoke and surprised us equally.

"I am not a boy. I am a girl. I have been traveling a great distance to get here, and I thought it best for safety's sake to appear as a boy. Please do not think me evil. I know it is wrong to wear the clothes of the other sex, but I was frightened and alone and I did not know what else to do," the child confessed, her voice quaking with a mixture of fear and shame.

"Does that not beat all, Rachel? SHE is quite resourceful. What is your name? How old are you? And where is your home?" I inquired impatiently, my arms folded across my body.

"My name is Mariana. I was named after the Blessed Mother of Christ. I am ten or eleven, Ma'am. I am not sure. What is the date? My day of birth is the first of September, but I have lost track of time. I have been traveling so long, it seems, but the weather is still fine, so it cannot be much past the middle of September, can it? My last home was with my mother in Salem, but it is no longer safe for me there."

At this, the child's voice cracked with tears. "And my mother, oh, my mother's poor soul lives in heaven with Holy Mary now. I have come from Salem to here to save my life. Hail, Mary."

"Now, here is a good one. We have a papist among us. Unlike the good English people of Massachusetts Bay Colony though, I don't find papists troublesome. My own departed husband was a product of his beloved Jesuit priests' teachings." I laughed as I remembered my past. "They got on so famously with the native people, they brought the French right to our beds." I looked up after a moment remembering where and whom I was with, and as the laughter left my eyes, I focused again on the child before me. This was not the time for this kind of talk. "Go on, Mariana," I coaxed, more gently now. "I am known as Dark Ray, and this is Rachel."

Rachel retrieved a hunk of freshly baked bread and offered it to Mariana who took it with shaking hands and immediately devoured it.

"When was the last time you ate?"

"A couple of days ago, I think."

"All right, then. We're listening. Eat up, Child. There is more. Were you caught up, then, in that witch craze those fool Puritans like to entertain themselves with?" I sensed a stiffening in Rachel's posture and addressed her directly. "Don't give me that look, Rachel. Do you really still consider yourself among their kind? A great lot of good it has done you! Get her a mug of ale before she chokes on that bread." I turned back to the child. "Go ahead, Mariana, finish your story."

Encouraged by the food and drink, Mariana, relaxed and appeared more trusting. She spilled out the story of her flight. When she got to the capture of her mother, she slowed down her frantic pitch and a sob escaped her lips. I remained still so as not to frighten the child even more, but Rachel went over to her and placed an arm around her shoulder. "Now. Now. There is nothing you could have done to save her, and she would not have wanted you to remain in Salem to be captured. Your mother wanted you to live. She was brave, and she wanted you to be brave. She taught you well if you have made it this far by yourself. You are not alone, though. Sometimes children do not have the good fortune to remain by their parents' sides as long as they would like," she concluded, and I realized that Rachel was still grieving about her own circumstances of last year.

When Mariana's story ended, I heated the water that Rachel had collected earlier, its intended use forgotten in order to prepare a bath for the orphan. I spoke gently to Mariana as I approached her.

"Now that you've eaten, we need to get you and your clothes clean before the men start arriving and looking for their mid-day meal. Rachel will help bathe you in that tub over by the fire." I pointed to the metal structure that was used for a variety of purposes—from mixing ingredients for ale to washing bodies.

"I will wash your clothes outside in the rain barrel bucket. I have no others to give you in their place. The sun is so warm today. They should dry soon if I lay them out on a bush. Until they are, you can go up to my bed and rest. You may have been able to have lived by your wits and survive your journey, but you are still a little girl. In time, we will have to make you another set of trousers. There will be no skirts for you, young one. I believe you will be safer here if you continue to dress as a boy until you are a little older."

Mariana's eyes clouded with fear, and her hands clapped her mouth, suppressing a gasp.

"Do not fret over my decision," I continued. "Here we don't spend time worrying over the naming of our actions as sins. We all do what we have to do to get by. Rachel, use that coarse soap you just made. She has layers of filth on her. I believe she will turn out almost as fair skinned as you when you are finished with her, even though her hair is as dark as mine."

Rachel and I helped Mariana undress. I held the tattered, dirty clothes away from me and walked outside to wash them. In a few moments, I returned and placed my attention on kitchen duties. Already the morning was advancing, and the mid-day meal needed to be prepared. While I would not have chosen to take in this new arrival if the choice had been mine to make, I couldn't bring myself to put the child back on the road. I resolved to keep her safe and put her to work. Besides, Rachel and I needed the assistance as the tavern business continued to grow.

****

(Mariana)

At the water basin, Rachel's tiny hands soothed me. No one had touched me since I lost my mother. I sat entranced by the gentle caresses of this beautiful fair-haired angelic creature despite the abrasive soap on my unwashed skin. Still timid though, I leaned forward and whispered so Dark Ray, who was stirring the stew at the fireplace, would not hear. "Does this mean I can stay for awhile?"

A smile brightened Rachel's face. She whispered back as if we were old friends. "I believe that if she did not intend to keep you here, Dark Ray would have sent you back on the path, even if it meant you would have had to swim over to the other side or drown. She is fully in charge here, and she expects to be obeyed. Do what she says, and you will get on fine with her. I think she likes you already. I have only been here a year myself, but I have come to know her well. And love her. Why, I would follow her anywhere. Like you, she took me in at my worst hour. She is a woman of strong words but of enormous generosity. You will see."

So I lived here. I lived here despite the goings on. Pray for us sinners. I begged Mary's forgiveness. But where else could I live once I became attached to these women who seemed to need me as much as I needed them?

Chapter 4

1693

The Trying Out

"Father?"

It was early morning when Rachel came down the stairs to prepare a cup of peppermint tea to soothe her uneasy stomach. Too many oysters. When would she learn? As she stirred the brew, she wondered why she uttered this word in her sleep after so long. Had she been dreaming of him? Her father's influence was from another time in her life when she paid attention to what others thought she should be. She was satisfied that she had grown into being her own person now, and while she missed him greatly, she hadn't made any effort to steal across the harbor to visit him these last two years. What good would it have done? It would only have caused the old hurt to surface.

Groggily, she looked over at the dining room and noticed a formally attired man smoking a pipe at one of the tables. He did not appear to be one of the fishermen. It was an odd hour of day for someone to be in there. Yet something about his carriage appeared familiar, but that person would be out of place here, and certainly that man would not have been smoking. She squinted to examine him further, and then taking in a deep breath, she whispered again but in complete disbelief, "Father?"

Elijah Sloane turned to look at the beloved daughter. At the sight of her, all resolution vanished, and he wondered how he could have waited this long to lay eyes on her again. He put down his pipe, stood up and went to her, enthralled by her new maturity and loveliness, conscious of the scant remnants left of the little girl he raised.

"Rachel."

She was unable to keep her body from trembling. She wanted to run into his arms in reunion; she wanted to run out the door and leap from the cliffs on the west side of the island to her death; she wanted to disappear before him like an apparition, her discomfort was so intense. Instead she remained perfectly still, unable to move. He advanced and slowly encased her in his arms. She was his little girl again; she was lost to herself.

"Rachel, I have missed you these last two years. Word got back that you were at this place—this is a small community, after all—the townsfolk know what goes on here even if they choose to deny it. I wanted to come to you immediately, but I succumbed to foolish, cold pride. It is my worst sin. I believe I will burn brightly in the fires of hell for it, God save me." He caressed her loose hair, twirling it into curlicues, even though when she lived with him, she kept it hidden under a modest cap, and he wasn't likely ever to touch it. Next, he examined each of the fingers of her small hands as if she were newly born. She was not completely uncomfortable in his familiar arms, but her heart pounded nevertheless at his presence in the room, in her new life. Her father did not belong here. She was not able to speak, but she momentarily slipped back into her former self as she allowed

herself to think: Do I belong here after all?

Elijah, however, couldn't stop the flow of words from

spilling out of his mouth. It was as if he had stored these words,

having rehearsed them over and over for when he would have the

courage to visit her.

"You were my whole existence after your mother died. I

prided myself on how well I had raised you when others counseled

me to marry again for your sake. You grew up the model of virtue

nonetheless. Again I was so self-righteous in my confidence that it

was my doing that produced the young woman you were

becoming." He stopped momentarily and then continued, breaking

away from her, so that he could pace while he talked, a habit she

recognized from her years of living with him.

"I was so blind. The last time we saw each other I was

harsh to you. But Rachel, you sinned despite all my guidance! I

had to have you out of my sight—as if your physical absence

would solve our problems. I could not accept your carnal

weakness because it reflected on me, on our family name. You

knew exactly how I felt. When I was informed a few days after you left our house where you had gone, I wanted desperately to come for you. But what was I to do? Bring you home in your condition? The neighbors do not sleep. Someone is always watching someone else's business and soon, they would have observed your growing form. And although you lost the child—yes, I heard that too—the law was against you."

Rachel's eyes darkened at this disclosure. She steadied herself against a nearby chair. Who could have passed that information along to him?

"You know as well as I that you would have been severely punished," he continued, unaware of her mounting stress. "Fornication outside marriage is an offense, you know this. You could have been whipped, forced to stand in the stocks to suffer the ridicule of the congregation. We would have been fined. But worst of all, after the punishment, the imprisonment, you would have been permanently labeled. No one would marry you! What else could I do but condemn your actions?"

At last he stopped speaking. As he began to weep, Rachel was startled by his display of emotion. Yet, she gathered her wits while his tears silenced him. She was conscious now of a growing indignation that had begun to form after she became accustomed to his presence and had been building within her the whole time he was talking. She was overcome suddenly by a violent desire to smack his face, but she controlled her base reaction. Instead, she stood up straight, free of the chair's false security, and looked up but not directly at him. Like her father, it was as if she had memorized the lines she was about to speak. They seemed to flow from her mouth effortlessly.

"Then, Father, if word from here can get to you so quickly, why did you not come to comfort me when I lost the child? Why did you stay away when I was hopelessly bewildered in my grief, not knowing where to go, or if I should remain and allow this island life to embrace me? When I was sure not a living soul on this earth or a God above loved me or cared if I lived or died? Was that pride as well, Father, that kept you from me? You were my whole world for so much of my life. Yes, I sinned. I fell in love with a man other than you. Is that what really made you reject me?"

Her father's eyes, which had been downcast until this last question, were now blazing as he made eye contact. "Rachel, you live up to your name: you have grown, I see, not only into a handsome young woman but a self-willed, petulant one as well. Please, do not be so harsh with me now. You cannot imagine how I grieved for you—for the loss of you in my life. But yes. Pride kept me from forsaking every tenet of religious conviction I had and coming to you. At times I was relieved the child died—surely, it was cursed by the devil—I was convinced of that. Two years of avoiding one's daughter. You cannot know what that means to a parent. You have been so close and yet, so far from me. I consoled myself to let you go because in my own grief, I also had no one to turn to for advice. You lost a child. So did I. And the way I lost her!"

Both fell silent and looked away. The tavern was strangely quiet, but not unusually so for this time of day. The whalers were down at the shoreline trying out their current whale harvest, their great fires burning the blubber into oil. Depending on the wind's direction, the noxious smell from the process found its way to the tavern. But the smell was tolerated; it was the smell of money.

On these trying out days, Mariana got to sleep a little later as she would be serving the men food and drink long into the night.

She was still dressing as a boy and so far, her female identity had gone undetected, but Mariana told Rachel several times how she yearned for the day that she could look and act like a woman.

Already it was a year since Mariana arrived at the tavern, and while she felt at home with Dark Ray and Rachel, she was nevertheless shocked by the conversation that awakened her that morning. She lay very still in order to hear the exchange between Rachel and her father. Mariana had not been told why Rachel had settled at the tavern. She had never thought to ask, but now she understood what Rachel had whispered as she soothed Mariana's uncertainty with every gentle stroke of her hand to clean Mariana of her traveler's dirt that first day. Rachel had said that children do not always have the good fortune to remain with their beloved parents. Now Mariana knew why Rachel had to leave her home. She had been a sinner. She had gotten herself with child. The Rachel Mariana loved did not fit this behavior even though it was obvious that she consorted with the men here. As Mariana continued to listen, she began to sort the pieces together that not only explained Rachel's life, but foreshadowed Mariana's future as well. She closed her eyes and prayed to Mary for strength, all anticipation of a virtuous life suddenly threatened at this place where rules of decency were nonexistent.

Downstairs, Rachel spoke after the uncomfortable silence. "So, why now, Father? It has been two years. Why did you care enough to see me now?"

"Rachel, I have always wanted to see you. I already explained how difficult it was for me to stay away. But I knew with those selfish acts of fornication, you were lost to me and my world forever. And look what you have become. Do you think I am not distraught knowing what you have chosen for your life? I have deliberated for months whether or not I could bear to see you in this environment. Believe me when I say that I am well aware of the goings on here. I know all about this place and you. Dark Ray keeps me informed. She is the one who got word to me when you first arrived."

Rachel's courage to look directly at her father returned. She squared off and stared coldly into his eyes. She put up her hand to silence him. "What business do you have with Ray? How do you know her?"

"Daughter, I have known her for years. Children, especially girl children, are not meant to know the dealings with which a father engages to support his family. I am sure you never even considered the activities that sent me out of our home to my place of business. Truly, have you ever wondered how I have made my money? I suppose you will exclaim that your ignorance is my fault again, but I never troubled you with my worldly affairs. It is not something one shares with his daughter—even with one he has shared most other discussions. Nevertheless, I will tell you now."

He paused briefly and again walked around the room, this time re-lighting the pipe he had dropped on the table. Her father performed the act so unconsciously, she wondered what other habits he had for which she was not privy.

"I have been a partner with Samuel Hawes in the whaling business. I helped him build this establishment. I am responsible for its maintenance while Hawes inspects the whale distribution, so the oil and other products are dispersed fairly to the town members. Since we built this place, Samuel and I, we have become quite wealthy. Because my end of the work revolves around the management of this tavern and its surroundings, I have had ongoing dealings with Dark Ray. While I do not approve of all the activities that take place in what was meant to be a whaling station, I do know she is a faithful tavern keeper who can be trusted. When you fled here, I worried for your mortal soul, but I also found comfort in the fact that you would be well taken care of."

"Taken care of!" Rachel exclaimed. "Both you and Dark Ray have deceived me. How could you do business with her this whole time, and I not know it? Why have I not seen you here before now?"

Elijah grew uneasy. "For a time, I withdrew from my business concerns, but Dark Ray worked doubly hard to keep this place running smoothly. She contracted some praying Indians to act as messengers between here and the mainland. They met with me on a weekly basis, and I saw to it that this place was adequately maintained from home."

"I must be honest." He placed his pipe back on the table. "I have only lately recovered from my shame. When you left, I was rarely seen in public. At church services, I could barely stand the censuring looks from the congregation. The one person who came to my aid was that wonderful young Deacon Sweet. I am sure you remember him well. You so graciously cooked extra food to share with him before his angelic wife arrived from England. Matthew observed my sorry state and befriended me. He offered to come here in disguise and secure you a trip back to England."

Elijah paused briefly and examined his daughter's face. "You seem startled by his generosity, Rachel. Have you forgotten how much you enjoyed discussing the Scriptures with him in Bible class?"

Although she never expected there would be a time to reveal the truth to her father, Rachel felt something close to relief for she had no desire or need to protect Matthew any longer. "Believe me, Father. Matthew Sweet is not a man to be forgotten. I will remember him until my dying day although now I wish him even more ill will knowing he sought to banish me to England— out of his gaze, out of his life!"

"Rachel. What am I hearing?" Elijah took his daughter's shoulders and held them tightly. "Surely, he was not…."

"Surely, he was. The irony!" The words all but exploded from her tongue. "The one man who wronged me in the end helped my father through the ordeal." Rachel laughed bitterly. "Please, Father, do not look so shocked. Sin is not solely the domain of impressionable young girls. We do require partners. How wonderful for him that his wife is angelic. Maybe she will save him from further indiscretions and the fiery pits of hell which is where I pray, when I pray, he will reside in the next life."

Elijah Sloane stepped back from his daughter as if slapped. "My God, Girl, you have turned bitter! What is to become of your soul?" He looked around the room wildly, "It is this place...."

"Father," Rachel insisted. "Stop. I beg you. Do you hear your words? The Deacon who lives closest to the Christian God was never influenced by anything outside the church walls, and he too sins."

Elijah sat down on a nearby stool, lowered his head and appeared distracted. His voice was quieter, less confident. Almost contrite. "You are right, Rachel, but please believe that I had no suspicion about the man." Then he remembered. "What a perfect fool I am. I was the one who sent you to his arms. It was my idea that you provide him with his mid-day meal." He looked up and into her face. "Your sin was mine."

"Oh, Father, I fed him all right. But alas, he was never full. He did not hesitate to forget me and marry as soon as the angel arrived on his doorstep. You can see that I have become a little less naïve, yes? A little more concerned about my own preservation? I have changed a great deal in these two years, Father, away from the two men I truly loved and trusted." The strain was almost more than she could bear. Her stomach, which ached upon waking, was now so tight, she wanted to bend her frame in half for some kind of relief.

Both of them suffered, but Sloane, the more practical minded of the two attempted to put his anguish aside because there was no gain in dwelling on it. He had other business to deliver. He stood up and said, "Rachel, let us not talk further of the past. Let us endeavor to move forward if we are to live with any peace in the remaining years of our lives."

"You asked earlier why I came today at last to see you. Here is the reason: business is going quite well at this whaling station. This enterprise continues to grow as the demand for more whale products increases. I was thinking I would move to Boston and continue to expand whale commerce in this entire region of the colonies." He grew self-conscious, and his face reddened. "And, I have met a woman. Goody Sweet's widowed sister. She followed Matthew's wife to Billingsgate after her husband died in England last year. The Sweets introduced her to me upon her arrival. They sought to ease my loneliness with you gone. Rachel, your mother will always remain in my heart, but Elizabeth and I are marrying."

At this news, Rachel's resolve weakened. She could not endure another moment of standing, and so she found the nearest stool and slumped down on it, her arms wrapped around her worsening stomachache. Elijah Sloane, however, seemed unaware of his daughter's distress. He continued headlong with a renewed confidence.

"Elizabeth is a generous and loving woman," he began but then stopped. "She encouraged me to invite you back into my home. We have plans to move to Boston at the end of the month. I was coming here to ask you to join us, but given what you have confessed to me, I realize it would not be wise to do so. The happiness of all would be compromised." And rather too quickly, he added, "Perhaps you should remain here. Despite what this place is, it seems to have served you well after all."

There was a pause before Rachel gathered her thoughts, but when she did, it was with a conviction stronger than she ever expressed. In actually forming the words, she was incredulous that they were issuing from her own lips. She had the uncanny feeling she was outside her body and hearing someone else speak. But her own voice resonating throughout her form confirmed she was indeed the speaker. And there was no stopping her now.

"No, Father. It would not be wise at all to invite me back into your society. Besides, I do not wish to live among the hypocrites with whom you so valiantly surround yourself. Matthew knows what he has done, and he hides behind his proper English marriage and his church. And you. You will forgive him and marry his sister-in-law." Her face turned scarlet with indignation.

"You need not worry. I will remain here and happily. My world has expanded beyond the dictates of your merciless church doctrine. I may have lost a great deal from committing a transgression, as you call it, but in the process, I have learned a great deal about myself. I enjoy talking to people freely about all matters of the world. I can no longer be some mousy woman in a cap who speaks only when she is addressed and then only about household matters and Scripture. I am even teaching others here to read. And let me be completely honest, Father, since now there is nothing left to hide. I enjoy a good time. I play cards, and best— best of all—I dance." Despite her aching stomach, she stepped off the stool and began to twirl in front of him speaking the whole time.

"When my body catches the rhythm of the fiddle, I am as happy as if I were up there in heaven visiting your God. So yes, Father. I will remain here, for wherever you live, these things that I love will not be mine to embrace. I mean to live my life on my terms, and you can thank Dark Ray for teaching me that."

She stopped twirling and speaking and looked at the face of the beloved parent who was father and mother to her, and briefly she faltered at the rushing recollection of the loving years they spent together across the harbor. Her tone softened. Now she saw how gray his hair had become since she left his house. Why should she punish him any longer with her actions and words? He made his life; she only wanted to make hers. She decided not to hurt him anymore. She reached for his hand, and with that simple act, she remembered how protected she felt holding it as a little girl.

"Father, I will always love you and treasure my childhood days in your company. I know I brought you pain, but so much of the pain we experience in life is caused by what others think. I have learned that here. Let the past go. Let me go. Have a life and a woman to spend it with you. I wish you well. You will always know where to find me. This is my home now, and I have no intention of leaving it."

With nothing more to say, Rachel turned from her father and ran up the stairs where she allowed herself to release all the held back tears she refused to weep in Elijah's presence.

Mariana, who heard the entire exchange and who initially was shocked by Rachel's actions and words, now only had sympathy and love for this golden-haired companion who showed her pure and honest love. She reached across the bedstead to touch Rachel who allowed herself to be collected in Mariana's arms and to be held as she rid herself of the last tears of shame and regret she would ever shed.

While the father and daughter had been speaking, Dark Ray had been out tending to chickens and hauling water from the spring in preparation for the long night ahead. By the end of the exchange between Rachel and her father, Dark Ray entered the dining room and sat quietly on the settle by the door. As Elijah Sloane turned to leave the tavern, he saw Dark Ray sitting there. Their eyes met, and then he looked down. Just as he stepped outside, Dark Ray spoke to him.

"Elijah, believe that what we give away comes back to us in another manner. You and your daughter are no longer the same people you were two years ago. For a little thing, she has deep soulful feelings. She will carry the remembrance of the good you gave her all the days she was growing up and pass it along in her own way to others. Is there more we can ask of anyone?"

Later that afternoon and long after her father left the island, Rachel emerged from her self-imposed isolation and found Dark Ray in the kitchen assessing the ingredients for the next day's meal. Though her eyes were still red from crying, she studied the older woman carefully before she cleared her throat and spoke.

"Ray, you have been like a mother to me since the first night I arrived. I will forever be grateful to you for taking me in and caring for me. However, like my father and Matthew, you too betrayed me. Why do all the people I love betray me?"

Dark Ray turned and faced her. "Betray? How? Because I didn't tell you I knew you were a Sloane the minute I saw you? Because I didn't tell you I had communicated with your father shortly after you arrived? Don't you think I may have had a reason for my actions?"

"But why did you not tell me these things then? What possible good did it do to conceal them from me?"

"I will tell you what good. When you showed up at this door, you were dangerously close to death. Don't ask me to explain. I simply knew what I saw. The best way to treat you was to allow you to think you were starting fresh with people who didn't know your name or your relations. You put yourself in my hands, and now you question my motives? Do not even suggest betrayal because I will tell you of a betrayal that will make you lose your mind."

Dark Ray observed Rachel's paleness and knew the daughter was still distraught from the father's visit. She continued. "Rachel, put this behind you, as you advised your father earlier today. I saw a very lost young girl, and I reached out to pull her back to health and a reason to go on. You have become your own woman these last two years, one who would never have realized her own worth in that world she left behind. Trust that I had your survival in mind when I did not reveal my association with your father."

The warm, brilliant smile with which she had become so beloved to the tavern dwellers and visitors illuminated her face, despite her tearful eyes. "Oh, Ray, I have been so angry with you all day, but you speak wisely and honestly, how can I not be anything but grateful to you?" As she said this, Rachel moved to Dark Ray's side and rested her head on the big woman's shoulder. "Seeing my father brought back all that pain, and I sought to include you in it, too. The past is behind us. We are here, and we are thriving. I cannot remain angry with the woman who saved my life. The woman who mothered me and made me whole."

Dark Ray allowed the moment to linger briefly, and then she gently stepped away from Rachel, wiped her clean hands on her apron as a gesture of finality, and said, "Let's get to work, Girl. I can hear the men on the path already. It will be a long night after this trying out day."

Chapter 5

1696

Oysters

Oysters. They were as plentiful as the rocks in Billingsgate Harbor, and Rachel loved them. When she was a squeamish Puritan girl, she would turn her nose at the slimy mass encased in its rippled pearly shell. At the tavern she ate them at least four times a week, sometimes more. Sometimes too much, and then her stomach rebelled. However, the time of day she consumed them did not matter; whenever the oysters were harvested, she would see that at least half a dozen passed her lips in the normal course of her day's work. They made her feel desirable, sensuous. And these feelings she came to prize.

On her twentieth birthday, she headed to the kitchen to bake some oyster pies to mark the day because she was so happy to be alive. She was five years at the tavern and harbored no remorse. After her father's visit three years ago, she cried out all her regret and sorrow and replaced it with joy—for having found a place where she could make her own decisions, for sharing her time with people who would not judge her.

As Rachel entered the low-ceilinged room behind the two front serving rooms on the first floor, she found Dark Ray already in the process of parboiling the shucked oysters in their own liquid. The crust had been rolled out on the bread table, and the seasonings and precious chopped currants and dates awaited the oyster mixture for baking.

"Why, how did you know I was fixing to prepare this dish today?" she asked the older woman.

"Rachel, it's no mystery how you feel about these slimy little buggers. We can't keep them stocked fast enough for your needs. Since it's your birthday, I thought to surprise you with these pies. But it seems there is no keeping anything a secret around here."

That is so sweet of you!" Rachel went over to bestow a wet kiss on Dark Ray's cheek. Any sign of affection towards this woman was met with a stiff shrug. Rachel and Mariana came to accept the gesture as loving if guarded acknowledgment. There was no pushing Dark Ray to express more than she was willing to show. They had grown used to measuring her love in other ways. For Rachel, the making of these oyster pies was one of them.

"With all to do around here, and you are baking special for me? And using what little store we have of the dried fruit?"

"Mariana has agreed to pick up what I haven't the time to do. Believe me, Rachel, keeping you full with oysters is good for business. That is all."

And that it was.

In the evening, when the fishermen were done with their work, the clay pipes filled, the tankards refilled, and the dishes cleared away, the music came out. Elisha found his fiddle in the corner of the serving room right where he left it the night before; he took it up, settled himself comfortably by the fire, and began to play. As she cleared the table scraps and tossed them out the door to the chickens, Rachel's body began to sway. By the time she removed the utensils and dishes, she began to hum. Her feet stepped in rhythm to the music, and before she completed the dish washing in the adjoining room, she couldn't help herself any longer. Wiping her soapy hands on her apron, she grabbed the first man she saw. Together they danced around the open space left clear for this purpose since she first arrived. She was the tavern dancer, and she loved that distinction. Tonight she was feeling an acute sense of balance and well-being. It showed in her dance.

She admitted to Dark Ray and Mariana once that she always wondered what it would be like to fly. She often dreamed about soaring through the air. But after she learned to surrender to musical rhythm, she declared, "If we cannot fly, we might as well dance." And so she danced whenever she could, and in her imagination, she experienced flight.

It was a warm summer night cooled down somewhat by the setting sun, but Rachel grew increasingly hot as she took up one partner after the next. By now, Thomas joined Elisha's fiddle playing with his mouth harp. The doors and windows remained open to catch the night breeze. The candles dripped unevenly from the swirling current created by the dancers' movements. The night was intoxicating.

Rachel flung off her apron. It landed on a nearby table just missing mugs and pipe dishes. She felt the liberation of removing weighty garments from her body and decided to dispense with another layer, but first she let her long, blond curly hair fall to her waist. Then still dancing but now by herself, she loosened her bodice. The left sleeve fell down her arm revealing the whiteness of her left breast. The men whistled and cheered Rachel on, begging for more.

She worked her way over to a table, took the mug right out of a man's hand, and drained the flip. She completely gave over to the music's rhythm as she reached for the hem of her dress and slowly shimmied it up to her thighs. The cooling breeze bathed her legs, and she felt the seduction creeping into her limbs. The boots were next to go as her feet could no longer remain confined in leather. She eased herself on a customer's lap and placed one foot then the other on the table, unlaced her boots and removed her stockings as he fondled the exposed breast and kissed her neck.

Barefoot now, she made her way to the dance floor and resumed her skirt lifting, this time more slowly. The blond hair framing her flushed face was dark with sweat. She licked her lips moist. She half closed her eyes. The others caught her spirit, and the place was wild.

With one swaying motion, she loosened her dress enough so that it slid down the length of her torso into a heap at her feet. Still swaying, she stepped away from the dress and caressed the nearly exposed parts of her body. Her underdress was loose and sheer. Sensing no reason to stop now, Rachel crossed her arms in front of her, grabbed for the hem of the underdress, brought it over her head, and threw it to the gathering crowd in the room. And still she danced. So seductively.

The music slowed, and her hips began to enact what all were thinking. She had to be satisfied. She had to have someone now. There was no more rational thought as to where. No time to get up the stairs to the usual place. It would be here. Right in the center of this room. The men understood her suggestion. They instinctively formed a circle around her. They threw coins on the table, vying to be her partner. Her eyes welcomed them all.

Dark Ray quickly estimated that Daniel was the highest bidder, nodded her head to him, and he joined Rachel as they slipped to the floor, writhing in anticipation. She felt his hands groping her everywhere. She directed him to the place where all ultimate pleasure resided. Her legs spread wide, and she drew him in, her neck arched back, her eyes closed, her hair fanned around her, her thoughts in flight.

When it was over, the room became eerily hushed. All were spent, having experienced the collective orgasmic moment.

Still lying on the floor in the center of the circle, Rachel focused her gaze around the room. As if a bright lantern shocked her into consciousness, she appeared confused and disoriented. She looked from face to face and couldn't recognize any of them. Her eyebrows furrowed in concentration. Dark Ray retrieved Rachel's underdress and bent down to give it to her. As she helped Rachel up, she broke the silence: "Give us some breathing room, good men, but first a toast. To our Light Ray—may she continue to dance through life!"

As the cheers subsided, Dark Ray announced that Mariana would be pouring the last round for the night. As they returned to their seats, Rachel looked around the room and located Daniel. He nodded to her, and then he smiled the broad grin of a satisfied man. She lowered her head, completely spent but a similar smile brightened her face. Mariana gathered Rachel's garments and placed them in her hands. Rachel signaled a good night and walked slowly up the stairs to the women's bedchamber and to sleep.

After the morning dawned and a ray of light crossing Rachel's face awoke her, she joined Dark Ray in the kitchen to prepare the day's meals. Because Mariana was not yet awake, the two women, who felt more comfortable discussing certain subjects without her often contrary opinions, spoke freely.

"You were in rare spirits last night, Rachel," Dark Ray began. "Those oysters certainly agreed with you."

Rachel smiled. "Yes, I do love them, but I am somewhat surprised this morning at how far they took me. Or did all of what happened come directly from me? From the person I have become?"

"Do you have regrets, Rachel? You didn't do anyone harm."

"No, I do not regret a thing, Ray. I have never been happier in my life. I was just thinking back to my earlier days across the harbor and realizing the woman who danced last night is not the same young girl who fled here a few years ago. That girl did not know who she was. She was everyone else's image of who she should be."

"And who is the woman she grew up to be?" asked Dark Ray.

"She is a woman who has grown into her true self. She makes no excuses for her actions. She gives as she takes. She will grow into old age living as she chooses."

Chapter 6

1698

Mary's Shrine

Behind the tavern to the west, the land rose gradually. Here the whalers perched from two lookout towers to sight the blackfish before they entered Billingsgate Harbor. One was for observing the northwestern water where the expanse beyond Provincetown led to the great wide sea. The other was for monitoring the whales as they advanced into Cape Cod Bay and proceeded to Jeremy Point, the sandy finger at the southernmost tip of the island. Once the whales were spotted from the first vantage point, the fisherman on watch alerted the others to prepare for the capture. By the time the fish reached the second lookout, the gear had been loaded onto the boats, and the whalers awaited the kill. This hunting strategy had long been in use. It served the *Nausets* for generations when they used the island. It served the English for years after the *Nausets* taught them how.

The watch towers also provided solace from the noise and the confining quarters of the tavern. Here a whaler enjoyed some time apart or invited one of the women to join him. If alone, he might bring his whittling knife and carve some scrimshaw. Between these two towers, the land dipped slightly and was protected from the wind that whipped across the grassy sands.

In this shelter, Mariana fashioned a shrine for her beloved Mary. Over the years, she collected driftwood, rocks, shells, and even the hollowed casings of horseshoe crabs and placed them strategically around a small plaster statue of the Virgin given to her by a Portuguese sailor who visited from Provincetown. In this dip grew the tiny blue flowers Mariana loved; it was one reason she set up her altar to the Great Mother here in the first place. When the season and her time permitted, she gathered other wild flowers to set in a tankard before the statue in loving tribute.

Mariana visited this spot daily no matter what the weather once her tavern chores were completed and before the evening serving began. On the nights of the full moon, she stole out to her shrine after everyone was asleep or gone, and she performed what remained in her memory of the monthly rituals of her mother's time. She believed her devotion to Mary strengthened her, nourished her soul. Showed her the right way to live. Protected her from harm. Most importantly, absolved her sins. When Mariana went to the altar, she smelled roses, and believed that despite some of the activities in which she was now engaged, Mary understood and blessed her. Forgave her. She needed to believe this, or she could not go on.

When she arrived at Great Island, Mariana was just eleven years old, and she quickly appreciated Dark Ray's decision for her to remain dressed as a boy. Now she was seventeen. Some of the men who spent time at the tavern frightened her, and she worried about how she was going to remain chaste, especially when both Dark Ray and Rachel were involved in occasional sex with the men. She could not imagine that she would ever be like them. She never once imagined exposing herself like Rachel did when she performed her oyster dance once a year on her birthday. She didn't possess Rachel's free and open nature. While her body had grown every bit as beautiful as Rachel's, Mariana reserved the viewing of it in private, and even then, she wasn't always comfortable with the exposure.

The day after Rachel's first oyster dance, Mariana came to her shrine and stayed longer than usual. She could not remove from her mind the image of Rachel writhing naked on the floor. Even when the light was faded in the west, she lingered. She wanted to scream, but she knew the others would hear her and come running, concerned that she was hurt. Instead she raised her hands to the sky and silently pleaded, "Mother, what do you want of me? How can I serve you here?"

At times like this, she couldn't bear the thought of remaining at the tavern, and she contemplated leaving; she'd plot for days and days, imagining she'd head south to a warmer climate. But just as soon as she made the decision to go, she dismissed her plan, for now she was clearly a woman, and a woman traveling alone would not be safe. Besides, what skills did she have? Who did she know? Unable to answer these questions, Mariana resolved to stay on the island. After all these years, she had come to love Rachel and Dark Ray. They were her family, and she would have to forgive their bawdy ways because she knew they would never hurt her; they loved her as well.

She thought that perhaps her mission at this place was to bring the other women to Mary, but she decided early on against approaching Dark Ray since the woman often expressed her distain of Christianity of any kind. Whenever the occasion allowed, Dark Ray would remind anyone who would listen that she never became a praying Indian and didn't ever intend to. While her adoption of some European ways enabled her to carry on business effectively, she was perfectly happy worshipping her own *Nauset* gods in private.

Rachel, however, seemed a better choice to join Mariana in honoring Mary. She had been raised a Christian; would she not be interested in learning about the Great Mother? After that first oyster dance, Mariana decided she had waited long enough and would speak with Rachel about the state of her soul. Once when

Rachel had been teaching her how to read on a late afternoon, Mariana put the book down gently and looked directly at the beautiful blonde woman who seemed to wear a perpetual smile.

"Rachel," Mariana said. "Do you pray?"

"I used to be very pious, Mariana, if that is what you mean. I knew the Scriptures well. You know I was raised a Puritan. Having lived in such an English household yourself in Salem, you understand how devout the members of the congregation can be. You also saw that their kind of devotion can lead to fanaticism and censure, and I can no longer abide that kind of thinking. Why do you ask me this question now?"

"I know of your past religious learning, and I was wondering if you would be interested in joining me in my worship of Mary. I miss not being able to share her with anyone here— Dark Ray will have nothing to do with my shrine or my beliefs. I thought perhaps since you were once a devout Christian, you might be more inclined."

"Dear Mariana," Rachel said as kindly as she could, putting her arm around the younger woman's shoulders. "As a Puritan, I would have scorned your idolatry. Worshipping a plaster statue!

Now, I have no desire to berate others anymore. I have denounced the teachings of my faith because they would have me do just that. Yet, I know you. Your heart is pure. While I will not judge your spiritual practices, they have no meaning in my life. I would like to make you happy and participate in your prayer and rituals, but I cannot. I am not that person."

"But," Mariana persisted, "do you not fear for your soul?"

"Fear?" repeated Rachel. "Fear is the cornerstone of faith, and I want no part of either. Living here I have learned to honor the goodness in people, to love them regardless of their gods. I suspect your Mary would understand that."

"She would, Rachel. Mary teaches nurturing love. Neither of us has a mother—She is the mother of all. Do you not think you would find comfort in knowing the love of a mother again?"

"Mariana, I understand that you wish to help me, but I do not believe I need help. The only mother I want is Ray. There will never be another who comforts me more. I am content with my life now, and that was not always so. She knew me the moment I entered the tavern—knew me when I did not know myself."

Rachel's right fist clutched her chest. "My heart was broken, and along with it, my desire to pray to any god or goddess. Ray taught me to believe in the goodness of people and to honor the wind and the sea and the earth. When the spirit moves me, I dance, and for me that is a kind of worship, too. I leave the praying to Mary to you for all of us if that comforts you."

She opened the primer to where they had stopped reading. "Now. Shall we get back to the task of teaching you to understand the words on these pages?"

While Mariana continued to perform the rituals alone over the years, she was comforted by the love of Dark Ray and Rachel. Although Dark Ray terrified her initially, Rachel's assurance that the woman was essentially a good and generous person was accurate. And Rachel was a sweet, loving woman whose beauty and warmth brightened any room she entered. Over the years, Rachel, who wasn't any taller than Mariana although six years older, smothered her with kisses and treated her with such kindness that Mariana soon lost all desire to be any other place. She believed Mary had guided her here for a reason, even if it wasn't to bring other souls to Her. She would do Mary's bidding; she just needed to figure out what that bidding was. She waited for signs, and the years passed. But she never gave up the hope that she would serve the Mother here in some way, at some point in her life.

Everything that her mother had taught her about Mary concerned love. Unconditional love. So Mariana determined that her responsibility was to forgive all, despite the behavior. When she was younger, she did not understand much of the goings on around her. Dark Ray blocked her from the adult activities, making sure she was busy assisting in the kitchen or up to bed before the ruckus below began in earnest and ultimately lulled Mariana to sleep.

Her routine and her impersonation as a boy lasted for at least three years, but when her body began to change, both she and the other two women knew Mariana's life would change as well. It was not difficult to fool the men. None would wonder where the young boy had gone and from where this new girl came. Although there were local regulars year in and year out, their business was to work the whales, and many of the others who visited the tavern simply arrived one day and left the next with no regularity at all.

People generally came and went randomly—no one kept track. Only the two Rays were constant presences, making this place their own, their home. And as the years progressed and Mariana grew up, she became attached to Dark Ray and Rachel, and this place became her home as well.

So when she took off the cap that held the luxurious, curly hair that she refused to cut after her first blood flow and began to wear dresses again, the two Rays alone registered the change. And as she grew into her sexuality, she struggled to keep her religious ideology intact, but she lost her virginity to the Portuguese fisherman from Provincetown nevertheless. He spoke her mother's native language and reminded her of memories she only half understood. The first time they were together, she was so fearful of the sin she was about to commit that she could not relax. He coaxed her, eased her mind, and answered her incessant questions.

"But, is it special?" She wanted to know. She needed to know before she allowed him to penetrate her.

Of course, it was special, he assured her with the infinite patience of a fisherman. It was special because they loved each other.

When he showed up one day with the plaster statue of Mary, she was hooked.

Chapter 7

1700

A Beaching

(Dark Ray)

When I found Cessie on the shore where her father had left her, she appeared confused and very frightened. Here was the third girl I did not ask for, and this one was far younger than Rachel and Mariana when they arrived. The tavern was no place for her. Yet, as I watched her little shoulders convulse with grief, I was not surprised by this silent plea from my people to care for one of our own. Even though I had established my life among

Europeans, I had kept silent ties with my *Nauset* kin. No matter how I lived my life, my ancestors were in my blood and guided me never to forget my people. And although we became quick friends with the English colonists after their first uneasy encounter many years back, our numbers dwindled due to the sickness the outsiders brought with them that *Nauset* medicine could not always cure. Maybe it was the soul sickness of English ways that destroyed my elders first, exposing their physical bodies to the disease as their will to live among the strange pale beings ensured the premature decline of our once strong and vibrant numbers. Those like me who survived seemed to have tricked the gods and found ways to prevail. We lived among the Europeans, and we learned their ways. Over time, we seemed more European than *Nauset*.

But seeming and being are two different things. In my heart, I was true to the old ways and practiced them nonetheless. Above all, I worshipped *Kiehtan*, the creator. I had been fortunate. My French husband respected my heritage. He embraced my beliefs, and I tolerated most of his. Even as a young girl, I knew the source of my strength. I might adopt some European mannerism or etiquette, but beyond surface behavior, I saw no inner substance from which to draw. So when I came upon the little girl sitting on the beach watching the canoe head back from where it had come, I knew I would be faithful to my ancestral responsibilities and raise Cessie as my own despite that fact that this was no place for a young girl. The other two—Rachel and Mariana—had been old enough to fend for themselves, even if they hadn't realized it early on. They never needed my attention once they got used to the goings on at the tavern.

However, this one had been sent to me for a reason. That much I sensed, and I would not question it. I would keep the girl safe from the diseases that ravaged so many. The girl's father believed I could do that, or he wouldn't have sent her to me. And he believed the ancestral island would nurture Cessie as well. Because of the island's current use, he may have questioned his decision, but he believed its sacredness remained—in the rocks, in the vegetation, in the fog—even if his people no longer wintered there. And he was right—the sacredness remained. Leaving her here, though, may have been his last resort and final hope. She must have been well loved.

I learned to love Cessie too even though her unusually large eyes registered no sign of understanding or acceptance of love. I assumed that since we were kin, Cessie would sense my feelings despite my reluctance to display affection to others openly. Rachel and Mariana both grew to understand that I would do anything for them, protect them from any harm within my power. Love did not have to be spoken. Or be physical. It could reside in the mind. Be shown through actions. I was sure Cessie would come to know me as well although she would have to come to know herself first. She seemed so fragile, birdlike almost, but her sorrow spoke of a huge, sad, hidden heart.

Cessie wouldn't speak the day I found her on the beach. I had been collecting rose hips that morning and had wandered along the shore where the rose bushes grew in profusion. When I placed my basket full of the hard orangey- red fruits at Cessie's feet, the child didn't look at it or up at me. So I sat down beside her on the sand as the child gazed across the water and watched the trail made from the canoe disappear. When I sensed it was time to return to my tavern duties, I stood up and reached for Cessie's hand. The young girl took it although I felt no life in her touch. Still, the child must have known that she had no choice and so, she placed her cold hand in mine.

I resolved as we walked up to the tavern to find ways to reach this child who hid her emotions even deeper than I did, but as time wore on, I was never able to access Cessie's thoughts completely. Neither could Rachel and Mariana, who both tried to welcome the child into our home. She rarely smiled, and when she did, it seemed she was just imitating those around her to keep them distanced from her inner life. She wasn't able to shed that despair that all children who believe they have been rejected carry with them. She was like the smoke from *Maushop's* pipe. No one can hold the fog in her hands, and I found I could never gain Cessie's complete trust. The child must have grieved for her people greatly, but she never spoke of them, even to me who would have known her relatives.

Still. She was so sweet. So sweet. I'm not one to cry, but I often wanted to cry for her. Maybe then Cessie would lose that pained expression she wore on her face when she thought no one was observing her. As the days passed into months and on into years, Cessie kept to herself but always did more than her share of the work. She seemed to thrive on giving. She didn't know how to take. She believed she had been given away. Thought she was never missed. Did not possess the capacity to know how much I and the others loved her.

Chapter 8

1702

Oil and Water

(Charlotte Primrose)

Oh, the stench! What is it about these men, lads some of them, that makes me stay here? Surely, I could do quite well elsewhere with what I have to offer. So far, this country is no better than England. It is just as dirty and even less civilised. In my work, I have spent time in far more lavish surroundings. Servants pampered me. The finest of silk garments adorned my body. I wanted for no material pleasure. Through my own efforts, mine had come to be a comfortable life.

Yet, I cannot fool myself. I know exactly why I stay. Even with the awful smell that accompanies the trying out of the oil, there is a wildness in the men that results from their whale activity. They become stimulated by all the blood that coats their clothing, the smoke that permeates their hair, the oil that seeps into their pores, the quick pace of the work itself. It is a ghastly business, this trying out. I refuse to watch them as they toil along the shore, slicing through the whale blubber, stoking the great fires. I will not watch. It repulses me. Instead, I wait upstairs—resting— because I know that once these men are finished with the wearisome work, they are not weary at all.

Quite the contrary. As Cessie heats the water that will bathe their faces and hands before Dark Ray allows them to take one step up the stairs to me, I too am preparing myself. I douse myself liberally with the sweetest perfume that a visitor from Spain gave me on his way to other ports. I brush my hair with a frenzy that produces static in the air around me. I wrap my body in anticipation with the best of my undergarments from London. I primp and preen in front of the one looking glass we have in our bedchamber. I know I am the men's favorite on nights such as this. We are well suited for each other. I am unlike others they have had. Rachel may be the dancer, and who knows what they think of that prudish Mariana, but I am their ultimate reward for a hard day's labor. I alone can match their savage wildness.

The trying out renders the oil out of the whale. The oil lubricates the hands of the men who work the whales. It seduces their senses. It prepares them for me as I so easily take up their sensuality in my two hands and give them the best part of the trying out experience. How I love these nights! They bring out the best in me—I glow, satisfied for a time that I can control my destiny. I am in charge.

Society belittles what I do, but I do not care about other people's opinions. Too much of this bitter life is starved of sensual pleasure. Not my life. I make my living with my body. I do not believe fornication is evil. All animals do it. Human beings are fortunate enough to be thinking animals. They can consort even when they have no intention of procreating. I just want to use my body for what it was meant. Why waste natural talent?

I suspected I would earn a living this way, even as a young girl in London. The women in the streets seemed to command a good price and lived better than most others in my class. My parents were destitute poor—I was a girl—economic circumstances and female gender meant no schooling for me. From the time I was seven years old and the oldest of five, I was forced to help support my family as a laundress. While I had no cause to think of myself with grand airs, I knew I would never survive as someone's servant. I was destined for more. I saw how men looked at me in the streets on my way home from work. Even through the filth of my worn dress, the tangled mess of my hair, I was beautiful. I saw approval in others' faces as they noticed me.

And knowing one's assets makes for a smart businesswoman. My eyes were a clear green, not hazel, but deep green. Later when I traveled, I saw that the color resembled the clear seawater along sandy Caribbean shores. Once my body began to take on the defining curves of womanhood, the glances my way became even more pronounced. They seduced me those looks, making me want to know what might come of them. Perhaps they would rescue me from my tiresome laundry work.

One young man—about my age at the time, thirteen—was persistent about getting my attention as he watched me toil at my laundry station, so I gave it to him one day. I simply stared back at him until he became bold enough to speak first.

"Take a stroll with me?"

"Where?"

"Oh, along the river here and around that curve."

"You would not be meaning to hurt me, would you?"

"Sweet girl, I will be as gentle as I can."

That was the day I learned what the dark, moist space between my legs was for. And I realised in liaisons that followed how much power resided in that place. First, the power to gratify my own growing sensual needs. Second, in assisting others in gratifying theirs. Third, in making a living doing both.

Not much after that first encounter, I packed my meager belongings in a cloth sack and found my way to a boardinghouse for women of like persuasion. The work was good for about two years, but so many other girls in similar situations were discovering a way out of their miserable lives as well. Lying down for a customer was much easier and certainly filled the purse faster than washing other people's filthy clothes. Competition became fierce and downright dangerous. It was tedious, and I had no patience for it. Soon there were so many girls walking the streets of London, my livelihood was threatened, and I was not used to such stress. So I decided it was time for a change, and I sought to try my luck in Massachusetts Bay Colony.

I had no sustainable family ties in England having deserted my crowded ancestral home years before, after I had grown tired of enduring chapped laundress hands to help pay their meager bills. My ma and da seemed to care little for me except as someone to support their miserable lives. They pushed me out to work as soon as I could feed myself. Soppy drunks they were. Drinking and baby making—that is all they were good for. I was happy to be done with them. How I inherited my brains and beauty was a mystery to me. All else around me was squalor.

The talk of the great city of Boston in the New World was everywhere in the publick houses of London. In the absence of light-skinned women it was said, native and African females serviced the European men. The market for young, adventurous, English wenches was open for business. Hearing that, I did not hesitate to book a crossing with one of my regular customers and to travel over the Atlantic to start a new life.

The stories of Boston were true. Having the means to present myself at the most reputable house, I soon settled into life among my fellow countrymen in Boston. Although the original English colonists—those fanatical folks—had established the place expecting to expand their righteous and godly way of life, I learned that they succumbed to desires of the flesh as well. They enjoyed a tumble as much as someone with less religious inclinations. My capital increased. My richer clients spoiled me with expensive gifts. My fortunate luck lasted until the century turned. By then, however, there seemed to be as many women of my profession in Boston as there had been in London when I left in 1691. Business was again cutthroat, and I soon found myself ready to move on.

It did not help that I was becoming old for the job at the ripe age of twenty-seven. Always one to trust my instincts, I decided it was time to locate less competitive circumstances. Bostonians talked from time to time about an island tavern across the Bay at Billingsgate on Cape Cod. Through bits and pieces of information from clients, I gathered that while a Samuel Hawes owned the establishment, a woman of unknown origin ran the place. She had a few girls working with her to satisfy the needs of the whalers and other fishermen who spent their time at the tavern in the off hours.

At first I dismissed the notion of re-locating there. What did I want with smelly fishermen? I was a city girl accustomed to comfort—warm baths at will, finely scented bed linens, servants to wait on my every need. The thought of finding myself away from such things made me cranky for days. I was not ready to give up my soft way of life. As a child, I was already acquainted with living more coarsely, and I had fled from that existence the first chance I got.

But something else ultimately changed my mind and caused me to pack my bags with firm resolution. I did not like to acknowledge this truth, but someone had been stalking me, it seemed, and while I feared no man, this one unsettled me. I did not know his identity, but I sensed his unwavering and constant presence. In the streets when I left on sunny afternoons for a breath of fresh air. In the publick houses at night.

It was not just Boston where I encountered him. I was aware of him even when I lived in London, but back then, I had dismissed those occasions as delusion, youthful innocence. And yet, shortly after settling in Boston, the stalking returned. I could not describe his looks because I never actually saw his face. He tended to lurk in shadows out of full view. At times, however, I did see wisps of red hair poking out of his cap. I wondered why he did not visit my boardinghouse. Everyone knew where to find me, how to secure my services. I was perplexed. If he did not want to fuck me, what could he possibly want with me? I was not schooled except for what I observed and learned by myself—one might say I educated myself. Yet, I surely did not think of myself as wifely material. And while he never came closer to me than hovering just outside my direct line of vision, I knew he wanted me. He was desperate for me. I recognise yearning a long distance off. I often thought of going to him. I am bold and never afraid to approach a man. But I did not approach him. In his quiet, watchful way, I knew that he was offering me something I was not prepared to accept.

So I left Boston, determined to escape his gaze once and for all. He seemed used to city life—he did not appear to be a fisherman. Surely, I could lose him if I left for a place that would not interest him.

****

(Dark Ray)

Buttoning my bodice as I made my way down the stairs, my eyes weary, my hair—still black as my girlhood days—more out of its leather tie than in it, I resolved once again that I must resist the temptation of consorting and stick to running this place. It was enough work in itself. Here I was, already thirty-four years old, responsible for keeping the tavern going while the others still slept, their only concern this early in the day that they got their necessary rest. Except maybe Cessie. But who ever knew what she was thinking? I shook my head at my own folly. When would I give it up? I wasn't sure. There were some men who favored a woman with some flesh on her bones, and Rachel and Mariana didn't qualify in that category. I alone possessed the abundance that some of them desired. And too, I had needs of my own to fulfill. Ah, well. I'd be too old soon to care either way.

As I rolled out the dough that would become the day's bread, I heard someone enter the tavern at the front door. Who could that be? Had one of the men returned for some reason? I left my work and entered the hall to find a woman waving an ivory fan across her face and waiting impatiently for whoever came with her up the path. Sure enough, seconds later, two burly men, short of breath, entered the room carrying a huge leather trunk between them.

I looked at the tall, well-formed woman to the men and back to the woman. I decided the woman was in charge.

"What brings you here at this hour of the day?"

"Well, my heavens. That is a fine greeting! Are you Dark Ray? I was told you might be ornery, and I guess my sources were correct."

"So." I reached for my clay pipe and started to work its contents for lighting. "What else did your sources tell you? And again, why are you here? You certainly don't look like someone who would seek an out of the way place such as this."

Which was true. Squinting through my pipe's smoke, I could see and hear that the woman was obviously not from the region. Her speech sounded more like the newer English colonists than those who had been living in Billingsgate for a while. She was dressed in fine silk and expensive lace. Her person seemed well tended. Her hands were smooth. This woman was not used to manual labor. She looked to be somewhere in her mid-twenties—not young, but far from ancient—and she was exceedingly beautiful although her skin was not as taut as someone younger. She was showing signs of that beginning fade from beautiful into handsome that would become more evident in the next ten years. But her clear light green eyes retained a youthful sparkle and playfulness that was completely arresting and would cause a man to look no further, unless he caught sight of her ample bosom, and then the whole body was up for assessment. And it was stately.

"It is dreadfully early, is it not? I am terribly exhausted from the travel." The woman haughtily motioned to the men who were still holding the trunk in mid-air. "Oh, sorry, chaps. You can place that down for now and go out for a breath of air. We will wait to see where this good woman puts me up. I will call you in when I need you."

"Puts you up?" I repeated. "Are you serious to think that someone the likes of you will feel comfortable with these accommodations? Look around you. The rooms are large, but these are all the rooms down here, except for the kitchen in the back, and the space upstairs is divided into two bedchambers—one is the common sleeping quarters for all the women, and the other is for entertaining our guests. Judging from your appearance, you are used to more private arrangements."

"You would be right about that. Mind if I sit down?" Before I could respond, she fell dramatically onto the settle. "But my current style of dress does not reflect accurately all the conditions under which I have worked. Come. Let us get to know one another. I am Charlotte Primrose, lately from Boston and originally from the streets of London where I can assure you my living conditions were far inferior to this tavern."

"I like adventure," Charlotte continued, "and I love my work, and I am quite sure I will be good for business. Why, I even have some customers from all parts of the globe who visit me wherever I go."

"I am still somewhat confused. You are thinking to live and work here? Forgive me, but you will not last a day with these whalers for all your worldly airs," I declared, letting a raucous laugh escape in the process.

Charlotte's eyes narrowed, and she stood up to move directly in front of me. I was a tall woman but not as leggy as Charlotte.

"Look here, good woman, you do not know me. How can you have any idea what I am capable of enduring? I would think, instead, that you would welcome a new woman to add some spice to a place like this, and here you are trying to discourage me. I will not have it!" Her indignation expressed, Charlotte paused and then switched to a calmer demeanor.

"It appears we are both wise businesswomen," continued Charlotte. "Suppose we agree to my staying here for a month in which time if I do not bring in more customers or at the least, keep the present ones content, then I will go. What do you say to that?"

Although skeptical, I considered. With more money coming in, I could afford to order those things Samuel Hawes' son, the current owner, would not purchase—he kept our allowance meager and refused to provide what he did not think was necessary. Yet, there were more of us living here now. We needed personal items he wasn't concerned about funding. He said my work was to run the tavern, but I also felt responsible for the women's well-being and made every effort to stretch his money and what small pittance some customers would offer us to cover all our needs.

So, I decided to accept Charlotte's proposal. What was to lose in letting this one experience the howling wind through the drafty walls, the whalers' crude jokes and their rough hands? That skin of hers was used to perfumed baths. Let her see what working out on an island with fishermen was like. I straightened up and extended my hand to Charlotte.

"Perhaps I misjudged you. I will agree to your deal, but I am warning you. You will receive no special treatment. You will share the common space with the other women. Here they are now." I looked up at the three who were standing at the top of the stairs, clearly curious about this new arrival. "This is Rachel, Mariana, and Cessie."

I returned to stare hard at Charlotte. "You will not put on airs with the hard-working fishermen who come in here for food, drink, relaxation, and some merriment. If at any time you make life harder for me than it already is, you will find yourself on the next boat to Boston or whatever other port will take you. Understand?"

Charlotte was visibly annoyed by this speech, but she was also tired and probably hungry as well. Maybe she had no other choice. No place else to go. I thought so because she cheerily waved up at the women, even though, after taking them in from head to toe, she seemed dismayed by their homespun appearance. Then she responded directly to me. "You have a deal, and you will see. I will make money for this place. I always do."

Part II

1703-1730

The Bonding

"Pilot whales form some of the most highly cohesive social groups in the world…. They take their name from their habit of following one or more dominant members of the pod. Mature females, generally the leaders, form a good matriarchy."

---from an article in <u>The Cape Cod Times</u>, July 30, 2002

Chapter 9

1703

A Proper Wife

Mariana removed the wilted flowers from the tankard and replaced them with a fresh supply of the season's first daisies. Her curly black hair fell to her waist. She wore it this way when she was not working in the tavern. Otherwise, she fashioned it in one long braid down her back. She heard footsteps behind her, and as she stood up to face them, he was there before her with his open arms, ready to receive her.

"Oh, Manuel! You have arrived early today!" she squealed, as she met his lips on hers. "I am so happy to see you. Look. I have just replaced last week's flowers with these daisies. Mary will be pleased."

"Silly girl. Are you pleased? That is all that matters." He said these things as he sunk his face into her wonderful hair.

"What a question. When you are here, I am pleased. And when you are not, Mary is always with me."

Still holding her against him, his lips reached her ear. He bit it gently, then whispered, "How would it please you to be near me all the time? Have you not missed me during these last three years when we have been apart and I cannot get here to visit you?"

She drew back and looked into his dark brown eyes that were framed with drawn lines from constant sun exposure. "What are you asking me, Manuel?"

"You know me well, silly one. I am asking you to come with me to Provincetown. I have secured a little house that awaits you. You can set up a statue of the Virgin in your own garden. You do not need to remain here where others can have you. You should not want anyone but me. I want you all to myself. I will be nearby working the fishing nets, and when the evening sun sets, we can be in each other's arms almost every night. It will be far better than living here and being subject to Dark Ray's orders. You can have your own home."

"Are you asking me to marry you?"

He looked away, acting like he was interested in her flower offering to the Virgin. "Come with me. In the eyes of God, we are already wed."

"Yes, of course, my love, but will we ask a priest to sanctify our union?" With her hand, Mariana gently directed his face back to hers. "Tell me, Manuel, does this mean we will have children, and I can stop protecting against their conception?"

He shifted his weight and stood apart from her, but he continued to hold her hands.

"Just come with me. It will all work out."

Why was she hesitating? Had she not she prayed to Mary for this very moment? A proper life with beautiful, healthy children running outside as she prepared the kale soup for when their father returned from fishing. Her life spent nurturing her own family under the protective gaze of the Great Mother Mary.

"Yes, Manuel. I want to go with you. You offer all I have prayed for these last three years. When can we leave?"

He embraced her again. "We can leave as soon as you can ready yourself. I have a shallop waiting to take us back to Provincetown today. The weather is fine for the trip."

"Now? Can you really mean it?"

"Yes, of course. I mean everything I say to you. Come. Let us not delay. I want you to see your little house before dark."

As he headed off to the beach to wait, Mariana ran back to the tavern to tell her news to Dark Ray and the others. When she saw the older woman tending to the chowder at the fireplace, she stopped. How could she leave another mother behind? Was her life a series of leaving the women who nurtured her and not looking back? What had her life been worth, though, living here? She had always felt remorse from her actions and the actions of the other women around her. They allowed themselves to succumb to their fleshly desires too easily. Had she only been playing at serving Mary here? Yes, she loved Dark Ray especially, and the others, but surely, she was meant to live a different life. A respectable one as a proper wife. Holy Mary, Mother of God.

Dark Ray looked up from the chowder pot and saw Mariana lost in thought. She knew life here had not been as suitable for Mariana as it had been for the others. As Mariana matured into a young woman, Dark Ray wondered why she stayed. She continued to remain devoted to her shrine and her fanatical prayers, but despite Mariana's resourcefulness around the tavern, she never developed an independent spirit—one that would give her the same confidence to seek a new life as she once did out of necessity as a small girl. Dark Ray put down her wooden spoon, reached for her clay pipe, and lit its contents as she motioned to Mariana to sit on the settle with her as she smoked.

"What is it, Mariana? You don't often look this disturbed. Is that Portagee fisherman distressing you? I saw him making his way to your shrine earlier. Say what you will, but I think that one is trouble. And yet, you choose to spend your free time with him whenever he is here. Just because he speaks the language of your people does not mean you should pick him out of all the others who seek your company. Other fishermen speak your native tongue, too." Dark Ray took a full drag of her pipe and then through her teeth, she added, "There is something about him that I don't like."

"You do not understand him, Ray. He treats me fine. Listen," she said impatiently. "This is what you read on my face. He wants me to go back to Provincetown with him. He has a house for me. He wants us to be together."

Dark Ray removed the pipe from her mouth and looked intently at Mariana's face. "So. Has he promised to make an honest woman out of you? Catholics like him are stubborn about such things. You of all women know that."

Mariana's eyes filled with tears as she voiced her conflict. "He says we can work everything out when we get there. Please give me your blessing, Ray. You are the only earthly mother I have. While I am so eager to be with Manuel, I am reluctant to leave a mother again. Hail Mary, full of grace."

"Dear Mariana, you don't need my blessing. You are a grown woman. Ask your Mary for her blessing, but not me. I will only tell you that you are free to choose your own path. All I ask is that you think about it, and if you still decide to go, then go with a happy heart that you made the decision for yourself. Remember also that—no matter what this place is—you always have a home here if you need it."

Dark Ray stood up and returned to stir the chowder and to stoke the fire. She added a log and refused to speak more. Facing the great brick hearth, she watched the flames ignite the new wood. She remained silent.

Mariana continued to weep quietly, and her voice exposed her confusion. She stood up but leaned against the threshold by the settle. "I cannot think any longer about it. The shallop waits. I must gather my things and go. Manuel is expecting me. I think I must go with him now or not at all. I am already twenty-two years old. Will I have another chance to make my own home?"

Silence.

"I am ready to go and start a new life, but I will miss you, Ray. I love you."

Silence.

Although reluctant to depart this way, Mariana ran up the stairs to collect her other dress, some undergarments, the warm winter shawl she'd knit from the sheep's wool. As she raced down the path to the beach, she slowed down momentarily to consider her plaster statue of Mary. She decided to leave it at her shrine to

protect her island family. Manuel would get her another for her

own garden.

Chapter 10

Big Momma

1703

(Dark Ray)

There were days when it seemed all I did around the tavern besides take in desperate females was to give the male customers an education in good manners. They must have believed because I was a woman, they could boss me around and call me names *they* found endearing. Sometimes I was not in the mood for their affection.

"Hey, Big Momma," one of the new men yelled across the bar one night. "Pour me a draught of your good flip."

I needed to hear that just once from this redheaded upstart. He was not like the other men. When he showed up alone a few days ago, I wasn't sure why he had an interest in this place because I couldn't imagine him capable of doing the whale work. There was something about him—almost feminine—and yet his features were manly, his size substantial. Charlotte, who never seemed particular about the men she bedded, would not go near him, and she especially liked to break in the new ones. When I thought more about it, when Charlotte first encountered him last week, she turned as deathly white as Rachel looked when she arrived years ago. Then Charlotte quickly turned on her heels and shot up the stairs faster than I'd ever seen her move. She didn't leave the women's bedchamber until the next morning, and then she was in a sour mood.

What frightened her I couldn't understand because there was kindness in this man's open expression, his freckled cheeks, his pale blue eyes. At Charlotte's reaction, he blinked, blushed, and watched her retreat. Yet, I saw affection in his gaze. But the night he called me Big Momma, he pushed the limits of my good nature, and I was not about to spare his feelings. I didn't move anywhere near his direction. I kept chopping the oysters, mussels, and clams for the chowder.

"Momma, you hear me? The flip. They say it is the best outside Boston. Has the right amount of sweet molasses, dried pumpkin, rum, and nutmeg spiciness—all mixed frothy into the ale. Or do you use cider as your base? I wager you would not share your recipe now, would you?" He leaned forward on the bar. "You fetching me some or not?" He looked around to see if he was making an impression on his new friends. They refused to meet his glances. They knew better.

I looked up from my chopping. Slowly. The knife still in my hands. I took him in with one slanty-eyed glance. I dropped the knife on the table, went to the flip barrel, pulled off a pint, and walked over to him, placing the mug within his reach. Then I waited. He looked lovingly at it, and right when he was about to swallow his first mouthful, I took my left hand and grabbed him around the throat. He didn't know whether to laugh or cry he was so surprised. My hand was so tight, he couldn't do either. All he could do was lose most of the first mouthful down his neck and shirt, the rest remaining in the cavity of his mouth, causing his gasps to sound a little like he was drowning instead of choking. I didn't grip his throat like this for long. I had no intention of killing him. My interest was to teach this fellow a lesson if he was going to hang around and whale from this site.

"I may be big, my good man, but I am surely not your Momma. If I were, you wouldn't be sitting here right now because I would never allow the puny likes of you to breathe on this good earth. Are you beginning to see who's in charge here? Show some respect, and we'll get along. I'm Dark Ray. That's what you call me. Nothing else."

I released his bony throat, and he coughed up the remaining flip from the recesses of his mouth before he could speak. He wiped his lips with the back of his hand. Stared at me. Cockiness gone and the blush of embarrassment creeping up his neck.

"I am so sorry, Dark Ray, Ma'am. I meant no disrespect, but I am from away—London and most recently Boston—and I still do not know the customs of this country. Can you forgive me, for fuck's sake? I truly did not mean to disparage you. Name's

Dodger. Jack Dodger," and he extended a tentative hand in friendship.

The other men at the bar watched this exchange with quiet amusement, their snickers muffled by their arm sleeves. I ignored them and Dodger's attempt at reconciliation. I would not accept his forgiveness yet, so I turned my back and returned to my chowder. But I believed I was going to like this freckly molly who clearly seemed to be enjoying my flip at an alarming speed given the sound of his slurping. There was something about him that I took to—I'm a sap for redheads, maybe. They sometimes act mouthy on the surface, but underneath that exterior attitude, there is usually a cuddly pup looking for warmth and affection. As time went by and this fellow's real reason for coming here unfolded, I complimented myself for having a true sense of him from our first meeting. Endearing names aside.

Chapter 11

1704

Spoiled Flowers

When the little blue flowers bloomed that summer on the island, it seemed they would grow unnoticed for Mariana was no longer there to herald their arrival. However, before the season passed completely, she returned, her long hair in a heavy braid down her back, her right eye as black as her hair. She entered the tavern, sank down onto the settle, and stared straight ahead at the dining room. She didn't seem to hear Rachel as she came up to the front door with buckets filled with water from the spring. Mariana sat like a lifeless statue. There was no danger of her spilling the water as she did the first time she entered this room ten years ago.

Leaving the buckets at the door's entrance, Rachel swiftly moved to Mariana's side. "Mariana! Why are you here? When you left so abruptly a few months ago, Ray explained that you had gone to Provincetown with Manuel. I was so happy for you—I knew that was your dream." She stopped speaking and examined Mariana's face. "What happened to your eye?" Rachel gently placed her small hand on Mariana's right cheek. "Oh, Dear, tell me what happened to you."

Through her sobs, Mariana related her story. Dark Ray appeared half in the dining room cellar entrance. She had heard voices above and came up the ladder partway to see the two young women and listened to Mariana's tale. They were unaware of her presence.

"He was already married. He even had children. I only just learned this, or I would have returned sooner. How could I have stayed? He set me up in a small cottage by the wharf farthest from the center of town. For a time I was happier than I had ever been. He did not always return in the evenings, but I know that fishermen cannot keep regular hours. He was always pleased to see me at home in his town, tending my small patch of garden, setting up my new shrine, preparing the simple Portuguese food he taught me to make. Despite all this happiness, I kept asking him when we were going to be officially wed. I so wanted to raise children with Mary's blessings. He gave me half answers and changed the subject." She paused. "That did not stop me from asking."

Neither Rachel nor Dark Ray interrupted Mariana; instead they remained quietly and allowed her to continue.

"Over time, he became irritated with my constant prattle of matrimony and began to leave the cottage whenever I pressed him too hard. And then the other day when I was at the market, I realized that other women were staring at me with disgust. I had never noticed this behavior before. Maybe I had been so distracted by my new life that I did not see the real truth surrounding me. One bold one spoke up, and because my Portuguese had returned from speaking with Manuel, I understood what she was saying."

Mariana hesitated, covered her face, and sat silently before she could go on. As she resumed her story, her voice became louder and cracked with emotion. "Pray for us sinners. She called me his whore. She cursed my existence with the cruelest of words. She said that I would burn in hell for the sins I was committing. She said that Manuel would burn alongside me for what he was doing to his wife and children.

"I hurried out of the marketplace, shocked at her words, ashamed that I had been all this time with another woman's husband. Ashamed is not strong enough a word. I was mortified. I felt dirty. That night when Manuel returned, he saw my red eyes and wanted to know what was wrong. I told him outright what happened that day. He started to deny the certainty of this information, but when I said he was lying because I had finally understood why he would not marry me properly—he could not— his punch to my face sent me across the room.

"I lay against the wall as he finally shouted the truth to me. 'What did you think you were, you silly ignorant woman? What are you if not a whore? I took you from a tavern where I may have been your first, but I was surely not your only. Do you think I would want any children of mine to come out of that place where other men have been? You should have been happy to get out of there. I secured you a place of your own. You should be grateful to me. Instead, you whine about everything. Marry you? Never!' And then he slammed the door and headed, I assumed, to the publick house at the end of the wharf. Or maybe he returned to his real home that his wife kept and where his children were being raised. He did not come back to me that night. That much is certain."

Mariana let out a sob and continued to cover her face. "I am ashamed beyond words. How could I have been so blind? I could not stay a moment longer, so I packed up the garments I had brought, stole the coins Manuel kept in a jar, and paid my passage on a boat that was headed in this direction at first light."

Achy from standing so long on the rungs of the cellar ladder, Dark Ray shifted her weight and sighed. The young women jumped at the sound and at last saw her. "Have no fear, Mariana," she began, "no one here will judge you. I told you when you left that whatever this place is, it will always be your home. If that scoundrel ever sets foot on this island again, I will personally drive him off. He is no longer welcome here. I don't think he will though. His kind move on to easier conquests when times get rough. Don't waste your tears on him. You are worth more than that." As she ascended the steps and entered the room, Ray lifted her arm and pointed to the direction of Mariana's hollow. "Go now to your shrine. You will find it as you left it. Seek solace from your Mary. We need you here, Mariana. We want you here. This is where you belong."

As Dark Ray was speaking, Rachel took Mariana in her arms and stroked her back. She kissed her lightly on her black eye and nodded her head in agreement with Dark Ray's words. Tears streamed down Rachel's cheeks. She recalled her own heartbreak with Matthew Sweet, his betrothed, and the lies she thought were truths. She believed if Mariana could move past this pain, she too would have a chance, as Rachel had, to make her own life.

Mariana looked from one woman to another, offered each a weak smile and stood up. She turned to the door and left, her feet taking her slowly along the comforting familiar path to her Mary, but she felt no comfort. Wondered absently if she would ever experience comfort again, feel joy again. She was a discarded flower, not fresh enough to be set before a shrine.

****

(Mariana)

My feet recognized the rocks and visible roots along the path to my shrine. It was small relief to see my Mary among the blue flowers because I remembered that Manuel gave me that statue a long time ago, and I was overwhelmed once more with sadness and shame. Only now that I was back did I recollect the haste at which I re-packed the bag that I brought with me to Provincetown. And as I recollected that most recent flight, I was reminded of my escape so many years ago from Salem. My heart was heavy with sorrow then as well. Was I just a common thief who took what she needed to survive without any thought of others? For I stole that knife then to cut my hair and those breeches to disguise my sex, and I stole Manuel's coins to pay for my trip back to Great Island. Perhaps I deserved to be punished for my sinful actions. All of them. Pray for us sinners. Now and at the hour of our death.

The men who brought me back knew me, had been regular visitors to the tavern. They were kind not to question my actions. They allowed me to sit off to the side of the vessel, alone in my thoughts, as I looked out at the horizon, watched the sea birds as they followed the boat in hopes of an easy meal. I supposed I would have to be kinder to these men in return the next time they visited us. Yet, I had no desire to be with men. I even wondered on the trip back if I should join my mother by jumping overboard to my death. But Mary would not have approved. She endured her son's death. I would endure my sins.

When we arrived on this shore, I did not feel the hope for a better life as I had the first time a boat brought me here. I was no longer an eleven-year-old girl in disguise expecting to find a life that suited me. What would have suited me now? I thought being someone's wife, someone's mother, would be all I needed to assure a happy future. Would I ever love another man again? I was inclined to believe Manuel. I was not worthy. But I prayed for my soul and for those of the women who loved me regardless of what I was, a common whore. And in time, I hoped I would learn to smile again and appreciate the simple things. My little blue flowers. The smell of roses.

Chapter 12

1705

Snowbound

The flakes began as large, fluffy, circles of lace that fell
from the gray sky and left large wet splotches on their clothes.
Two hours later, the storm had increased in its intensity and
reduced the flakes to harder, more compact designs that stung the
exposed faces of the last of the whalers who were putting back to
Billingsgate shore. They knew the look of this sky, and those with
families were eager to return to town to be sure their loved ones
were safe. They took the single, stray men like Jack Dodger with

them. For the first time in a long while, no one stayed behind to keep the women busy.

By mid-day, every man was gone. Now it was a place inhabited solely by women. From the mainland, the island was not visible at all; the snow was falling so thickly, the tavern, even lit, was lost from sight. All alone behind this wall of snow, the women at first felt restless, not used to the quiet or the pace. Here they were, the five of them, left with nothing to do. The livestock had been secured, the bread was baked, the rooms were swept, the chamber pots emptied, the wood brought in and stacked by the hearth. They were sitting in the dining room, their stools and benches forming a semi-circle around the fireplace as they placed their stockinged feet precariously close to the flames.

"Is there something else to be done?" Rachel asked Dark Ray. "Have we forgotten anything?"

Cessie sat quietly by the hearth off a bit by herself and not too close to the adult women. She'd been living at the tavern for five years since Dark Ray found her alone on the shore, and during this time, she had never quite grown used to her situation. She spoke only when she was addressed, and she found ways to avoid the company of others. She made it a practice to keep to herself and to stay busy—so busy she dropped exhaustedly into sleep as soon as Dark Ray sent her to their upstairs bedchamber. Dark Ray tried to encourage her to spend more of her hours with the other women, but Cessie did not made an effort, and now she wasn't sure she was going to like being cooped up with them during this storm.

Her immediate fear was that Charlotte would become bored and start to pick on her. Of all the women, Cessie trusted Charlotte's motives the least. Often she had the misfortune of being in Charlotte's line of vision when she wanted something and expected someone else to do it for her. If Cessie could feign invisibility today, maybe Charlotte would ignore her, so she attempted to make herself small against the bench she sat on.

Dark Ray looked over at Rachel. "No, we're as secure as we're going to be in this storm. Those lily-livered men bolted out of here in a hurry as soon as the flakes changed. Only Jack Dodger was willing to stay behind, but thought better of it when he realized he would be the only one of his kind remaining. I suppose you were relieved about that one's leaving, eh Charlotte?"

The formal and stately Charlotte always sniffed before she spoke. "Whatever do you mean, Ray? Why would I care one way or the other about that one?"

Dark Ray just shrugged and laughed, but Rachel couldn't resist the taunt. "Oh, come now, Charlotte. You blanch every time the poor fellow walks in the tavern. You have never once attempted to be friendly with him. Why is that?"

"All right, if you must know," Charlotte huffed. "He makes my skin crawl like it is covered with vermin. I just do not like his looks. That is all!" But her words were superficial, and they all sensed it.

"You do not like his looks?" Mariana joined in uncharacteristically, but the absence of men made her feel spirited. "Are you trying to tell us you prefer that smelly old William Oates whose breath is enough to straighten my hair? Why, that man reeks of his beloved garlic, and yet, I know you have entertained him upstairs a time or two. I would think you would take Jack over him any day—he seems very gentle, but he does not seem interested in any sporting although something tells me he would go up there with you. When you are in sight, he will not take his eyes off you."

"Well, Mariana, that is the justice of this place. Ray does not force us to take anyone we do not want. Believe me, I have been at establishments where the women have no choice whatsoever in whom they entertain. And yes. William has been up there with me, but not every man wants the same thing from us. You all know that, I trust." She paused and decided to offer more information to the unenlightened. "William is actually very easy to accommodate."

Rachel dragged another bench over to the semi-circle to form a plank long enough to support her entire torso. She settled on her stomach, her hands cupping her face as she looked up at the women.

"Ooh. This is getting very interesting. Do tell us, Mistress Charlotte, what William Oates likes!"

"I declare. Is there no privacy here? Ray, must I continue?"

Dark Ray, highly amused by this banter and enjoying the rare free time, wouldn't mind hearing herself. "What's the harm,

Charlotte? There's a snowstorm raging outside. We won't see another living soul much before tomorrow afternoon. Let's put our guards down and relax with each other, shall we? Who knows when we'll ever have this chance again to sit still at the same time and in the same place?"

She stopped and gazed at the flames in the fire. "This day reminds me of the old times when my people wintered here, and the elders told us stories around the fire to pass the time." She turned to Cessie. "It's a pity, Cessie. You're too young to know those times." When she got no reaction from the young girl, she changed the subject. "Would you mind fetching us all a pint of flip? I think I'll light up my pipe as well."

Relieved, but momentarily surprised at being seen after having tried so hard at invisibility, Cessie straightened up and wordlessly left the room. Mariana prompted, "All right now. Tell us fast before that young one returns with the flip. Hail, Mary. She is only eleven, and I worry about what she sees and hears around here. Quickly, Charlotte!"

"I do not like being rushed, Mariana, but here it is: William Oates likes to watch me pleasure myself. That is all."

"Whatever do you mean, 'that is all'?" repeated Rachel. "Does he not even whip out his prick and relieve himself as he watches?"

"No. He sits upright at the edge of the bedstead just like the gentleman he is, says not a word, makes not a move, and smiles broadly when I am finished. So there you have it," Charlotte concluded just as Cessie entered the circle with a serving tray of filled pints.

Rachel burst out laughing.

"You are joking, yes, Charlotte? A gentleman? No wonder the poor man walks around here like he has a load in his pants. He does! I swear, at times, I have noticed his breeches looking a little wet around the crotch. I had been thinking all this time the poor 'gentleman' had trouble controlling his water."

With this last remark, pandemonium reigned. Hands went up in the air, hands held stomachs, hands got slapped on knees. Flip spilled. Tears of laughter dripped down cheeks. Even Charlotte couldn't help joining the fracas; only Cessie was on her guard as the grown women became boisterously loud. She'd never seen them act this way without customers.

Once again, Rachel stole the show, and the display of mirth among the women inspired her. She quickly sat up and said, "I have an idea. Let us play a game. Everyone has to tell a story about the worst partner she has ever had, but the tale does not have to be true. It is up to all of us to guess whether the story is real or fake. What do you think?" Before anyone could respond, she continued. "Wait. Before we begin, I am all of a sudden very hungry. Suppose I ladle out the stew we made this morning, Ray, and we can play while we eat?"

Charlotte stood up and yawned as if to indicate that this activity was beneath her sensibilities. "I suppose I am willing to give it a try, but if I get bored, I am going straight upstairs to bury my head under the covers and sleep through the storm."

Usually the most reserved of the women, Mariana gave Charlotte a frown. "Come now, Charlotte, it is a game—a bawdy one, but why not? We have time on our hands. Let us play for once."

Ever since she returned from Provincetown last year when she learned the truth about Manuel, Mariana avoided male company and devoted her time to such activities as mending the women's clothing, assisting in the kitchen, and spinning wool. However, she was feeling restless and tired of her routine, and Rachel and Dark Ray were heartened by Mariana's interest in participating. Rachel had always been able to bring her out of her private gloom, and today was no exception.

Dark Ray nodded her head in agreement with Mariana. She walked over to the door and opened it a crack to see the snow piling up against the building. She bolted it tightly and faced the group. "Sounds fine to me. It doesn't look like we're going to see anyone else today. Let's amuse ourselves instead. I'll fetch a bowl of bread to go with the stew and more flip. Or do we want something stronger to wash down our meal?"

"I would not mind some of that sweet wine from Portugal, Ray," said Mariana. "I will go down to the storage cellar and bring up a few bottles. I feel like getting sloppy today. It has been a long year. Holy Mary, Mother of God."

"Good enough, then," said Dark Ray, relieved to see Mariana so light-hearted. She had been morose and withdrawn, refusing to socialize with the customers since her confrontation with Manuel. This day would be good for her. Then she spotted

Cessie leaning against an exposed beam, her large eyes wide as she took in the situation.

"Cessie, you don't need to stay with us. Perhaps you should go upstairs to our bedchamber and play with your poppets and cat's cradle. You never have time for them. Take a bowl of stew up with you."

The young girl nodded, and thankful to be truly out of sight, she hastily ladled the stew into a bowl and disappeared to the second floor.

"I will begin," Rachel declared. "Let us see. Yes, I have one. A couple of years ago, I was on my way back from the spring, and Zachariah Smith was at the first lookout tower watching for whales. He saw me approaching and offered to carry the buckets back here if I would visit with him for a while. So I said, 'Just for a few minutes. Ray needs this water for cooking.' He said, 'It will not take long, Rachel.' I could tell he had been hoping one of us would come by because his breeches were practically down at his ankles by the time I finished climbing the ladder to the landing. Keep in mind that the man is a bit far-sighted. He immediately proceeded to lift my skirt, fumble with the underdress, and even though he was close enough to insert himself in the right place, he missed completely and found himself stuck in the knot hole of the plank that I was leaning against.

The more he tried to pull himself out, the bigger his prick got. Thinking he was enjoying himself, I stepped aside, lowered my skirt, and said, 'You will not be needing me, Zachariah. I will bring the water to Ray myself,' and left before I burst out laughing. I did not want to hurt his feelings.

"So. True? False? Pass me that wine, Mariana."

Rachel looked around as she swigged the liquid right from the bottle. Charlotte was the first to speak. "I say false. I know that knot hole, and I know Zachariah, and he does not possess what it takes to fill it!"

The women snorted with laughter. Even Mariana, who had decided to keep one of the Madeira bottles to herself, was relaxed and enjoying the day. They continued to tell their stories, real or fake, throughout the afternoon as the snow piled up against the building and outside all was a quiet shush of falling snow. They ate to their hearts' content. They drank until they were giddy. They laughed uproariously throughout it all. Charlotte stayed.

Mariana loosened up. Dark Ray and Rachel were themselves—only more intoxicated.

By the end of the evening, they even attempted to play music and dance. Charlotte picked up Elisha's fiddle, Mariana found a left-behind mouth harp, and Rachel and Dark Ray danced to the cacophony of what sounded like music to them. Having returned to the dining room, Cessie sat with guarded amusement and watched the women make the most of being snowbound.

When the snow finally ended that night and the moon broke through the remaining clouds, it shone through the windows on the contented sleeping forms of the tavern women strewn every which way across the dining room furniture. Nowhere to go. No need to be anywhere else. Tomorrow would be a slow, headachy day, but this snowy day they bridged differences, and their bond would sustain them.

Chapter 13

1708

The Tide

Her life as she knew it was over. It was all about to change. Last night she was awakened by a warm thick wetness between her legs. For a moment, Cessie thought she had peed in her sleep, but when she got out of bed to examine her bedclothes, she could see in the moonlight that the wetness was dark. She knew this meant—that at fourteen, she was officially a woman. Dark Ray told her this day was coming. She did not feel like a woman, and she did not want to be one, either. She did not like what women do with their bodies—have sex, bear children. She wanted none of that. She wanted her body simply to be the vessel that housed her mind and spirit. She did not want her physicality to count for anything beyond that. She continued to yearn for invisibility.

But she was not. And the next day as Cessie sat alone on the shore where eight years ago she was left by the people she loved, she knew her fate had gone from bad to worse in one night. Her thoughts went to Dark Ray who surely needed her help. This time of morning was the busiest; preparations must be made for the mid-day meal, the rooms must be swept, livestock tended, so many things, and then of course, if they desired, the older women were available for the men later on.

She knew it was inevitable that soon the men would notice her. Her body had started to fill out. Already some of them had watched her more intently than in time past. They had begun to reach for her buttocks as she served up their food, but she managed to slip out of their grasp. They laughed at her reluctance and told her someday she would like their attention. Would she? She knew that Charlotte thrived on it. She knew Rachel danced for it. She knew on occasion Dark Ray indulged in it. Even Mariana, who lived and breathed the teachings of her Mary's divine love, couldn't help herself and succumbed to it, although afterwards, she seemed sad.

Cessie stretched her legs in front of her. She lifted her skirt and examined the space between her thighs. What did it feel like? If she tried it once, would that be enough to know? Would she want more? When this bleeding subsided, maybe she should, although she became sick at the thought of a man entering her most private of places, a part of her that had truly remained invisible up to now.

****

A week elapsed, and her first menstrual cycle ended. Cessie thought of little else, but she would not share her musings with the other women. She paid more attention to how the women looked after their time with the men. Mariana visited her shrine in the hollow between the two lookout towers and kneeled in sorrow before her Mary statue the morning after. But then she returned to the tavern, and there was only the look of peace on her face. Ray seemed completely unaffected, but she didn't usually show emotion of any kind. Rachel smiled more brightly. Charlotte behaved like a well-fed cat. What then could be the harm? Did she not yearn for someone to touch her? Hadn't she herself begun to finger these parts that had a new sensitivity to her touch just before she fell off to sleep? She would do it, then, but not up there where they all went. She would take that young *Nauset* boy who came to work here lately, and she would lead him down to the beach where she liked to go to be alone. He would be the one—he was one of her people.

It was twilight. Most people were relaxing in the downstairs rooms. The pipes were lit, but the music had not yet started. Outside, Cessie secured the chickens in their shed to keep them safe from foxes, and then she returned to eye the tall thin *Nauset* boy as he sat alone in a corner observing this relatively new surrounding. He caught her gaze. She tilted her head to the front door. He lowered his eyes, waited until she left ahead of him and then followed her out. From the chicken yard, she walked southeast, avoiding the main path and taking one favored by the sheep. Although he was right behind her, they did not speak.

When they arrived at the beach, she took a sudden turn and walked to the dune where there was a recessed hollow. Without looking at him, she reached behind, grabbed his arm, and pulled him into her secret place. He lost his footing, and together they toppled onto the sand. They were too close to avoid eye contact, and he stared at her in the dimming light, waiting for her direction. She had none, and she looked back at him questioningly. Surely he knew what to do. Knew what he wanted better than she knew herself. Timidly, he brushed her lips with his. Again. This time more forcefully. They continued like this for a while, but then she felt his hand reaching up her skirt, and she knew it was coming.

She thought she would be able to calculate every move, but for the first time, her mind gave itself over to her body. It was her body that articulated the moment. It was her body that orchestrated her mind's commands. Now the two were straining to get closer, skin on skin, clothing aside. They were seduced by the feel of the other's partially exposed flesh. He rolled her to her stomach and lifted her onto her hands and knees. He was most familiar with that position. He had seen women taken this way from behind in his village. Imitation served them. She was unsure of the next step, but as he straddled her from behind, her fingers and toes dug into the sand for balance. She felt his hardness, and when he entered her and took her, first she was blinded by the pain, but then a warmth, joy, the touching, the rhythm, like the tides—in and out—and she loved it. And she hated it. And she loved it.

She hated it.

Chapter 14

1710

Value

One year spilled into the next and then the next, and Cessie was sixteen and no more at peace on the island than the first day she arrived. The other women, although different in temperament, formed close bonds; they seemed content with the course their lives had taken. Cessie couldn't stop believing that she would have been content, too if only *Kiehtan* had granted her the good fortune to have remained with her people. Although Dark Ray treated her as an adopted daughter, Cessie had not been able to give any love back. From time to time, she thought of returning to the mainland to locate surviving loved ones, but her instinct warned her she would find no one there. So she kept herself slavishly busy and tried especially to avoid the one she walked in on this morning.

"Cessie! Where have you been? Did I not tell you to clean the sand from these shoes? You know how I hate the grit against my stockings! I swear," Charlotte murmured more to herself than to the young girl who was standing at the room's threshold wishing she could turn and run. "I must stop agreeing to visit the whalers when they go to the lookout stations during the day. How I ever get talked into it, I do not know. But sometimes I become so bored waiting for the evenings. This place can be so dreary."

When she was in this kind of restless mood, Charlotte yearned to be off to other more comfortable and stimulating surroundings. But she was well aware that her youth had been spent, and she sensed her arrival would not be welcomed at other establishments where younger more supple bodies could be had. Also, she had given up thinking she could escape Jack Dodger, who even in this confined space, had not approached her but had followed her there nevertheless. Theirs was an acknowledged and unspoken co-existence, a delicate arrangement that neither one of them seemed eager to disturb.

Charlotte paused to massage her feet and looked up at Cessie. "I am tired from working the afternoon and evening customers from yesterday. But then, you do not have to worry about such things, do you? When was the last time you were with one of the men?" Charlotte pulled on her stockings and sat on the bed, dangling her feet and waiting for Cessie to retrieve her shoes and brush the sand out of them.

Ordinarily, Cessie would have ignored Charlotte's taunting and even carried out her demand if only to silence her, but today she had the worst cramps, and her normally subdued temper flared. She so rarely spoke that the sound of her voice first came out squeaky but then strengthened to shouting.

"Look here, Charlotte, I am NOT your personal servant! You walk around this tavern thinking the rest of us were created to serve your demands. I may not be sought after like you, and I do not wish to be, but I have also not been put on this earth to see to your needs."

She took Charlotte's boots and tossed them over to her. "Clean your own shoes. Do you not see that I am trying to remove the linens from this bedstead? Will you please get off it? I follow Dark Ray's orders, not yours, and these linens should have been airing an hour ago, but you have only just decided to awaken and bless us with your nasty presence."

The two were upstairs in the visiting bedchamber, but their voices could be heard downstairs in the cooking area. Dark Ray waited before deciding to intercede as she generally did when Charlotte was demanding of Cessie. Today, however, Cessie seemed to be managing for herself. Her menses always made her testy—she did not like to be reminded of this most basic, primal function of her being—and on the first day of her cycle, she was sullen and disagreeable. How this behavior manifested in so quiet a creature, Dark Ray didn't know. What she did know was that Cessie was not comfortable in her body the way the other women were. The way she was. She was stunned, however, to hear how well the young girl was handling herself today with Charlotte. She had never heard Cessie speak up in her own defense before.

"It is the bed linens you are after," Charlotte proclaimed. "I wondered why you were in this room. Remember what it looks like? How the feather bed feels? I know. Here is a treat for you. As you scoop up the linens, be sure to bury your nose in them so you get a good hearty whiff of the man scent that clings to the fabric. That might just change your mood. Or would it? Maybe you like women instead? You are the one who is nasty! I see how you stare at Rachel with those cow eyes of yours."

Cessie stopped pulling at the bedding and glared at Charlotte. "Is there no decency in you? Why must you constantly deride me? You cannot possibly want anything I have."

She paused, not sure if she had the nerve to continue to speak her thoughts aloud; she had already said more than she was accustomed. But she was feeling cranky this morning. Why shouldn't she be honest? So, she said what she really thought. "Unless you begrudge me my youth."

Even Cessie herself was startled by the words that escaped her mouth. Charlotte's aging body was not something anyone had the courage to ridicule. All the women were aware of how a remark like this would send Charlotte into a tantrum. Once

Rachel, in her innocent way, suggested Charlotte sew some lace over her bodice so as not to expose so much flesh in the daylight as her low cut dresses revealed, and Charlotte left the island for a month to visit old friends in Boston.

"Your youth?!"

Charlotte started to strip the bedding herself and hurled it at the younger woman. The bundle missed and landed at Cessie's feet. "I would die first before I envied *your* youth. I would not be caught dead walking in your skin even if it meant being younger!"

That last remark was enough for Dark Ray to hear. She charged up the stairs, unsure which woman she would handle first. Her eyes noted the bed linens strewn on the floor, and she picked them up, shoved them in Cessie's arms, and said, "Get these outside to air. You will be having to put them back on the bedstead before much longer. Go!"

Charlotte slumped back onto the straw mattress, spent from the verbal exchange and stung by Cessie's references to her age. Dark Ray moved towards the bed and towered over her.

"Explain to me what gives you the right to torment her so. Have you ever considered that she might do more for you if you treated her with a little kindness?"

Charlotte responded by keeping her eyes firmly fixed on the ceiling. Her obstinate behavior did not silence Dark Ray. "You've been here for going on eight years. I have left you alone against my better judgment to structure your own time, and you have been a steady worker. The men favor your company—there's no question about that. This place has profited from your industry. Yet, I will tell you now. You have not been an easy person to like.

"I am warning you for the last time: stay away from Cessie. You knew when you came that this tavern was not like some of the other lodgings where you have worked. This place is here for more than what you provide, so do not think that you are the center of what goes on. You can be replaced. Never think you can't."

She paused briefly, thinking to stop, but she decided she might as well keep going. These were words she had wanted to say to Charlotte for a long time. "Charlotte, the problem with you is that you insist on living in the world of men, whereas, the rest of us here live in the world of women. We look out for each other.

We don't compete. We live to suit ourselves. You have attempted to join us from time to time, letting your guard down and socializing with us. You might try more often. You might be surprised at how pleasant that can be."

Charlotte appeared only to be half listening to Dark Ray. Throughout, she played with the lace on her undergarment as if Dark Ray's words were not valuable enough for her full attention. But Cessie's outburst had exposed her worst fear and left her feeling raw and unsettled—her body was aging. What would she do when men avoided her like they did Cessie? What would she be worth then?

Chapter 15

1713

No Value

It was no use. Cessie had lost her way and couldn't find a safe haven. Even her secret place where she now sat, where, already five years ago, she took the *Nauset* boy for their first time no longer provided the comfort it once did. She had never felt at home at the tavern, especially in the upstairs bedchamber where the women entertained. After that first time, Dark Ray, who had eyes as sharp as a hawk's, sensed that Cessie might be ready for the men and asked her if she was interested in their attention.

Cessie said, she supposed so, not knowing what else to say—feeling trapped, not only within her own body, but by the circumstances of this place as well. Nevertheless, she attempted to use her body for pleasure. The men sought her out at first, always looking for a fresh experience, but as the months went by, she was clearly the least favored. She didn't seem to mind. Lately, she was hardly ever in their company, having discouraged their advances. She didn't even seek out the *Nauset* boy any longer, and he showed no interest in her, either. Her body was of no concern to him or to any of them. Her body was of no use to her. It bled; it ached; it was not handsome, nor graceful like the other women's bodies. She was relieved that the men didn't want her. She couldn't put her heart into it. She tried to belong, to deal with the life *Kiehtan,* the creator of all, willed for her, but at every intimate encounter, she was reminded of how poorly she was made, how unloved she was.

Cessie's mind returned frequently to the day she was left on this shore. She was haunted by the scene—dim now that she was no longer a child, but not faded enough to be forgotten. The lapping waves against the canoe. The sad eyes of her father. The memory of her grandmother's arms wrapped warmly around her. Even though those arms as her grandmother's body lay on a pallet had grown cold by the time she and her father reached this island shore, she felt their comforting pressure on her skin. She still didn't understand why she couldn't have stayed among them. And if she died of the disease that took her beloved relatives, then she would have been happy to have followed them so quickly to the afterlife.

She wanted to blame someone. Dark Ray came to mind first; yet this woman had provided for her since her father left her on the beach. Her bond with Dark Ray was unspoken and sure, but not one that sustained her with any lasting warmth. All these years she kept to herself, fixated on the memories of her grandmother's love. She did not converse and mingle with people; she only served them. She felt sorry for Rachel who, in her warm and loving radiance, continually tried to reach her.

"Come, Cessie," Rachel urged one day, "Walk with me out to the Point. We have some free time, and it is a lovely day. Let us walk along the shore and let the lapping waters soothe our feet. We both could use a break." But Cessie mumbled that Dark Ray wanted her to mend a basket of stockings, and she turned away and headed to their bedchamber, leaving Rachel alone to watch her retreating back.

Yet, supreme loneliness was building like an angry storm in the smooth curves of her mind. It was enough to drown her. And as she sat that day with the mending in her lap, she wondered why she couldn't give herself over to that sweet woman. But she couldn't. It was not in her nature.

As Cessie lingered at her secret place contemplating the accumulated loneliness, she absent-mindedly picked up small rocks. She felt their smoothness in her hands as she rolled them around her palm, and then one by one threw each to the shoreline to be picked up by the next wave and returned to the ocean or heaved back onto shore depending on the rhythm of the tides. She stacked in piles the shells that her wandering hand found to adorn the entrance of the hollow. These shells once held the food that voraciously hungry seagulls feasted upon.

One of the shells was jagged, and as she placed it on one of the piles, the sharp edge of the oyster shell sliced her thumb. She took her wounded finger and put it in her mouth, sucking the blood from the cut. In the pain, she realized she felt a comfort, a release as soothing as the memory of her grandmother's hands braiding her hair. Retrieving the shell from the pile, she examined its shape. Like all the others along the beach, it was smooth on the inside where the oyster lived and rough on the outside of the shell that faced the world. Not unlike Cessie herself.

She slumped down on the sand and put her finger against the sharp edge where the shell broke unevenly from an impatient seagull's urgency to get at its contents. She lifted her skirt and began to move the jagged edge against the front of her left thigh. The pressure from the shell drew a red line across her skin. Fascinated by the sensation, Cessie increased the pressure of her hand against the shell. Blood rose to the surface in little beads along the edge of her broken skin. She tried again, and the second line produced the same feeling. With each scoring of her flesh, Cessie experienced a growing contentment so lacking in her life all these years. The blood felt seductively warm as it dripped from her leg. By inflicting these wounds on herself, she sensed a slow release of the deep pain she had carried within. Like an exhausted lover, she was spent. She fell back against the sandy wall of the dune. She wanted to sleep, a quiet unbroken sleep. She was satisfied at last however lonely.

Chapter 16

Evil Eye

1715

(Dark Ray)

People say that because my eyebrows grow straight across the bridge of my nose, I've been blessed with special powers. I'm not sure what physical appearance has to do with being able to see beyond what most don't recognize, but if that's what keeps them from messing with me, then I am fine with the story—I get power from my eyebrows.

What nonsense.

I don't need to be told from where my power originates—it was passed down to me from my mother's people who believed that *Kiehtan* the Creator bestowed his gift of extra sight on those strong enough to make use of it. The leather pouch I wear around my neck holds medicine long used by certain female members of my line. The words and the rituals that accompany its contents must be kept secret, are only passed on to others at specific moments in the year. Otherwise, the power gets lost in the telling. I guard my knowledge with the passion of a warrior in battle, and I keep the pouch under my dress—close to my skin. Men have seen it, have felt it graze their chests, have sensed they better not ask.

I refuse to put the evil eye on anyone myself because I believe power should not be used for harm. People may think otherwise, but that mistake only serves to keep them from becoming bothersome. I recognize, however, when the evil eye, cast by those with less honorable intentions, is present.

When Rachel arrived in 1691, I saw immediately that the young woman was carrying a child who was never going to survive. The story of Rachel's condition was visible on her face. There were the telltale shadows around Rachel's eyes. Her skin was ghostly pale—transparent, robbed of blood flow, the life force. Rachel was carrying death within her when she thought she was bearing life. I tried to keep her healthy in preparation for the imminent expulsion of that deathly mass, and she thrived despite her burden. But I was determined to learn who had set out to threaten Rachel's life because I never met anyone less deserving of such injustice. Only good and light radiated from Rachel.

I was aware that Rachel was a Sloane the moment I saw her. Rachel looked like her father, and I had known that self-righteous fool for years. He had been one of the investors in this whale station. Although he was harmless, I never liked him, but I realized that he loved his daughter dearly when I spoke to him shortly after Rachel's arrival. He begged me to care for his child like she was my own. I assured him I would. He was not to blame for his daughter's state, although I have known fathers who were.

My suspicions rested on the deacon instead. I generally don't have a good opinion of the servants of the Christian god. They wear specially ordained frocks that designate them as holier than their congregations, but those garments sometimes serve as useful masks to hide their corrupted souls. Based on Rachel's rendering of her relationship with her beloved deacon, I suspected him. However, I could not dismiss Rachel's supposedly helpful friends who provided her with measures to avoid pregnancy that worked only so long. First I needed to determine who had more to gain from working the evil eye—the deacon or the friends?

After some gentle questioning about the young women, I decided that foolishly jealous as they may have been, the friends might have aided Rachel's pregnancy, but they would not have the desire or evil nature to kill her—public disgrace being more along their line of thinking. That was why my suspicion fell exclusively on the deacon.

I needed to work fast if I was going to save Rachel, but I harbored no hope for what she was carrying. During that first week after her arrival, Rachel stayed close to me, performing every task with enthusiasm as she hid her torment well. I had heard Rachel's sobs more than once when she thought no one was listening. Rachel's growing trust enabled me to prod her about Deacon Sweet. If I could uncover his motive and method, I could work against the evil. Without that knowledge, any attempt at saving Rachel would take more time than she had to live.

"Why did he leave England, I wonder. Was he assigned to his post? Did he have family or friends already in the Colony?" I questioned as simply as I could. It was more my manner to speak openly and frankly without any pretense, but that style would not succeed in this case.

"Matthew never wanted to talk of it when I asked. He would quietly say that Divine Providence had brought him to Billingsgate and to me."

We continued to speak as I tended the lamb stew on the fire and Rachel spun wool nearby.

"You know, Rachel, I've never been inside the dwellings of the Christian clergy, but I pride myself on being familiar with European customs. Is it different from the homes of other European folk?"

"How do you mean, Ray? That is a strange question! Of course, all people have the same needs. There is a fireplace for cooking and heating, naturally, and a small bedchamber, a modest sitting area, storage shelves, a chamber pot." At this last item, Rachel giggled and put her hand over her mouth.

"Well, yes," I replied. "Europeans require those things, but are there, say, poppets or items of decoration different in their houses? And what of books? Are they all of a religious nature?"

"Yes. The books are surely religious although Matthew had some works as well by William Shakespeare, a very popular English poet and playwright. He treasured these volumes, but he assured me that most god-fearing Puritans would scorn his ownership of these texts as there was much paganism in the lines. These he kept out of the congregation's sight."

Rachel paused to think further, and as she did, she went over to one of the tables and placed a crust of bread in her mouth before returning to the spinning wheel. Chewing vigorously, she added the following information.

"He also had an early draft of a work by a Cotton Mather, I think. A friend of his. I took it down from his bedchamber shelf one day, but he quickly pulled the pages out of my hands. He said they spoke of issues I would not understand. I questioned him on it because he was always willing to instruct me on subjects in which I was ignorant." She brushed crumbs from her mouth. "But he acted strangely and said the writings were about matters of the invisible world, and it would do me well to remain in the visible one, for surely, that was where he wanted me."

At last Rachel had told me something useful, and even though I could read, I had no idea where I could procure a copy of this work in time to save Rachel. I was beginning to think I couldn't save her at all when she made a most startling statement.

"And he did seem to enjoy seeing me, Ray. After our lovemaking, he would just stare at me, his eyes taking in every inch of my being—I'm embarrassed to tell this part to you."

"Rachel, nothing you say can shock me. Please go on."

"Well, Matthew used to say his eyes could not get enough of me. Even though he might burn in the fires of hell for saying it, he told me I was elixir to him, and his eyes could drink me up. He wanted to consume all of me—my body, my mind, my soul. And I allowed him every scrap of myself. I lay there as long as I could possibly stay without my father wondering where I was, and I let him possess me with those different color eyes of his."

"Different color eyes? What do you mean, Rachel?"

"Matthew has one green eye and one blue. They were beautiful," Rachel broke off and for a moment was lost in her memories.

Like my straight across eyebrows, people with different color eyes are said to have the skill to cast the evil eye. I was sure I had uncovered the source of Rachel's declining health. Had she not become with child and so escape his control, the wretch might have succeeded in causing her death. Had Rachel been some cruel experiment to him that he could compare with his friend's writings of the invisible world?

At least, she was out of his gaze for good, and I could deal with the evil he had already inflicted, and then, she would be free of his power. Maybe my straight across eyebrows did alert others to my power, but they were not its source. The deacon's eyes had shown me the way to his power although the evil resided much deeper within.

Later that night as Rachel slept beside me, I lay a cold steel knife across her forehead. Then I gently licked her eyelids and spat the evil away from her. Rachel was a sound sleeper, so I didn't disturb her rest. I'd been taught this method from an Italian sailor, and I wanted to use all the practices I'd heard of in case the ones I learned from my people did not take on Europeans.

From that day until I was sure she was free of Matthew's spell, I made Rachel wear a medicine pouch around her neck, the contents of which I would not reveal but which I was sure would protect and save her. When Rachel protested out of Christian fear of the unknown, I assured her the pouch was meant to give her strength like the nettle beer I persuaded her to drink for a healthy delivery. And while the delivery came early and produced even worse than I expected, Rachel had survived and was free of Matthew Sweet's spell.

The evil eye has existed since human beings have told stories. Running the tavern brought me in contact with strangers from all over the earth who saw our lights at night or caught a glimpse of us by day. I heard similar stories from the tongues that my toddy loosened after one too many. I've seen goat horn amulets worn around the necks of the Italian sailors and the blue eye beads carried by the Turkish merchants. Men from all over what they call the European continent who have passed through here have worn protective charms. Even the seemingly fearless

African pirates adorn themselves with magical jewelry to ward off evil spirits.

From time to time, I speculated about the common fear that these men possessed. I knew the solution to fear was simple: for evil to exist, there must be an imbalance in nature. If the human spirit roams too far from the natural world, then evil abounds. Power tumbles out of the imbalance and can be seen in the eyes which some have defined as the windows of the soul. The eyes, then, reflect the spirit. Vision is the sense that establishes harmony or discord among people. And discord between the female and the male creates evil. That is what happens when men do not believe in the power of women. That is what happens when women do not believe in themselves.

Chapter 17

1715

A Call

Over the years since the settling of the European visitors, the numbers of native peoples dwindled severely, and as a last effort to preserve themselves and their way of life, the *Wampanoag sachems* determined that the healers of the separate tribes in the region must come together in prayer and with practical advice to seek ways to avoid the complete destruction of their peoples by European disease, religion, and greed.

Although Dark Ray lived at the tavern among the Europeans and worked for them, the remaining *Nausets* across the harbor remembered her healing powers despite her absence from their village and chose her and her childhood friend Solosana to attend the meeting. There were so few of the old ones left. Though Solosana still lived among their people, they didn't object to Dark Ray's decision to live apart from them. They knew she protected their beloved island, keeping it safe. They knew her heart remained loyal to her ancestors who lived among the grassy dunes long ago. That was why they chose to put Cessie into her care so many years ago.

While she hesitated at first to leave the tavern and her responsibilities, Dark Ray answered the call to set her daily work aside and participate in this sacred and necessary event. She believed her counsel would be of use to the gathering. She had been called to represent her people—the few pure bred left—and there was no greater honor. Rachel, who had shown her ability to assist Dark Ray in every way, and Mariana, who renewed her steadfast loyalty to her place at the tavern since she returned from Provincetown, would maintain the business in her stead during the fortnight she was gone. During the time *Kiehtan* had chosen for her to meet the faraway island man, the keeper of her soul.

****

He too had been summoned. He knew this even before his *sachem* called him away from his clay and told him he had been chosen to represent the *Aquinnah* at the gathering of *powwaws* on the mainland at Mashpee. He knew this because he dreamed it two nights ago. Since then, he remained silent, planning the long trip in his mind, mentally choosing the provisions he would bring so he could travel lightly and swiftly. In his dream, he wore his ceremonial breech clout, painted his face, re-colored his body drawings, and donned his eagle feather in the tuft of hair at the top of his otherwise shaved head. He saw himself sitting among the other healers of the *Wampanoag* federation. He saw the woman among them. Large but exquisitely graceful with a strong, beautiful heart and gentle, expressive hands. Deep black midnight eyes that pulled him into the core of her being. He knew from this dream that he would be traveling far across water and land to meet her. She too would travel over water and land from her smaller island. He saw her living among the Europeans already, but he also saw that her spirit remained uncorrupted. They shared the same purpose in attending this meeting. They shared a common destiny beyond it.

Chapter 18

1715

Promises

(Dark Ray)

I returned to the tavern saddened, rejuvenated, awed. My

heart was burdened by the knowledge the *powwaws* shared of the

diminishing numbers of *Wampanoags* all over the region. Even

those of us who refused to fight in King Philip's War long ago lost

people far too rapidly to re-populate our tribes. The European

illnesses had stricken so many of the young ones along with the

elders who could not fight the wracking coughs, the raging fevers, the pain of the skin rashes. I knew these things to be true among my own *Nausets.* Cessie's relatives were victims of these illnesses, but to hear that the same fate existed throughout the land was almost too much to bear. The stories we shared brought tears and wailing.

The devastation crushed our spirits as we *powwaws* mourned our common losses, but we refused to remain broken. In the end, we swore to survive these earthly tests. We determined to pray to *Kiehtan* with greater intensity, but after much arguing and protesting, we also agreed to encourage the remaining pure bloods to associate more closely with the Europeans, to add their bloodlines to ours for strength.

I was not shy and became very vocal in this regard. When those who opposed me became louder than I, the man I was later to love more deeply than any other walked up to my side and quietly waited for the taunts to become as silent as he. Some knew of my previous partnership with my deceased French husband, and while there were those who had scorned me and supported only the purity of their dying blood, the majority acknowledged that to survive, their people must do this. Many like me had consorted with the Europeans since they first arrived. It would not be difficult to continue to encourage such relationships that would result in our conjugal joining. We *powwaws* left the gathering knowing that as the years progressed, we would no longer be pure *Wampanoag*, but we would exist. We would not fade out of earthly existence as fast as our ancestors had.

That was my sadness because while the solution ensured our survival, it also acknowledged that a way of life and a people would never be the same. My rejuvenation came from being back with my own kin for an extended time—recounting old stories, dancing around the great fire, chanting with drums. I had already made the step toward the blending that the others faced, and I believed my example was the greatest help I could give them. My life had not suffered from my affiliation with other people of lighter skin and different ways. We had much to teach each other if we would only listen.

I also felt rejuvenation from being away from the tavern work I loved but needed to escape for a while. Upon my return, I was comforted that Rachel and Mariana proved they could run the place handily without me. However, the relief in their faces when they greeted me at the island's shore did not go unnoticed, and in that regard, I enjoyed reuniting with my English and Portuguese sisters and hearing their stories of our time apart. From all our years of living together, we had formed bonds that transcended bloodlines.

My awe. I was not young any longer, and so it was with great mercy that *Kiehtan* saw it in His divine power to grant me the chance to love a man again. I believed that this gathering, beyond its sacred purpose, would yield more than a meeting of the *powwaws*. I sensed the man before I saw him, and when I saw him, I knew we were meant to be together. He sensed it, too, and during our stay in Mashpee, we wasted no time in getting to know each other. For the two of us as old as we were—in the fourth decade of our lives, there was no time to waste.

After the first council meeting, old acquaintances wandered off to sit around the various fires and talk of the past. My childhood friend Solosana turned to me about to suggest we do the same, but as she continued to tug on my sleeve, she realized my attention was elsewhere. In the shadow of the central fire, Anawon, as I later learned he was called, waited for me with more patience than a man on a mission usually possesses. As we watched each other without moving, Solosana finally understood my silence. She giggled, stood up, and went her own way. Now that I was alone, Anawon came around the fire towards me.

He quietly took my hand and helped me stand up. Never much of a talker as I was to find out, his actions communicated all that he needed to say. We walked side by side down to the shoreline, as the voices behind us diminished. When he believed we were sufficiently removed from the group, he removed his hand from mine. It then traveled across my shoulder where it rested awhile before it gently pushed down, and by that, I knew he meant for us to sit. And then lie. And then discover each other—all without words.

The words came later on the walk back to the camp. I burned to know about him, and so in his tender way, Anawon told me about his life on *Noepe*—his island out in the great sea—and his place in his *Aquinnah* village as *powwaw* and potter. He said he needed his hands to be at work to be content, and working with clay was the most satisfying. Until now. Before his hands had touched me, he had not known true contentment. His hands exposed his nature, I was to learn—gentle but strong. Able to knead the right places, caress the rest.

When the meeting disbanded several days later, Anawon and I prepared to return to our people and share the outcome of the gathering. That last night though, we clung to each other like the youthful lovers we imagined ourselves to be. At our parting, Anawon promised to take the even longer journey from *Noepe* to my island.

"I will return to you," he declared as we lay in that same spot he had found along the shore that first night and every night after. "It may not be as soon as we would prefer, but you will see me before long. We will be together again before we leave this earth, and our souls take their final journey west."

"I want that," I said—now I was the quiet one—and told him the course he would have to travel to find my smaller island and home by drawing the directions on his naked back with my finger. Then I kissed the places where my finger had traced, but I did not stop there.

"I will find you. Look for me walking up the path. To your tavern," he gasped as my kisses traveled further.

I acted like I believed him, the other half of my self. I listened to his every word, every promise, wanting nothing more than what he said to be true, but I am a practical woman, and I never expected to lay eyes on him again. Besides, I reasoned with myself, the powerful memories of our time in Mashpee would serve me well. I could live with them alone and be happy. I never imagined I was destined to be with any one man for very long, anyway. My French husband and I lasted three years until his death, and all the men in between did not matter. And now here was this magnificent man, a distant relative of my own people, promising we would be together again.

I suppose stranger things have happened.

Chapter 19

1716

Anawon's Gifts

His return to the mainland the following spring was not on tribal business. Feeling somewhat selfish about leaving his people, he rationalized to himself that he was fulfilling a promise to the woman, but it was also his own need to be with her again at the heart of it. They were not young. They did not have much time left. Anawon put aside some of his pottery tools for the journey along with hard bread, deer jerky, a hunting knife, a blanket, his beloved flute, and two of his finest bowls made from the magically colored clay that he collected at the Giant's Cliffs in *Aquinnah.*

Although he was a tall man and muscular, he was wise enough to know that to travel light at his age would assure his endurance. He would take his wooden dugout from his island shoreline to Mashpee and store it with some friends he made there at the *powwaw* gathering. Then he would travel on foot across the Cape until he reached the shores of the bay. There he would barter using one of the pots—the other, his gift to the woman—to secure a boat ride across the bay water. He would work for his passage if the bowl was not enough payment, but he didn't think he would have to do that. His pots were unique and exceptionally beautiful. He heard that only in the far southwest of this land were pots similar to those he made, and those were not often available for trade in this area.

****

When he walked up the path from the beach, he saw Dark Ray working with a young Indian woman to turn over the sandy soil on each side of the tavern's front door. His woman was so focused on her digging that she did not look up at his approach as the younger woman did. Anawon stood still and watched the smooth curve of her strong back arching over the shovel. He waited, placing his travel bag at his feet. It was only the fact that the staring younger woman had stopped working that Dark Ray ceased her digging and addressed her helper.

"What, Cessie? Are you giving up already?"

As Dark Ray straightened herself, she realized that Cessie's eyes were fixed on something behind them, and she finally turned around. Her shovel dropped to the ground with a clatter when she saw him. Without a word or hesitation, she wiped her hands on her apron, stepped to him, grabbed his hand, and all but dragged him down another path beyond the tavern that sheep had cut over their years of island habitation. Although exhausted, he was more amused by her reaction to his coming, and so he followed along silently. He submitted, content with the knowledge that he would not wish to be anywhere else. With anyone else. The long months of waiting to see her again dissolved into moments, and he felt as if he had never left her side.

Dark Ray finally stopped when they reached a sheltered hollow well removed from the tavern, lookout towers, and activities of the island. In this place, they were quite alone. Even the sheep had chosen another part of the island to graze that day. When she looked up at him, he found her eyes wet although her mouth had broken into a radiant smile. Their embrace re-kindled the magic of the previous autumn. As they sank onto the sand, his exhaustion completely forgotten, her duties cast aside, they joined body and soul in the precious moment of their reunion.

Afterwards, on their slow return walk to the tavern, they were comfortably quiet, that time in the hollow having satisfied any need for talking, any need for explaining the reunion. But as they approached the building, he asked, "That young woman. Your daughter?"

"No. Well, yes, she is an adopted daughter. Her *Nauset* people left her here in my care some sixteen years ago when the European spotted illness killed her mother and grandmother. She's been with me ever since, and so, yes I have cared for her as a daughter. She's not always easy to understand as she communicates little. But she never complains, so I believe she is content enough despite her refusal for society of any kind."

As Anawon picked up his deer hide bag where he had dropped it earlier and slung it over his shoulder, his expression registered doubt.

"Content? I am not so sure of that. I read pain in her large eyes, Woman."

"Oh, and are you telling me that you know the moods of young women, Old Man?" She playfully bumped up against him.

He laughed and admitted, "Maybe not, but it is unfortunate that the girl has not learned to imitate your ways after all these years with you."

"True, she still needs to find her place. I've tried everything so far but food preparation. That's what we were beginning when you arrived."

As they approached the tavern, she paused. "We are going to expand this garden spot. That mound of soil over there has traveled over the wide seas, the gift of many a passing sailor who misses the gardens of his home. Over time, I have collected the rich earth that this island lacks to improve this sandy soil. Cessie will learn how to harvest and use the plants we grow. She seems interested, but then she would do anything to remove herself from social activity. She is a loner, that one."

"It seems that I have arrived in time to help. I also will teach her what I know of medicinal plants."

This talk about Cessie kept them from discussing the questions plaguing their minds. Is he staying? Does she want me to stay? How will I fit in here? Are we two crazy old fools thinking at our age that we can trick time and behave like young people? But none of these questions got answered immediately. They simply allowed the warming spring days and the natural course of life's cycles to carry them where they needed to go.

****

The days and months unraveled easily and smoothly into years, and he stayed, helping her in ways she never anticipated. For one, he re-kindled her Indian wisdom into her everyday life, a life so filled with European circumstances. On his first day there, when he pulled out the multi-colored clay pot he made for her, she gasped at its beauty.

"I've never seen clay like this before. Where did you find it?"

"Maushop the Giant created the sunset-colored cliffs of *Aquinnah* where this clay can be found. Our stories also tell of him transforming people into water creatures."

Anawon's strong attachment to his island stories made her ashamed.

"Living among these Europeans, I have forgotten so many of my people's stories."

"I am sure that your stories have not died within you. You can recall them if you put your mind to it. We can never lose our stories, or who would we be?"

A few days later she related her story of *Maushop* whose pipe smoking created the fog. And that recollection triggered a treasure of stories they found they both shared.

Another way he brought her back to her past was his refusal to join with her or to take his rest in the tavern. He declared he could not abide by restrictive, angular space for long.

He was convinced he would never be able to dream in such squareness. The sun was round; the moon was round; the womb was believed to be round; therefore, humans were meant to live in the roundness. So she helped him build a round wigwam with the discarded bark of the few remaining trees on the island, and she slept with him there whenever the tavern duties allowed. When the weather was particularly fine, they made love outside in the hollow where she had taken him the day he'd arrived.

He repaired stools broken by rowdy guests. He built new benches with the wood that she ordered from the mainland. He experimented with the clay he found on an excursion to the beach dunes along Billingsgate's ocean boundary, but he complained that the quality of the clay was inferior and dull compared to his beloved *Aquinnah* cliffs. He helped with the slaughtering of the sheep. He hunted for deer on the mainland. He fished along the island shore. On some of his trips for clay, he returned with a robust tom turkey he met fortuitously along the way.

And he played his flute—sometimes alone in the quiet of the day when she was preparing the tavern for the evening activities and sometimes at night when he accompanied the

European fiddles and mouth harps of the whalers. He was not a talkative man. The soothing sounds from his flute, however, spoke of his love of all living things on the earth, of his respect for all that was in spirit, of his own place in both realms, of his devotion to this woman. His flute playing, she said, was a sound she could die happy hearing.

He became a friend and a teacher to Cessie, spending hours with her as they explored every part of the island in search of medicinal plants. They made cuttings, collected seeds, and cultivated her garden. He was one of the few people with whom she could look directly in the eye—she trusted him that implicitly. He was the only person she could bear to be physically near. He was one of her people.

Charlotte warned Dark Ray more than once to be careful Cessie didn't steal Anawon away from her, but Dark Ray laughed and said the relationship between Anawon and Cessie was not that kind. Charlotte refused to accept this explanation. She didn't believe there was any other kind of relationship between man and woman. But Dark Ray knew Anawon was like a father not a lover to Cessie and ignored Charlotte's prattle. She was grateful to her man for being so generous with his time since Cessie never looked so alive before his arrival. Understanding the pleasure of silence, Anawon did not interfere with Cessie's need for solitude unless he wanted to teach her something new. They rarely spoke as they worked.

"Come here, Cessie," he directed. "Look at this plant. What do you see?"

She edged closer to where he was standing and leaned against him. They examined an outcropping in the remaining island woods of a plant whose red root was topped with a small white flower. "I have never seen this plant, Anawon, but it does not look like something we would eat."

He patted her shoulder in praise. "Good observation, Cessie, but plants do not only produce food or medicine. This red root has a sap that will dye clothing and even skin. I have used it here on this marking," he pointed to the red wolf paw etched into his right arm. "Let us take a few roots to add to your garden—we will put them in the shady part along with some of this rich wood soil for planting. Then I can teach you how to make the red dye, and we will brighten up that tavern some. Sound good?"

Cessie giggled as she watched him gather the red root and soil. He always had a playful way of reminding her that he too found the tavern lacking in some manner. He was always whispering to her that it was far too European for his tastes.

He did all these things, and he loved Dark Ray with the passion of a younger man. Rachel and Mariana had never seen their old friend so content before his appearance. They observed the couple's behavior with admiration tinged with longing.

When they were alone, Anawon gave Dark Ray wildflowers from his explorations with Cessie. Dark Ray washed Anawon's feet in lavender water when he returned after long hunts. He combed out her hair with his fingers. She massaged his back. He licked her everywhere. She respected his maleness. He honored her femaleness. They spoke of reciprocity and their relationship to all things in the universe and believed that even the rocks possessed spirit. They loved.

Chapter 20

1717

Dark and Stormy

Dark Ray yelled from the back kitchen. "Be sure to latch that door well, Mariana. That wind is blowing up harder than before. This promises to be a stormy night." Although she would rather have been snug in Anawon's wigwam nestled in his comforting arms, Dark Ray remained in the tavern while the customers waited out the weather.

After Mariana secured the door, she went to the kitchen and found Dark Ray instructing Cessie to double the pot of stew she was preparing. "Perhaps we should bring up another barrel or two of ale from the cellar, Ray," Mariana suggested.

"Yes," Dark Ray agreed. "The men won't be venturing far this night. They missed their chance to leave hours ago."

Later on, the roaring of the wind and rain all but drowned out the sounds of the music inside the tavern as its inhabitants stayed dry and distracted through the nasty storm. It seemed a perfect night for storytelling, and Josiah, a mixed blood praying *Nauset* who like Dark Ray, lived in his blended Indian and European world, was the best teller of tall tales among them. Usually, Charlotte lost patience with the nature of his stories and coaxed one of the men up the stairs. Tonight, however, the storm unified the group in its intensity, and Charlotte remained only somewhat unwillingly in Josiah's audience. No one ventured in, out, or up.

Cessie sighed with exasperation, sure she was alone in thinking of the chamber pots. They would be overflowing by morning because no one was budging to relieve himself outside. She would be the one most likely to empty them. Maybe she could convince Ray that she had too much work in the kitchen to attend to chamber pots as well. Let Mariana and Rachel see to them. Charlotte would never consider doing such a task.

"And then the wolf stopped in its tracks," Josiah explained, "because it smelled human scent. The moon was full as the creature advanced to the place by the side of the dwelling where the man had exposed his prick to make water before re-joining his friends by the warm fire. So absorbed was he in emptying the copious amounts of toddy that he was not aware of the animal's nearness.

"Yet no sooner did the man look up from his golden stream, but the wolf was upon him. I have heard tell that he never got a chance to place his prick back in his breeches, so there it dangled, swaying in the breeze, as the wolf lunged at the man's neck and sucked a pint of his juicy blood. The man, being so drunk, reacted slowly and was no match for the thirsty wolf."

Some of the men groaned at the mere suggestion—of the exposed organ, not the neck.

"Now, remember, this was no ordinary wolf. This was a shape-changing man who was drawn to his animal craving for blood on moonlit nights. By day he was a law-abiding citizen. By the light of the full moon, well, my God-fearing friends, he was something else. His hands became paw-like—his fingernails growing hard, his whole body covered with fur, and his teeth. Ah, his teeth changed into blood dripping fangs, and his nose resembled a wolfish snout. That is what helped him to smell his prey before they knew he was upon them. Yet, he had no intentions of killing the pissing man. He just wanted a taste of rich, dark red blood.

"The shape-changer got what he wanted because the man did not protest. He was too terrified to move or twitch in defense. He had also had his fill of good toddy, which was why he was out there in the first place. Truth is, the fellow was bloody well numb with too much toddy. The large, powerful creature staggered off like he had just gotten into his own barrel of flip, his taste for blood satisfied for the time being.

"As the dazed man remained on the ground, he reached up to his neck and felt two deep puncture wounds. He next looked at his hand and saw it was covered with blood, but he did not wince in pain. Instead he smiled wolfishly—all his teeth bared and gleaming in the moonlight. Because, ah. You will think this impossible, but the man realized that he could see in the dark. And even stranger—he craved blood."

Suddenly, Josiah jumped up from his seat. "Hark! Who is that at the door? For fuck's sake. It is a wolf man!" Josiah drew back from the door and reached up to cover his neck with his hands.

Mariana let out a shrill scream, while Rachel sought the nearest lap and cuddled in the arms of a fortunate fisherman. Cessie hid her large eyes in fright. The tipsy crowd was slow to react. Should everyone run for cover or burst out laughing? Dark Ray settled the matter.

"All right, you scoundrels. You've been served your last pint for the night. Find whatever accommodations you can in these two rooms. While you're at it, keep the fire going—it's chilly for April. No one is going out there tonight, and in here, the candles are about to be snuffed. And no one takes a walk up the stairs, either, for a visit. I'm going to need my women tomorrow to clean up after you swine, so they will not be wasting any more energy on you this night."

****

The next morning dawned still windy but clear and crisp. Dark Ray set out a bowl of warm bread, several jugs of ale, and mugs for the men to help themselves. Anawon came in as she worked, looked around at the still, sleeping forms, and whispered to Dark Ray, "Had your hands full last night, I see." He reached for a hunk of bread and leaned over across the bar to place a kiss on her cheek.

"Oh yes. We had Josiah telling his stories again." She nudged closer. "I would rather have been with you."

"Yes. I missed the warmth of your body as well. It was a fearful storm out there." He straightened up on his stool in an effort to change the subject. "I intend to stay here with you tonight. I was across the harbor already this morning, scavenging for downed tree limbs, and everyone was talking about a shipwreck last night over the ocean side of Billingsgate. They suspect it was a pirate fleet under the command of a man called Black Sam. They say he was on his way to parts north, but he wanted to stop by and visit his woman—one by the name of Maria Hallett. Have you heard of her?"

"A shipwreck, you say? The whole town must have been on that beach early this morning. I don't know if the folk on *Noepe* behave this way, but here, a shipwreck is cause for celebration."

He shook his head and replied, perhaps too smugly. "I have tried in all ways to avoid the company of Europeans on my island."

Dark Ray chose to ignore his tone. She knew his disdain for Europeans, but he accepted her work with them, and that was enough for her. "Well here, I can tell you, at the first news of a downed vessel, the beach crowds with the townspeople gathering what they can as quickly as they can before the magistrates appear to claim what's left of the booty for the crown. A shipwreck brings out all the folks who condemn greed at Sunday services. Hah," she snorted. "By now even the rings and other jewelry on the dead will have been ripped or cut off those drowned souls."

She answered his earlier question. "I do know of Maria. She is a handsome young woman. I would like to have her working here, but the town has banished her to live on the dunes overlooking the ocean, although she is not willing to leave, anyway. She has been waiting for her lover's return, so they can go away together. I have heard she is ready to become a pirate herself just to be with him."

As she spoke, Dark Ray continued to lay out food and drink. "Now that I think of it, the man she waits for is known as Black Sam. She had a child by him, they say, the last time he visited. The babe died, though, a few days after he was born. She still grieves for it. The townspeople also suspect her of being a witch, but that's mainly because she assists Solosana, one of our *Nauset* healers. Do you remember my old friend from the *powwaw* meeting?"

He nodded. "I do remember the woman. I remember more the first time I saw you."

She paused, recalling also their first meeting in Mashpee. "I'm happy you are staying tonight. There is more to your story. What is it?"

He took a long draught of his ale before he spoke. "While over a hundred dead bodies were found on the beach after the wreck, there is talk that some of the men are alive and roaming the area. The story is there were two ships. The one called the *Whydah* sank but had two survivors, and they have already found their way to Samuel Harding's house. They claimed to be honest sailors who had been forced into piracy or face death, and so, he took them in. However, the other boat that is smaller and simply stranded called the *Mary Anne* had several survivors. Some have already been arrested, but all are not accounted for. I intend to be near you in case they make it here."

Dark Ray scratched her head, and her brow wrinkled in disbelief. "Surely you don't think men who have just been in a shipwreck will make it this far. Besides, won't they be seen traveling the roads to the harbor and create suspicion? Word travels fast in Billingsgate and some are already captured, as you say."

"Woman, we are talking about pirates here—men not beholden to any laws but those of the high seas. What do they care of suspicion? They will be strong men, resourceful men. They will be armed. They will make it here. This place is known. What better refuge?"

"Are you saying they will be dangerous? Should I send word to Samuel Hawes' son? By rights, he is the one responsible for this tavern and whaling station now that his father has passed on."

"No. I think we can handle it. I will ask some of the whalers to stay again tonight. They probably will not need much coaxing." At that, he grinned.

****

Dusk arrived on the island along with seven unknown men, looking weary and dirty and determined. Four of them were African; the rest were of European descent. They bragged that their pockets were full of gold and silver coins from various parts of the globe. All were heavily adorned with precious metal: gold hoop earrings, thick neck chains and amulets to ward off the evil eye, several ornate finger rings, wide wrist bands. Their skin was tattooed, mostly with images of sea creatures and seductive women although one or two displayed a Christian cross on his forearms. Their faces were prematurely wrinkled from long days in the unrelenting sun. They appeared to be friendly, but they wielded daggers in the air as a reminder that they were in charge.

"Who runs this place?" bellowed a short stout man with a thick black beard. "What? A woman? Well, serve us up, Wench, or you'll not see the light of a new day." He looked around for protest, but receiving none, he settled down on a stool. A scowl remained on his face.

Dark Ray silently blessed Anawon's intuition. Earlier that day, she commanded the other women to the cellar, threatening to hurt them herself if she so much as heard a sneeze rise up from the floorboards. Against Anawon's wishes, she decided to remain where she could always be found this time of day—behind the bar. She reasoned with him that it would seem odd to strangers if they arrived here knowing there might be women and finding none at all. Besides, who other than he, an old man himself, would want someone the likes of her? Why she was probably old enough to be their grandmother. He sighed and told her once more that she would be shocked at the men who would desire her. She laughed boisterously, clearly enjoying his attention but not believing a word he said.

Dark Ray had served many men for many years now, and she knew what it took to get them drunk. In addition, she had summoned Cessie earlier to prepare tinctures of valerian and poppy that she could slip into their bowls of stew or chowder when and if the time called for more drastic measures. All in all, she believed the situation was under control. Some of the more robust whalers were hovering nearby, and Anawon sat quietly in the shadows in a far corner of the sitting room with his eyes watching the men but always keeping Dark Ray in his line of sight. She was reminded how wolf-like her man was—those penetrating eyes, that strong but sinewy stealth.

"What kind of tavern is this with no women? We were hoping for some female company. The word is that women work here," slurred one of the strangers. He looked menacingly at her as she served him another pint. "You call yourself Dark Ray? Why is that? Where are your women?"

Another who sat whittling a piece of wood, scoffed at his fellow pirate's request. "Damned if we need any women. It was the need for a woman that got us stuck here in the first place, was it not? If Black Sam had not insisted on seeing his mistress, we would still be on our way north."

Dark Ray did not appear at all intimidated, but slowly reached for the leather tie around her neck that held her medicine pouch. She fondled it with her hands as she spoke.

"Sorry, my man," she addressed the first pirate. "You heard it wrong. There are no women here. I run a whaling station is all. I feed and water the fishermen when they are not working with the whales. These men are God-fearing Christians. Many of them have wives and children across the harbor. In these parts, they would find themselves in the stocks if they committed adultery, so why would I tempt them here?"

She paused. "What else did you ask? My name? Hmm. You will probably think it strange, worldly men like you, but some folks around here think I can bestow the evil eye on my enemies. And I guess you could say that my name has something to do with that."

Dark Ray made an impression on everyone with her size and surprising grace, but whether or not the men had already had too much to drink, she seemed to grow threatening before their eyes as she continued to fondle her medicine pouch. Her heavy eyebrows were the color of crow's wings. Her black eyes stared into the pupils of the man who questioned her, and he could not break the gaze. He could not turn away. He was like stone. A bit of drool drizzled out of his open mouth.

At that moment, a loud pounding noise came from the front door. Eight militiamen from Billingsgate stormed in with muskets and easily arrested the pirates. They had no chance to defend themselves because they were sedated by the rum and Madeira wine served continuously since their arrival. Dark Ray never got to use the valerian and poppy mixture. She was almost disappointed. However, she was suddenly exhausted by this farce and sat down on a stool, relieved it was over.

As the militiamen chained the pirates together and herded them down the path, Dark Ray overheard one of the officials remark that the men were likely to meet the same fate as the two men befriended by Samuel Harding—hanging in Boston. She stood up and latched the entry at their retreat and then took a deep breath. Anawon came to her side and wrapped his arms around her. They lingered a while.

Slowly she loosened her arms around his neck and moved to the cellar door to free the women. When they saw the light from above and heard Dark Ray telling them all was safe, they stretched, Mariana and Rachel sighed with relief, Charlotte yawned from the confinement, and Cessie seemed thankful to finally put some space between the others and herself. As soon as she climbed off the ladder steps, she headed right to the kitchen.

Rachel spoke first as she and the others settled in the sitting room. "What happened? Are they gone so quickly? We could not hear a thing down there. Were you not frightened, Ray?"

"Frightened?" Dark Ray joked. "Josiah's stories are more frightening."

Anawon, however, retreated to his shadowy corner and slumped down on the bench he'd occupied throughout the evening. His head in his hands. His knees a bit shaky.

Chapter 21

1719

The Leaving

Anawon's going was a great wound she knew would never heal in this lifetime. Yet Dark Ray understood his need to return to *Noepe*, his faraway island home. Unlike her, he had not been able to make the transition from the old ways to feel comfortable among the Europeans. He had even been shy around Rachel and Mariana although he saw how they and Dark Ray loved each other and that pleased him. But Charlotte positively unsettled him and while he also sensed a mutual respect between his woman and this most self-centered of the women, he usually managed to remove himself from the common rooms of the tavern when Charlotte was present.

Dark Ray's head accepted Anawon's leaving; her heart did not. Could not bear to let him go. At the news of his going, Cessie too began to return to her former sullen nature. She completely avoided the women's company. Anawon's presence these last few years had softened her towards the others, but now she went off by herself again and returned exhausted, from what Dark Ray couldn't figure out.

But Anawon knew. He followed Cessie to her secret place and first watched from a distance as, unaware of his presence, she once again scored the meaty flesh of her thighs with her broken shell. The day of his leaving, he visited her and sat quietly by her side as she watched the blood ooze from the new wound. For one so isolated, she seemed comforted by his nearness. He saw the smile brighten her somber face as she absorbed the bittersweet sensation. He took her hand—the one with the shell—removed its contents, raised his shirt, and cut his chest in complicity. He looked directly at her as he returned the shell to her still open hand

and saw the silent tears erasing the rare smile. He told her he was leaving, and he felt sorrow for her pain. He would pray to *Kiehtan* for her safety and her long life—for, he told her—she must go on. She was needed.

She did not believe him.

It was not Cessie though that Dark Ray was thinking about as she watched him pull together most of the few items he arrived with three years ago. He was, of course, leaving the multi-colored clay pot that he brought her as a gift. He picked up his flute from the hearth where he kept it. He was about to place it in his pack, but he hesitated and put it back in its accustomed spot on the mantel. He could make no more music after he left her, but his commitment to his people was greater than his own selfish needs.

They had been talking of the leaving for weeks. While he loved her, needed her with a depth he didn't know was possible, he had to return to his home. He had been gone long enough. His job was to train the next *powwaw* if any of what he knew was to be passed on among his own people. He reminded her that they had always known he would leave someday. It was no consolation.

And now spring had arrived again, and it was a good time to travel. In the springs before, he knew he should have left, but he couldn't allow himself to go just yet, so he lingered. Told himself that Cessie needed him. Convinced himself that he could put aside his tribal allegiance and stay with Dark Ray as long as he lived. Now he knew if he stayed another year, he would never return— would not have the strength or will to make the trip alone, and he could not be thinking only of himself. He had already thought too much of his own needs by coming at all when a younger *powwaw* was just starting out and requiring the old man's knowledge. That young man he promised to teach, and he would not go back on his word. Had never gone back on his word to anyone.

They walked to the hollow for the last time. The day was milder than usual for early spring. The sky was deep blue like the water that surrounded the island. They marveled at the new shoots of grass already visible through the sand. In observing the nature surrounding them, they were borrowing time. Then they embraced as lovers, as friends, as partners, knowing that when their earthly end came, they would see each other again in the life that followed in *Kiehtan's* underworld. This last coupling would have to sustain them until then.

They took extra time, so that they would remember each caress, each touch, the feeling of skin on skin, the sweet sad glory of the orgasmic moment. They held each other long afterwards, so long that their aging bones creaked when they finally loosened their hold to lie on their backs and look up at the brilliant sky.

Without words, they spoke. What these brief years meant. How the rest of their lives they would feel alone despite the existence of the people who lived around them. Why they should be grateful that they had this time at all. When he walked down the worn path to the beach where one of the whalers secured him a boat for the trip down the bay, he did not look back, preferring instead to see her in his mind's eye where she would always be smiling at him. She didn't know, but he remained along the shores across the harbor for a day or two, reluctant to leave, watching the soft tavern lights appear on the island in the evening, contemplating what part of her he was taking away with him. None of it was material. She was part of his essence, his spirit.

She did not watch him recede slowly out of view. She went immediately back to work because it was the only thing that would keep her emotions under control, but she was aware already that a piece of him had stayed behind with her. As she placed her apron around her waist, she smoothed her front with gentle, loving strokes. He had left a part of himself right there.

Chapter 22

1720

The Remains of a Dead Blackfish

After months of constantly thinking about it, Cessie decided to take her life even though she knew it would not be an easy way out of her unhappiness. Yet, she ached for the final suffering. She welcomed it. Bodily pain had made her feel alive all along, but now even the cuts stopped easing the emptiness she felt each day.

Taking her life would require planning. Force her to make a choice—live or die in one last wave of agony. Perhaps if she suffered severely at the end, her pain would not travel with her along the road to *Kiehtan's* underworld. It would stay here on this earthly plane and let her know peace at last. Oh, the peace that would come from shedding this life like so much snake skin.

When Cessie set out to arrange her end, she had a difficult time deciding how she wanted her body discovered. In death she would no longer need to be invisible. She spent hours imagining all kinds of methods to terminate her existence. In the end, she chose a way that would be remembered. Although she knew the medicinal properties of most plants, she didn't use them. A carefully drunk essence of wolf bane, not a drip on her chin, not a drop left in her mug, but all finely and deliberately swallowed would have worked sufficiently. At which point, she could lay her sorry head on her pillow and fall seemingly to sleep—never to awake again.

Not memorable enough. Not visible enough.

Her desire was perverse—to be visible in death—if she couldn't stand to be in life. Remembered with vivid recollection. After the discovery of her scarred, useless, dead body, the conversation in the tavern might go something like this.

"Her? She was a bold one after all, she was. No one would have guessed she had it in her. So quiet yet cheerful as she went about her duties. But there she was. There they found her. Down in the cellar among the whalebones.... She had taken one of the towing ropes, hoisted it through a floor beam, tied knots as good as any sailor, placed the noose around her thin neck like some ornate necklace, tightened it to fit, and calmly stepped off the chopping block.... They say Dark Ray found her the next morning when she went down to cut some whale meat. Later when they were preparing her body for burial, they saw the deep, scarred lines on her legs, but when Dark Ray first saw her, she was stiff, ramrod straight, a mocassin dangling from one foot.... In her misshapen blue face were those eyes—those piercing eyes. They still seemed to see."

Cessie fantasized for days about what they would say, and she chose hanging because she believed the pressure from the strangling rope would emphasize her most memorable feature: her eyes. Yes, hanging it would be.

Life had become such a wearisome burden. She did not want to carry its weight on her back any longer. Although Dark

Ray had treated her kindly since Cessie's abrupt arrival, the older woman never understood Cessie's feeling of displacement. Dark Ray witnessed and observed everything, and yet she never saw Cessie's pain even when it was visible all over her face. As a child, she so wanted to be noticed, but when she realized she would never be the center of a loved one's life as when her grandmother lived, she imagined herself invisible. But Charlotte would still see her and make her life miserable. There seemed no way to hide from her, and since that woman's arrival, Cessie had rarely felt safe from Charlotte's taunting gaze.

Even Anawon, her friend and teacher, left her, so she believed she couldn't have meant very much to him, either. He was the only one to see her scars—to know what she did to stop the pain. She had to suffer. Although he even cut himself in an effort to convince her she wasn't alone in this world, she didn't know how to believe otherwise.

Cessie never felt like she belonged anywhere, to anyone once she arrived here. When her people left her on the shore of this island, she sat stunned, her eyes smarting from the vision of the canoe heading back home. Discarding her here like the remains of a dead blackfish. She too had been gutted—the heart ripped out of her as she watched her father become smaller and smaller in the distance. When Dark Ray lifted her from the sand and held her in her great arms, she might have been comforted if she had not just been removed from the cold arms of her beloved grandmother.

There were no other children as she grew up. To keep her busy and out of harm's way, Dark Ray gave her endless tasks that filled her life. Feed and water the chickens. Collect their eggs. Place flowers in the rooms upstairs. Sweep the dining room. Bring in wood for the fire. Wash the dishes and drinking utensils. Empty the chamber pots or "looking glasses" as some of the coarser men called them. Whatever she could handle at the time to assist in the up keep of the tavern was assigned to her. She was everywhere. She was nowhere. She worked hard to make the hours slip by, but each day resembled the one before and after.

Cessie rarely felt the touch of another as she grew, nor did she seek it out. At times, Dark Ray would smooth hair from Cessie's face and then as her arm slid down, she would rest her hand on the girl's shoulder, squeeze it gently if she had a mind to linger. Cessie did not begrudge her ways. She understood Dark Ray did the best for her, given that Cessie was not hers to love in the first place. Dark Ray cared for her physical needs. She never went hungry. She was clothed in fabric and skins to suit the season. Most times she slept with Dark Ray who no longer troubled herself with the men as she grew older and the younger women took her place. And once Anawon got here, she had no use for other men at all.

By the time Cessie became a woman, she tried to take her place. She did try to consort with the customers. But unlike Charlotte who seemed to enjoy the men as much as they delighted in her, she viewed this activity as just another chore although it did keep her out of the weather on nasty days unless someone wanted her company at one of the lookout towers. Then she would return to the tavern just as soaked as if she had been sent out to check on the new lambs in the dunes. She never refused; she accepted it as part of life's pain. A kind of punishment for living. Even though she was clearly not the favorite, she would occasionally receive a token for her trouble, yet what good were foreign money and trinkets to her? She never left the island.

Dark Ray told her many times that she was fortunate to have found her way here, that this land always was a sacred place to their people. Cessie never felt one way or the other about it. She was just here, and she wanted to be dead like her grandmother or at least return to what remained of her people, but Dark Ray had gotten word years ago that they had succumbed to the European diseases. All Cessie had left were Dark Ray and the other women. And Anawon for too short a time. They were not enough to ease the constant pain she bore, the pain that she eventually failed to ease with the cutting.

As she aged and her eyes continued to dominate her bony face, the ridicule of the whalers became constant. Dark Ray tried to silence them, but once out of her earshot, they persisted. When they came around for some sporting, Cessie was always the last to be desired, her thin, shapeless form incapable of stirring a man's loins, much less his imagination. They joked mostly about her large eyes that never seemed to blink. Sometimes in the height of their passion, she could feel them staring at her as they came, wondering if she truly possessed lids capable of shielding her hideous eyes.

They did not want her. Eventually, Dark Ray would have no more of this treatment and took sympathy on Cessie, putting her to work instead in the kitchen where she would not be seen. The invisibility suited her for a time. She cooked, and at last, she learned she had skill at something. Her meat stews were praised for their deep, hearty flavor, her chowders for their light, delicate taste. She kneaded the dough of the bread she made daily with the unbridled passion that lives in one who has immense stores of unused love but has no place to put it. By the end of the day, her energy was spent. She would stumble up the stairs past the merriment and great light from the fireplaces and collapse in the private bedchamber used for sleeping. Her days of frequenting the other room were limited to removing the bedding for airing on a clear windy day.

Cessie was miserable in the evenings, and over time, as she lay alone in the bedstead or at the beach in her secret place, she became obsessed with thoughts of death. And so, at twenty-six, when the other women were sleeping, she quietly left the bedchamber, tiptoed down the stairs, lifted the floor latch to one of the cellars, located the rope she had stashed a few days ago, and secured it.

Chapter 23

1720

Life Cycles

(Dark Ray)

I never expected my spirit to break in half when I went to the cellar to fetch some whale meat for the day's stew. The growing babe within me had caused my already large size to expand, and the going was slow, the stepping awkward as I made my way along the wooden ladder steps. Yet mid-way down, I sensed something was wrong. A shadowy vision clouded my thinking. The image of the little wisp of a girl I had found on the beach twenty years ago flashed before me. "Cessie?" I called out. "Are you down here? Has your candle gone out? Where are you?"

First I saw the moccasin that had fallen off Cessie's left foot and landed on the sandy floor below her. Then as I removed myself from the steps and went forward into the cellar, my candlelight exposed the other one dangling from her right foot. My voice caught up with the horror I was witnessing, and I cried out when I raised the candle, as inch by inch, Cessie's torso revealed what she had done to herself. When the light reached the poor girl's face, my legs could not hold me up any longer. My great body folded in a heap on the floor. Cessie's big luminous eyes stared at me. I could not read them then any more than I could when Cessie was alive, and I wept at my ignorance.

****

As Charlotte steadied the ladder from above, Dark Ray allowed Rachel and Mariana to ease her up the steps because she had no strength in her legs to help herself. The scream that resulted from her raw discovery startled the other three women awake, and they had come rushing to her aid. Now Rachel and Mariana were weeping as they guided Dark Ray's body out of the cellar, through the kitchen, and up the flight of stairs to the women's sleeping quarters. Dark Ray's water broke on the journey between floors, but she was not conscious of the matter that spilled between her legs and soaked her clothing. Her mind was still in the cellar, probing its dark corners for some answer, some explanation.

How could she have missed the signs? Why was she not able to save that fragile girl from herself? What good was she as a *powwaw* when, right in front of her, the girl's troubled mind had deceived her for years? These questions burned unresolved, as Dark Ray's head cleared abruptly from a sharp contraction. Suddenly someone else needed her more as the first searing wave of pain gripped her in the gut and would not let go. She put thoughts of death aside. Life was beckoning her. She was in labor.

Labor. What an appropriate word for what her body was doing. It was preparing for the birth of a new life to fill the space where another life had recently departed. She had never delivered a child to full term, but her aging body was handling the assault of her lower torso as her pelvis widened to make room for the baby to pass through. And because her body had taken charge of the moment, her mind relinquished its burden and experienced awe in the wake of the imminent birth. Labor? Yes. This was work, she thought, and her body was working to compensate for the mental anguish of the cellar discovery, but it was also fulfilling her soul's needs. How soothing Anawon's flute would sound.

She wanted this baby even now in her advanced age when she thought she was no longer capable of conceiving. In the past with her Frenchman, she had miscarried and after she took over the tavern, she was no longer interested in mothering a child. How could she have been a mother and run this place? On the other hand, if her French husband had lived, her life would have been different. She would not be living on this island. They would have tried to produce more children until they succeeded, but that did not turn out to be her fate. Yet, *Kiehtan* had given her Anawon for a time, and for those few years, to have had him was worth the price of her existence. For him to have fathered this child was beyond her imagination.

Kiehtan too led her to be with these women who were tending to her now as she had done for them when they arrived. Try as she might to understand it, she knew in the deep recesses of her being that they were meant to find each other. One after the other, they came with their own troubles trailing behind them, but unlike the youngest of them, the rest had thrived. She herself had thrived as she managed the tavern, grew to love the women, and spent her precious time with Anawon. As these thoughts of her life's journey unraveled between waves of contractions, she sipped the blueberry tea that would help her through this lying in time. Mariana, who had taken charge, placed the mug at Dark Ray's lips and whispered soothing nonsense to distract her.

She knew exactly when she conceived—what she was thinking—and doesn't the belief go that children manifest their mother's thoughts at conception? If that were truly the case, then this child, this girl—she knew she would deliver a female—was the daughter of the earth itself. For when she coupled with Anawon for the last time, they lay in the hollow far from the tavern, the sandy hollow in which they were protected from the incessant northwest wind. They reveled in the premature warmth of the day, their blood knowing that other past seasons in this region were not so accommodating. The evidence of new life surrounded them. It was a cloudless day in March, and signs of an early spring were everywhere especially in that hollow. The shoots of grass were already turning green, the sun felt warm on their bodies.

She remembered opening her eyes to the sky at the very instant of penetration and pulling in to her being all the beauty, harmony, and promise of that natural moment with her beloved. She knew right then that this child would grow to full term in her womb, and she would name her Terra, for the land. Her daughter would find her *Nauset* name for herself as she grew, but she would be known to all by an English name, for surely she would be living among Europeans.

Dark Ray pushed. She pushed for the precious child she was about to deliver from her body. She pushed again, knowing her life was inextricably bound to this little wonder in ways no other life had been tied to her very essence. She wanted so much to bring into this world this new life that began on that early spring afternoon. She wanted to raise this child born of an extraordinary love. Always the matriarch, she was now unabashedly maternal.

With her forearm, Mariana pushed her long thick braid behind her. Over the years, her black hair had become streaked with strands of white, but it was still lush and beautiful and perhaps even more striking in its variegated state. "She is coming, Ray. A little more and she will be out. There is the top of her head now. Go ahead. Take a small rest, oh Holy Mary, Mother of God," Mariana coached.

She wondered what it would have been like so long ago to have delivered a child of Manuel's as she stood up for a moment and smoothed her curly hair off her sweaty forehead. The weight of her braid was a nuisance today as she leaned in to monitor the birth. She had not cut it since her menses began two years after her arrival when she appeared dressed as a boy, and the two Rays accepted her into their circle. While this existence had not borne ill fortune, it had also not borne all the circumstances she thought might fill her life. And now at thirty-nine, Mariana knew she would never experience giving birth herself.

Even though Dark Ray was older than she and in the throes of delivering, Mariana believed such a miracle would not manifest itself for her. There were no men in her life other than the rare occasional fisherman. There was no promise now of a sanctified union in which to produce a child. She would only assist others as she did in the past when her mother was the midwife. At her mother's side, she learned what she was doing now and in this way, Mariana was humbled to carry on her mother's legacy. Because she believed this work was part of Mary's plan for her, she accepted it. How could Mary object to her bringing new life into the world?

As Mariana remained lost in her thoughts, Dark Ray slumped back on the feather bed, exhausted and knowing she did not have much strength left in reserve. From the bottom of the stairs, Rachel called up anxiously. "What is going on up there? Oh! Why must I be stuck down here with these impatient men? Keep your breeches on, Josiah. I will get your ale in a minute. Do you not realize we are having a baby up there?"

Before she answered, Mariana thought, yes. This baby belonged to all of them. And in that thought, she found peace and renewed hope. She was also relieved to have heard this collective ownership from Rachel's mouth. Throughout Dark Ray's pregnancy, Mariana worried that Rachel might become sorrowful as she remembered her miscarriage of years ago. But Rachel seemed impervious to sorrow and constantly referred to Dark Ray's growing form as "our" baby girl, for they all believed a girl it would be.

"Rachel," Mariana called, "all is going well. Stay where you are though. We need you downstairs. Charlotte is here if I need assistance. We will call you as soon as our baby is delivered."

As Mariana turned her attention to Dark Ray, her voice became gentle again. "Here we go, Ray," she coaxed. "This little dear is ready to join us. Get ready: push! I wish Cessie was here to help us," she said before she realized her folly in mentioning the name of the dead especially at this crucial moment.

But upon hearing that name, Dark Ray's eyes darkened with the conflicting pain of childbirth and loss. As she envisioned the scene in the cellar, her chest heaved with mixed sorrow and infinite joy, and she pushed away death and embraced life because that was all she could do.

"That is it! Here she comes—Charlotte, will you please get over here and help me? I need you. Come. Stand right here and get ready to take this baby while I finish up with Ray. Charlotte, are you listening? I need you!"

This day had been too much for Charlotte's sensibilities. First that crazy Cessie's suicide, and now this grisly birth. She was reminded of all the times she chose not to deliver a child. What would she want with one in the business she was in? Besides, she told herself, she never had an interest in being a mother, her own sotty parent not offering much of a positive example. And yet, she was dizzy with the spectacle of it all. As she advanced forward to stand next to Mariana who was about to catch a new life in her hands, Charlotte was mesmerized by the amazing transformations of Dark Ray's body. To think her own private part that had brought her so much pleasure would have unfolded like this had she ever remained pregnant—like some beautiful grotesque flower. To think from that flower emerged life. She had known the procedure of childbirth, had been in the room when her own mother delivered Charlotte's siblings, but there was never much joy in those occasions. Now she was paralyzed with wonder.

"Here she is. Hail Mary, what a little beauty. Look at our daughter, Ray," Mariana proclaimed. "Let me put her at your breast. Charlotte is apparently useless."

All that existed for Dark Ray was this child. She enclosed her baby in her arms and could not think beyond her little girl's toes. Her entire world was right here—no other world existed. She stroked the baby's cheek, the crown of her head, the tips of her fingers. In her baby's almond-shaped eyes, she saw Anawon. She was in love.

So this was it. She believed her whole life had been leading up to this moment. Now she knew why the one whose name she can never again say aloud came. That one was to be her supreme lesson from the gods. She was to have learned how to mother for this moment. While her heart ached from her poor attempt at mothering the one who passed on, she promised not to fail again. She would be vigilant as a cat with this girl *Kiehtan* brought through Anawon and her. She would do anything for this child—even if she lost her own life doing it. This was what she was here for. This was why she lived—for this moment.

"Charlotte, you really must help me now. Take the child. Wrap her in that clean cloth you see over there after you have wiped her up a bit. I must attend to Ray. She needs to expel the afterbirth," Mariana instructed.

While she waited for Dark Ray to complete the birthing process, Mariana went to the top of the stairs and yelled down, "It is a girl! Everyone is fine!" There were a series of excited exclamations and, of course, the propitious opportunity for a fresh round and a toast.

Charlotte advanced to the side of the bedstead. Her quivering hands reached out to remove the baby from Dark Ray's breast. Their eyes met, and despite their differences, they offered each other a smile and an assurance. With the baby at last in her possession, Charlotte sat and tenderly placed the child on her lap. She wiped mucus and blood from the little one's face and proceeded to clean its body. Then she wrapped it tightly in the smooth woven cloth that Dark Ray had set aside in anticipation and cradled the infant in her arms. She was overwhelmed, a little embarrassed, and suddenly regretful that the birthing experience was not hers. She turned away from Dark Ray and Mariana. She did not want them to see her tears.

Mariana was too involved with guiding Ray through the expulsion of the afterbirth to observe Charlotte's reaction. But Ray sensed them. As she heeded Mariana's directions, her eyes followed Charlotte's back as it began to sway. Before long, Mariana as well noticed Charlotte's gentle rocking and heard an original song that Charlotte composed as she rocked Dark Ray's baby to sleep in her arms.

"Baby girl, oh baby girl. How can such a wee little one steal my heart so soon? Baby girl, oh baby girl. And how did you know how to teach me to love?"

It was a melody that Terra would connect in later years to her nurtured childhood. It was a melody that Charlotte would sing to her at night as Terra was put to bed. Eventually, all the women would adopt the lullaby and employ it whenever the little girl required soothing.

Completely weakened, Dark Ray laid back on the bedstead with her eyes closed. As she did, Mariana cleaned her and removed the bloody blanket that had been hastily thrust over the featherbed that too was soiled and would eventually be burned. But she did not remove it now because Ray needed rest for the other matter that awaited them. Charlotte continued to busy herself with the infant. Despite the horror of discovering Cessie and the exhaustion she felt attending to Terra's birth, Mariana found herself amused by Charlotte's transformation from hardened harlot to tender nursemaid. Maybe there was hope for that woman, after all. She had tried for years to bring Charlotte into the Virgin Mary's fold and failed miserably.

Luckily, this baby arrived at a time when the tavern was not so busy handling the needs of numerous whalers. It was near the end of December, when the whales should be plentiful, but in the last few years, the schools had decreased in number and frequency in the harbor. The fishermen had quit coming to the island with regularity and returned to their families on the mainland or to wherever they went when the whales were scarce.

When she completed all the cleaning she could do until Dark Ray awakened, Mariana sat quietly with her hands folded on her lap and gave a silent prayer of thanksgiving. Charlotte was sitting across the room, still holding the baby, and she too closed her eyes but not to pray. She was thinking that when he returned— oh, God, let him return—something of a prayer after all, she would approach him with an answer to the question only his eyes had asked.

The uncharacteristic quiet and the deepening cold of the fading light of the day's sun caused Dark Ray to awaken. As she shifted her body to its side, her groan of discomfort startled Mariana and Charlotte out of their separate reveries. At some point, Rachel's duties downstairs had finished, and she was now standing at the doorway. They looked from one to another and seemed to remember at the same time the event that brought them together that morning. And as they recollected, each moved to Dark Ray's bedside and sat around her great body. An arm across a shoulder, another around a waist, a hand caressing a cheek, a daughter sucking at her mother's breast. And the tears. The tears spilled unchecked.

Chapter 24

1721

Found

(Cessie)

They buried my body in the garden, and I am grateful to

them for doing that. I loved my garden. Once Dark Ray put me in

charge of the kitchen, I devoted myself there as well creating ways

to improve the flavor of food. The more I learned about the natural

properties of plants, the more I wanted to know. Anawon, Dark

Ray's man from *Aquinnah*, understood the bounty of the earth

better than she, and his arrival about the time I started working in the kitchen proved beneficial to us all as he taught me daily what I might never have learned without him. Maybe because he reminded me of my father, I did not feel self-conscious around him. Or maybe it was just his way of making me feel wanted. Necessary. Before he left, he discovered my secret, and I was not sorry he found out.

When he was not spending time with Dark Ray or working with some clay that he complained was inferior to that which he could find at the Giant's Cliffs on his island, he was my beloved teacher. He said he did not want his skills to die with him. He needed to pass them on to those who appreciated them. Although he had an apprentice waiting for him on his island, he wanted to teach me while he was here. I loved when we would hunt for special plants. The excitement on his face when we found a rare one was a sight that filled my days with contentment. To be so alive—to so love the earth and its offerings—he was good medicine for me, and while he was with us, I stopped cutting myself.

And so my body became the nourishment that fed the plants that they would gather to sustain themselves in the days and years ahead. And I would sustain them--I owed them that. My spirit hovered over that birthing room, and I saw at last, now that I was truly invisible, the depth of their love for each other—even me. They cried for me.

In life I was so tormented by my own misfortune, I never considered their feelings. Except for Charlotte, they were kind to me. Never tried to hurt me. I was the one who refused to be their friend. I displayed a dutiful disposition. Responded to every request without complaint—that was as far as I could extend myself. But I could not reach out any more than that. I hurt so much inside, but I kept the pain to myself.

In death I realized that I should have trusted the women. My spirit continued to linger a few days around the tavern. I observed their tears, and I heard them speak so lovingly of me. Even Charlotte, who cares little for the feelings of others, seemed subdued after my death. Now I regret that I caused them so much sorrow by my selfish act.

What I learned in death—my stick-like frame and bulbous eyes really did not measure my worth after all. The part of me that lives on and is the best part of me is my soul. I should have remembered what my grandmother taught me. The *Nausets*—my people—believe that each person possesses two souls. When I departed this earth, my one soul moved on to be with the sacred ones—the other appeared to Dark Ray in her dreams on the night after I died. Now that I finally knew her, my other soul remained at the tavern to guide Ray, to protect her and those she cared for, to pay tribute to the mother I never realized I had. The island mother who insisted on blackening her face and shaving her head in mourning and who, out of respect, never spoke my name aloud again after I was gone.

****

With her newborn at her side, Dark Ray welcomed sleep the night after Cessie had died. She needed the strength because she would insist on leaving her confinement and attending to the burial the next day. Right now, she was exhausted in every possible way, but she told the others she was going to be there when Cessie's body was sent on its journey.

While Dark Ray slept, the other women tended to the few customers they had—Charlotte too, who seemed to have changed somehow since Terra's birth, also put on an apron and did her share of the work. It was Rachel though who couldn't bear to leave Cessie's body hanging, and so she cut the rope and lay Cessie's body on the cellar table. When she had Dark Ray settled, Mariana went down and helped Rachel prepare the body for the next day's burial.

Dark Ray was prone to unsettling dreams on nights that follow hard, stressful days. Although she was overwhelmed by the warmth of her baby's presence, she had trouble ignoring a nagging feeling of responsibility for the death of that adopted daughter whose despair she had not seen, but whose sorrow Anawon had read the first time he met Cessie. Dark Ray at last realized his observations had been accurate: Cessie was a troubled being, and none of them—except him—had paid attention.

Dark Ray went to sleep expecting to see birds, the messenger beings, and she did. As she gave in reluctantly to sleep, she expected crows to visit her, to peck at her eyes, to identify and expose her blame. Instead, in her dream a most magnificent red-tailed hawk flew across the path where she was walking to the spring to fetch some water with her baby wrapped tightly across her chest. It came so close to her she could see its piercing eyes. Their gazes locked, and she knew that she had seen those eyes before, but she had never looked long enough into them to see the deep wells of anguish that they held.

Even in her dream, Dark Ray began to understand its meaning. Cessie had been living alongside her for twenty years, but Dark Ray had been blind to the young woman's most essential need. She began to cry, but the hawk in its wisdom consoled her. She walked up to the tree limb where it perched. She was so close, it must have felt her breath on its feathers. She was not fearful of it hurting her baby. It didn't appear to want to bring Dark Ray harm. As her body grazed the branch, the bird stepped lightly onto her right shoulder and stayed.

She heard the hawk whisper, "I had thought all along that I had been abandoned. I never realized that in being abandoned, I had also been found." The feathers of its wings brushed against her cheek, and she felt the most amazing sense of protection and love emanating from the creature. Her heart wanted to burst with the joy she felt at that moment, a joy that erased the deep remorse she had been feeling. Dark Ray believed this messenger bird came to her in the supreme sorrow and joy of that day, and she felt comforted. And loved. And forgiven.

The next day, the women buried Cessie's body in the garden in the old *Nauset* tradition. Gently they bent her knees to her chest as they placed her on her side facing southwest, the place, Dark Ray explained to her European sisters, from which all nourishment originates. In the grave, they put Cessie's kitchen and garden tools beside her body as was the custom. The hoe, pestle, and spoons would assist her journey through the next life. Dark Ray asked *Kiehtan*, the great god of all others, to watch over her soul as it made its journey. Mariana placed the blue fabric she had wrapped around her statue of Mary on Cessie's head. Charlotte offered a favorite fan. Then they sprinkled the dried rosemary that Cessie had preserved last autumn over her silent body. Rachel told them that in English stories the herb symbolized memory. The fragrance would always, when they smelled it afterwards, remind them of Cessie. As they concluded the burial ceremony, all but Dark Ray began to place soil on top of the departed—they refused to allow her to do any more work—a hawk hovered overhead.

Red-tailed in its splendor, it had come to reside near Dark Ray and protect those she loved. From that day forward, it never left the island until she died, and then the two souls flew off in consummate understanding.

Chapter 25

1721

At Last

He arrived with the others even though the whale work had

not been lucrative these last years. Those few men like him

without families or ties to anyone but themselves would wait out

the winter months at the tavern hoping for whale sightings, or on

Chequesett Neck across the harbor where recent Irish immigrants

would put them up for companionship and for helping with the

meager farm chores. If the whales didn't return this year, they would be forced to consider the growing business of hunting the whale off shore.

In the years to come, many would find their way to another island—Nantucket. They would rarely inhabit that island although their families would take root and flourish there. Instead the whalers would reside for most of their remaining years on large ships that would take them to parts of the globe they never dreamed existed, let alone see with their own eyes. Many would be lost at sea out on the strange oceans and never reunite with their loved ones again.

He scanned the shore as they approached. If the women had the time and interest, one or two would be waiting to greet them as soon as their small boats touched the sand. Charlotte had never been one of those women. It was beneath her to show that much interest in the likes of these men other than what they gave her upstairs. The men knew this well. For years they tried to engage her in idle talk. She wanted none of it. And yet, there she was, alone, and waiting for him, it seemed. Her eyes followed every movement he made as the rowing ended, and the boat skidded to a halt against the sand. The other men were amused.

Was that their Charlotte blushing at the sight of a man she had made sure she stayed clear of for years? They never realized that Charlotte could blush.

One leaned in at him as they walked up towards the well-worn path that Charlotte's body now blocked. He whispered, "Say, Jack, my man. I believe she is thinking of separating you from the herd."

Now there were two blushing people on the beach although given his ruddy complexion, Jack reddened easily. He attempted a protest, but they paid no attention. They were more interested in Charlotte.

The men snickered into their woolen coats and passed around Charlotte to pick up the tavern path. She didn't even meet their glances, much less match their taunts as she was so accustomed to doing. She focused exclusively on Jack Dodger. Confused by her gaze, he tried to catch up to the men, but her gloved hand grabbed his coat sleeve and held him in place before her. Her eyes were the green of an approaching storm at sea.

She cleared her throat to speak, but an uncharacteristic shyness caused her voice to crack. She stood up straight, threw back her hair, and tried again. "I believe this meeting has been long overdue."

"What would you be meaning?" he asked stupidly as he studied his feet.

"I am meaning that we are too old for games. I am in my middle forties, and I suspect you are as well. You have been living around me almost my whole life. Did you think I was not aware of you back in London? Did you think I did not know you were around in Boston too? And you have been here off and on for years. Why have you never approached me? And yet, why have you always been near me?"

He stammered. The one moment he fantasized his entire adult life was here, and he couldn't speak. He was stunned that she had finally spoken to him, declaring her awareness of his presence from the beginning, even in places not so obvious as on an island where no one could really hide.

"You speak true," Jack began. "I have watched you all these years. And watched until I thought my heart would burst at your nearness. You will never know how I have wanted to come to you, to speak to you. Yet I always shied away. To touch you—

I have dreamed my whole life it seems, of touching you." At this remark, Charlotte allowed a curled smile of satisfaction to brighten her face. Jack continued. "But, I am not a man you would want."

Charlotte bristled and laughed. "Ha! What man would I turn away? I am not in the business to turn men away."

"If you knew more about me, you would." He paused. "For fuck's sake, this is far more difficult than I had imagined it would be." He started to turn from her. "Let us not speak any further. There is no use to speak more on this."

But Charlotte grabbed his sleeve even harder this time and shouted, "No! You will stay here with me. You will tell me why you have lived near me, watched me, and yet never approached me. I would think when I was younger and more beautiful than I am now, you might have tried."

"Charlotte," he spoke her name aloud for the first time, and those two syllables felt delicious, seductive rolling off his tongue. "It would have been even harder then for me to come for you. You were the most beautiful young girl I had ever seen—those clear green eyes, that abundance of golden hair, that sensuous body, even when you were living in the streets of London. And as you matured," now he couldn't contain himself and the words spilled out, "you only grew more beautiful in your self-assurance. I had nothing to offer that you wanted. I still do not, I think. But I cannot be away from you. It is as simple as that. I have been prepared to follow you wherever you go. To be somewhat near you has kept me from doing away with myself." He regretted his last words as he recalled too late the news of the events of the last few days on the island—the burial of that quiet one after she hanged herself. However, Charlotte did not seem to be offended.

She sat down on sand hardened by the winter cold and was momentarily silenced. His honesty unnerved her. She hadn't been prepared for such dedication, devotion. Although the sun shone upon them, the wind was biting, and it found its way through their layers of clothing. She saw him shiver but neither retreated. He slumped down next to her, quiet again as if he could only retrieve his thoughts in sporadic intervals. All he was conscious of was her nearness, her shoulder leaning on his as they looked straight out at the harbor. He marveled at the eagerness in her shoulder to press against him hard.

"And what do you think I want?" she asked.

"Why you want physical love, I think. You thrive on it. You glow."

She laughed lightly, but even lightly her laughter made him wince. "And you cannot provide me with that? You are a man, are you not?"

"I am a man, surely, but you need more of a man than I am."

"What can you possibly mean? Have you not got something dangling between your legs?" She reached over and touched him. "Is it not getting hard as we speak? As I touch it?"

Jack remained completely still. She would know soon enough. Why suffer the words to tell her?

Charlotte sat up straight as she carefully removed her hand from Jack's soft crotch. She folded both hands in her lap and spoke with an urgent determination.

"Tell me. You need to tell me everything. Now."

Jack knew one day he might actually be speaking the words to explain the one incident that irrevocably altered his life. Now that it was here, he wished he didn't have to reveal it, but there was no escaping the truth that had shaped his coming and going throughout his manhood. She was right. They were too old for games.

"I had an accident when I was a boy of twelve. In London I delivered potions for our local apothecary. The old man took a liking to me, and soon he had me assisting him in measuring out ingredients for his medicines. I was in the habit of sitting by his side on a stool and opening bottles of tincture—sometimes their lids were tightly bound, and I would squeeze the bottle between my legs in order to get a good grip."

He paused. "One day, I was opening a bottle, and the lid opened more quickly than I had anticipated. Before I knew what happened, the bottle tipped and the acidic contents burned right through my breeches and seared the skin on my private parts. The pain was so severe, I thought I would die."

Remembering the incident silenced him briefly, but then he continued. "Perhaps I might have if I were not right there with the apothecary—he did all he could to help me, but I was nonetheless deformed. The feeling has never returned completely with what is left to allow me much pleasure."

Jack paused to reflect on his circumstances. "I suppose I am lucky to be alive, and although at times I have wished for nothing more than death, I have tried to live in all other ways as a man. You have helped me do that, Charlotte."

"I? But how?"

"I have loved you since the moment I first saw you on the streets of London. I was still whole then, and I dreamed of making you my wife. My family was poor too. The first time I saw you, I was on my way to deliver some medicines to an ailing family, and you were collecting the laundry that you would wash that day. I vowed to take you away and make a better life for both of us. We would have children."

Jack stopped and looked down but saw nothing. "But then the accident happened, and by the time I healed and returned to my work, you had found a way to make more money than washing other people's clothes. I was heartbroken, but over time, I told myself this was the life Fate handed us. I would never be able to please you physically as other men could, so I watched you meet others imagining every time that I was the one in your arms that night. I have desired no other woman—not that any other would want me any more than you would. You have been my obsession. I have lived imagining your most intimate experiences. How terribly perverse! As I confess to you, I see what a wretch I am, have always been!" His hands dart up to cover his face, hot with humiliation.

Charlotte barely absorbed any of his explanation. Her mind stopped processing with the first words of his story. She removed his hands from his face and held them in hers. They turned to look at each other for the first time. How their lives had run parallel to each other for years, never touching, never talking, yet always running on some strangely familiar plane.

She realized suddenly how comfortable they felt together, sitting on the hard sand, unmindful of the cold.

"You. Love. Me?"

****

From the moment they walked back to the tavern hand in hand, it was clear to everyone that Charlotte and Jack had reached a mutual understanding. They entered clutching each other awkwardly and breathlessly like first lovers. Dark Ray with Terra strapped to her chest was serving the whalers. She placed the jug of flip on a nearby table, put her hands on her hips, and flashed a rare smile.

"Well, I never thought I'd live to see the day. Charlotte, you look positively innocent! And Jack. Jack, my boy, you don't look like a virgin anymore!"

The whalers looked up stunned. Seeing Charlotte and Jack still clutching each other, they let out a shout of good cheer mixed with dismay at their anticipated loss of Charlotte's time. The couple stood there numbed by the moment. Dark Ray attempted to ease the awkward situation by offering them two stools by the bar. She set two draughts in front of them, poured one for herself, raised it in the air, and declared, "To Charlotte and Jack—may they live long in each other's company!" Then she wrapped her arms around her baby and held her close, remembering Anawon and seeing him in their daughter's wonderful brown eyes.

Rachel and Mariana left the kitchen at Dark Ray's bellowing declaration. They were as stunned as everyone but Dark

Ray, it seemed, but they too joined in the moment by filling their mugs anew.

Before the week was out, Charlotte and Jack departed from the tavern although they could have left sooner. The day after they finally spoke, a vessel from Boston, arrived with fabric and other supplies, and Jack was prepared to secure them a ride on the return trip to the city. But after a passionate twenty-four hours—the two hardly leaving each other's sides, Charlotte became temperamental and uncharacteristically indecisive and found every excuse to delay the journey. It looked like snow. Perhaps they should stay on until spring when the weather was more pleasant for traveling. Her ankle was still sore from having twisted it coming down the stairs last week. She would never be able to travel with it feeling so painful. With the crazy one buried, maybe Ray needed Charlotte to remain at the tavern a while longer until a replacement could be found.

Jack began to worry that their union was doomed after all. The two of them moped around the tavern until Dark Ray couldn't take another minute of them. Jack sat at the bar all hours of the day drinking and whittling every piece of whalebone he could get his hands on. The size of the piece didn't matter. One day he carved the image of a man's head wearing a cap from a bone no longer than two inches in length. While Jack was thus engaged, Charlotte had taken to bed most of the day, nursing her perfectly fine and still handsome ankle and only feebly offering to help Dark Ray in the kitchen. Her eyes were perpetually pink from crying, an activity in which Charlotte had never allowed herself to indulge.

"All right, that does it." Dark Ray roared after Jack returned from going upstairs and looked like a rejected puppy.

"You up there. Get your lily-white ass down here. I will take no more of this behavior. Are you mad to think this game can continue? Charlotte, now!"

With a quilt wrapped around her shoulders, Charlotte limped to the top of the stairs.

"What is all the clamor, Ray? Are you so anxious to be rid of me?" she whimpered.

"Rid of you? No, Charlotte. I never thought I would say this, but I'm actually going to miss you. Terra will too. So will Rachel and Mariana, I warrant. But it's time for you to go. You have a chance to enjoy the rest of your days with a loving partner, one who obviously has been faithful to you since I don't know when. What are you afraid of? Companionship doesn't hurt as much as regret, and regretful is how you will feel in your old age if you let this man go now."

Although Charlotte had never been more frightened in her life, the weight of her indecision was lifted by Dark Ray's straightforward words. What was wrong with her? Jack was now out of the shadows and in the center of her existence. She knew she could never let him go. She had been oddly linked to him all these years, and it had been a comforting experience despite her refusal to acknowledge it. The truth was, her life changed with Terra's birth. Something in her died that day. Something in her was born. It was the ability to love another. And now she could never go back to just loving herself.

Resolved, Charlotte burst into new tears, torrents of them, and raced blindly down the stairs on healthy ankles into Jack's arms. The force of her body against his landed them both on the floor.

"Oh, my Darling," she sighed. "Forgive my foolishness. Ray knows me too well. I was simply frightened that I might not be able to adjust to this sudden change in my life. But how could I give you up now?" Still on the floor, they kissed passionately after which Charlotte bounced up as Jack remained dazed and looking up at her.

"I can be ready in an hour if we can find the transportation out of here. Shall we go, my Love?" Jack beamed, the freckles on his face hidden by the ruddy blush that had crept up his neck as she spoke. Standing up now, he took her face in his hands and kissed her mouth again to the cheers of all who witnessed it.

Within the hour, they were gone. A boat from Plimoth was waiting at the beach. They could get a ride across the Bay, and then travel the rest of the journey to Boston by carriage. Over the years, Charlotte found her way to the hearts of all the women, and their parting caused a great display of wailing, hugging, and promising to visit.

Mariana removed a small figure of the Virgin from her apron pocket, a gift from a visiting sailor, and closed Charlotte's fingers around it. "May this image of Mary protect you, Charlotte, and may She in Her wisdom draw you finally to her." Another time, Charlotte would have scoffed at Mariana and declared that she needed no protection especially from one of Mariana's papist idols. But today, she took it graciously, finally understanding the impulse behind Mariana's gesture. It was love.

With her tiny hands, Rachel stroked Charlotte's cheeks, then cupped her face and drew it close to her lips. She kissed Charlotte squarely on the mouth, stepped back, and said, "When you get lonely for us, Charlotte, think of how we danced. Keep the music in your head, and dance a step or two for remembrance."

Dark Ray, while more reserved than Mariana and Rachel, brought her baby over to the huddle the three women formed and placed her arms around them in silence. Terra was nestled in the center of their circle. Her baby eyes searched their wet faces, and when they saw her quizzical expression, they all smiled broadly and cooed at her, the lodestone of their advancing years. The men, including Jack, stood aside and watched as the women turned back to Charlotte, their petulant sister, bid her farewell and ignored all around them but each other.

Chapter 26

1725

Cat and Bird

Dark Ray woke up drenched in sweat. She sat upright pressing her left hand across her mouth so she did not scream and startle her young daughter who was asleep beside her. She had just experienced the most unsettling dream of her long life, and since she placed great import in them, she couldn't help recognizing that what had unfolded in the dream was a cautionary tale. She didn't know who was in danger, but she knew she herself was somehow involved.

After she gently lay back down, Dark Ray started to sort out the message. As in many dreams, this one came to her in symbols, and she fought an uncomfortable feeling as she pieced them together to make meaning. There was a large cat, like the bobcats that used to roam the woods across the harbor. In bright sunlight, the feline stalked an unsuspecting grouse as it foraged for food. Quietly, so quietly, it gained on the smaller creature. It was so close. A drop of saliva moistened the fur along the outside of the cat's mouth. Its yellow eyes held the small creature in a ferociously penetrating gaze. Its eyes staked out the plan that its legs were about to execute. The feline pounced and captured the bird in one unbroken movement. With its strong jaws, it ripped the prey apart in seconds. The blood from the grouse oozed onto the ground, leaving a red slick upon the fallen leaves. The grouse had not even had time to cry out in fear. The cat took what it wanted and left the remaining feathers behind as a token of its presence.

Why would she dream of a cat and a bird? Incidents like this occurred everyday in waking life. It was the natural order of things. Yet what she dreamed did not appear natural. There was a quality of bizarre truth to it. She was frightfully aware that danger was not lurking in the shadows but in the safety of the sunlight.

Someone would get hurt. She would be called to do something she

never thought possible with the stealth and speed of a cat. Life

would never be the same.

Chapter 27

1730

Repository

(Terra)

Was I spoiled? Yes, I was pampered beyond measure. When a child has four loving mothers, what else can be expected? As the years passed, and I grew from baby to child, I was made to believe that no one like me had ever been born on the island. On this great earth. I was shamefully doted upon, not only by my mother, but by the other women as well. My memories consist of Momma feeding me the best portions of every meal with her own strong fingers and telling me about the father I never knew. Of Rachel playing with me on the floor like another child or twirling me around in dance. Of Mariana taking me on walks to her Mary shrine as she taught me the names of the wildflowers and the wonder of her Mary's love. Of Charlotte, perhaps the most devoted, coming to visit from Boston and bestowing lavish gifts of special soaps and fine impractical dresses at my feet—and always humming a tune as I hugged her, one I associated with her and seemed to have been born knowing.

Being raised among grown women, I matured early. I was a sharply observant child who spoke her mind, and as a result, the women confided in me in ways most children do not experience. As I grew, I became the repository for all past wrongs and regrets, all present difficulties, all future dreams. The women stuffed me with their stories, filling my mind to bursting with tales of profound sadness and utter joy. I loved their stories.

"Terra," said Mariana. "Did I ever tell you about the time when I was forced to dress as a boy? Do not laugh, little one. I might not be here today braiding your hair if I had not done so.

Stop laughing and stand still while I finish. It was at the time when I lost my beloved mother."

Mariana paused, and the brush went limp against my scalp. "There is not a day that goes by that I do not think of her. She was everything to me like your mother is to you." Mariana resumed brushing. "She had hair like yours—straight and dark. How I miss her some days and wonder what my life would have been like had she lived to raise me beyond your age. But then, I might never have met you, my dearest, and my life really has been blessed after all. Mary has watched over me and all of you. Holy Mary, Mother of God. Pray for us sinners"

"Yes, Mariana, you have told me all about your mother and your Mary—many times—but why did you dress like a boy? Did you look silly?" I could not stop giggling, and Mariana had to put her hands on my shoulders to hold me still.

"Terra, I have no idea if I looked silly, nor did I care. It was a frightening time, and I was simply trying to stay alive the best way I knew how. What would you have done?" Mariana asked, as she began the second braid. "I felt safer on the road as a boy, so I cut off my long hair to here."

One of her hands held the braid in place while the other indicated the shortened length of her hair on my neck. "Then I stole, Mary, forgive me, some breeches and a shirt, left my dress behind in the yard where I stole the boy clothes, and ran. My disguise worked because I got here safely some weeks later. I do not know how long it took me—it seemed like forever, but then I was a young child like you, and time does not mean what it does to us older people."

"I understand, Mariana. You did the best you could. I'd have done the same, but I'm sure I wouldn't have been as brave." I knew that Mariana was feeling sad about the memory and wanted to soothe her. Mariana had always treated me like her own daughter, despite what I thought about her odd and constant habit of visiting her statue, weaving words from a prayer she tried to teach me into her conversations, habits I never fully understood. My mother had told me years earlier that it was Mariana who'd delivered me.

"Terra," exclaimed Rachel on another occasion when I was helping her sweep the dining room. "It is about time you learned to dance. Everyone needs to dance. When Matthew married another—I have already told you about him—I thought I would never laugh again. Then I lost our baby. But one night, a good-hearted young man brought me to my feet, showed me the simplest of steps, and from then on, I knew that dancing was my salvation. Dancing brought me back to life. Dancing is my passion. I need nothing else in life, except you, your mother, Mariana, and Charlotte. Come now, watch me and learn." And Rachel moved gracefully across the room with her broom as her partner, lost in the sensuous movement of her own private rhythm.

I tried to follow Rachel's example, but I didn't have the natural skill Rachel possessed, nor could I hear the music that was only in Rachel's head and inspiring her moves. Rachel laughed at my attempts, put her broom down, took my hand, and slowly moved along with me. It was fun, I thought, but not something I cared much about. However, I didn't tell Rachel who was so gentle and good. I would not hurt her for anything. I loved Rachel almost as much as I loved Momma. Instead I looked up in Rachel's radiant face and smile, letting her think I was enjoying the motion as much as she was.

"Terra, my sweet girl," crooned Charlotte on one of her visits. "When I come next, I promise to bring you the fan my first suitor gave me in London when I was so young and oh, so beautiful. You will never know how stunning I was." Charlotte's hands went up to the sagging skin of her neck. "I despise that I am growing old. You only know me as this wrinkly-faced woman, my waist filling out to rival your mother's. Thank goodness Jack loves me as I am. What would I do without his constant attention? Dearest, if you must get old, be sure you find a man who looks beyond your advancing imperfections and still sees with young eyes."

Old, I thought? Mariana was right. I was still too young to imagine myself aging, but I went to Charlotte and hugged her waist, breathing in her sweet perfumed scent and said, "Charlotte, you are beautiful. How could you have ever been more so?"

Charlotte squeezed me more tightly to her. "Oh, you charmer. You know just what to say to please me."

Each woman thought she was the only one who confided in me. A child was never so frequently hugged, bestowed with thousands of kisses, given all the sweets she desired. My mother would warn the women to stop feeding me sugary treats. She said I would become too used to the confections, and surely my teeth would rot in my head. None of them listened, and I consumed their sweet gifts with abandon. My cheeks were constantly pink from pinching. I was surrounded by the unconditional love of women, and I lived in a world of perpetual goodness and light for a time that I wish had lasted my whole life.

Chapter 28

1730

Friendly

"Terra!" Dark Ray called out to her daughter, who at ten was as dependable as any adult. And beautiful. Dark Ray was amazed that she had produced such a creature. She believed Anawon must have come from some handsome lineage for this child's stunning beauty was his doing, not hers. "Go see where those sheep have gone off to, will you? It's time to butcher one of the new lambs. I, for one, am tired of whale meat." With a love that almost suffocated her on a daily basis, Dark Ray watched

Terra as she sat on the settle by the tavern's front door tying up her boots.

"All right, Momma, but please let's not kill the new black one. I have already given him a name. I call him Friendly. I want to keep him always."

"You have named a male? We already have a good ram. Don't get too attached to him. We can't keep more than one. They will fight each other for the females. The young rams go in the stew pot. You know that. Name all the ewes if that's a pleasant game."

Dark Ray patted the top of Terra's head. "Now go, while you still have the daylight. Once you have found them, secure one in the holding pen. It doesn't have to be your Friendly this time."

"Thank you, Momma. I'm going now," said Terra as she raced out the front door towards one of the popular sheep haunts.

The flock had wandered to the far west side of the island where the grasses were plentiful. The lambs calmly nibbled the green shoots as Terra sat and watched them at a distance, especially the black lamb she called Friendly. She sat quietly, so mesmerized by their tranquility and the warm sun that she did not sense the man until he was upon her. She couldn't scream because he had covered her mouth with his left hand. With his right, he wrestled her skirt above her waist. Her strong young legs kicked, but he was stronger and now getting angry at her protest, so he removed his hand from her mouth and smacked it, causing one of her teeth to cut into the inside of her cheek.

She began to whimper. "Please, Hezekiah, don't hurt me. Why are you doing this? I thought you were my friend."

The man replied by smacking her again, this time silencing her and splitting her lower lip.

Terra knew him well—a frequent visitor to the tavern since she could remember. He lived across the harbor in town. He boasted of his twelve children and how his wife was not done yet producing offspring for him. He loved children—the more the better. Since Terra was young, he had a way of coaxing her onto his lap. A wonderful storyteller, he recited tales that he said he told his own children—of such creatures called goblins and trolls and of beautiful princesses. She developed an easy affection for him and looked forward to his visits to the tavern. Aside from the women she lived with, he was the only customer who paid much attention to her.

But of late, she had begun to feel uneasy around Hezekiah. Last Saturday she sat on his lap, and she felt his maleness harden under her legs as he pressed her down with increasing firmness. Since then, she was reluctant to go near him. His hardness confused and unsettled her. She no longer felt comfortable in his company. That last time she was on his lap, she had trouble releasing from his grasp, and she welcomed her mother's call to help serve the dinner.

Since then, she found ways to avoid his touch, hurrying off to help Rachel gather eggs at the chicken house or to assist Mariana with food preparation in the kitchen. She wanted nothing to do with that hardness. She didn't understand it. The hot stiffness of it against her young thighs felt like a violation of some kind. It felt powerful and dangerous, and she was used to being in control of her surroundings.

Now though, he had caught her. He was forcing that same hardness between her legs, only this time it was exposed. She was so frightened she felt sick and wanted to throw up. The hardness was tearing the soft flesh where she peed. Because he was meeting with such resistance, he backed away from her and went down on her, licking the place where he was having trouble entering. Feeling it sufficiently moist, he returned to straddle her, and this time he was successful in thrusting his maleness all the way up inside her. Her eyes remained clamped shut. She was vaguely aware of the colors inside her eyelids. The burning sensation between her legs was almost more than she could bear. It was unlike any pain she had felt before, but when he finally fell off her body, he let out a sigh of fulfillment. She was not sure if she would ever walk again. The pain traveled down her legs and up her entire body. She opened her eyes, but her body felt paralyzed with trauma. Her sobs escaped, anyway. She sensed a sticky wetness covering her thighs. She wondered if she was going to die.

He dressed quickly, sliding his breeches over his now limp maleness and buttoning them securely. He spit in the sand and wiped his mouth with the back of his hand. "Do not breathe a word of this to anyone, you hear? This is our little secret." He reached for his upturned hat lying on the ground beside her. She winced at the nearness of his hand. "Ah, quit crying. Admit it: you know you liked it. And if you did not this time, you will come to like it. I will show you how."

With these words, he turned and retreated down the path to the tavern. Along the way he looked from side to side, his steps wary and slow, examining the walkway before him, like a bird in search of its next meal.

Terra continued to lie in the sand on her side, her legs tucked up against her chest. She lost all sense of time, but as the light began to fade, she knew she had to find the strength to return home. Her mother would be worried about her. She saw that the sheep had returned after being frightened away by Hezekiah's violence and now were grazing at a distance from where she lay. Their presence reminded her of the errand that sent her to find them. She would return home empty-handed, but that did not disturb her now. She felt so unclean, so ashamed. How could she face her mother and the other women?

With her underdress, she tried to wipe the dry blood and discharge from her thighs. She used saliva to clean the blood from around her mouth. She straightened her braid, her skirt, her mind—to clear the horror from it. She didn't want anyone to know what happened. And now she was deathly afraid of Hezekiah. Yet, she had to maintain some control over her emotions even though all she wanted to do was cry.

When she entered the dining room, Dark Ray called out from tending the fire, "Where have you been, Terra? Did you take my request to locate the sheep as an excuse to get out of work? Don't get too attached to that young ram of yours. He's going to be in the stew pot before too long."

Her mother straightened up and faced her. "It's getting dark. I was beginning to worry about you, my girl. Did you secure one of the lambs?"

"Sorry, Momma," she said with an evenness that astounded her, for not only was she addressing her mother, but Hezekiah was over in the corner watching her every move. She avoided his gaze. "I was not able to catch one today."

"Come then," said Dark Ray. "You can try again tomorrow. I have some hearty chowder that Mariana made while you were off chasing the sheep. You must be hungry. Did you bite your lip? It looks a little swollen. We'll put some of that betony salve on it after you eat."

Terra carefully nodded her head in agreement, and her silence caused Dark Ray to examine her daughter more closely. Something was wrong with her. Maybe she had worms again. She'd have to treat the child for them tonight. Once again, she thanked the one who died on the day she gave birth to Terra for her garden still yielded a ready supply of medicinal teas, ointments, and potions. The one she still regretted never understanding and whose name she would never speak aloud.

That night before they retired, Dark Ray set about brewing a pot of nettle tea for Terra's worms. As she entered the sleeping room with the drink, she noticed that Terra had already removed her daytime clothes and was under the covers in her nightdress. The garments were in a heap on the floor, and as Dark Ray picked them up to hang them on a clothing hook behind the door, she smelled a familiar scent coming off the coarse fabric. Then she noticed the bloodstains on the underdress as well. She stood rigid, glued to the floor. Waves of nausea assaulted her stomach. Her mind was numb except for the repetitive denial coursing through her thoughts. *No. No. It can't be. No. No.* Then after what seemed like hours, *Who?*

Slowly she willed her body to move toward the bedchamber where she sensed that Terra was only feigning sleep. Gingerly, she slipped under the covers and drew her daughter to her. She whispered in her ear, trying to exhibit a false calm, "Terra, tell me about it. I must know what happened to you today." Then she waited.

First, she heard the sobs that her little girl must have held in all evening. Then she heard the hiccups that usually accompanied Terra's excessive bouts of crying or laughing. Dark Ray waited a long while before Terra became composed enough to recall the incident, and while she was waiting, she was frantically thinking about what she must do.

Finally, she listened to the story she never wanted to hear from her baby's voice—a story that no mother ever wants to hear her daughter tell. At the last before she fell off into an exhausted sleep, Terra asked, "Am I going to die, Momma?"

Tears rarely fell down the cheeks of Dark Ray's face. But now they spilled over her lower eyelids, sliding down her cheeks, and collecting in the folds of her neck. They were hot tears—of sorrow, of anger, of revenge. For years, she had protected the other women and avoided this fate that had fallen on her daughter. In her despair, she thought, why couldn't this have happened to me instead?

When she could speak, she whispered, "No, my dear one. YOU are not going to die." And with that statement, she knew what she had been called to do.

The next morning she left Terra to rest in bed longer than usual. When she awakened, her mother took time from the daily tavern chores to wash her in a warm, soothing lavender bath. As gently as a sea breeze in scrub pines, she washed every crease and fold of her daughter's body, removing the man smell. When she exposed the flesh between Terra's legs and saw the bruises, she wanted to scream. Although she felt like cursing aloud in fury, she forced herself to hum Charlotte's melody to Terra in an effort to keep them both calm, and she again assured her daughter that she was safe, that no one would hurt her again. As she helped her dress in clean clothing, Dark Ray said, "Terra, I want you to work very closely with Mariana and Rachel today. I have some business to attend to off island, but I promise to return this evening."

****

Dark Ray didn't often go to the mainland. All she needed was right here on the island or was delivered by boat weekly. After the mid-day meal, she borrowed one of the vessels at the shore and rowed over alone to Billingsgate dock. She stowed the boat away from the busy port, grabbed her leather bag of worn knives, and headed for the home of Hezekiah Cobb, the town cutler. When she knocked on his door, his wife, accompanied by the three youngest of his twelve children, greeted her. Although their much-mended worn clothing displayed the poverty that was their life, the woman was not happy that Dark Ray had brought her husband business from the island where she believed all manner of impropriety occurred. She did not invite Dark Ray into the squalid house but simply pointed to the shed behind the dwelling where her husband was working in his shop. Then she slammed the door in Dark Ray's face.

As Dark Ray entered the shed, she was shocked to see that Hezekiah was smaller in height than she anticipated, but then she realized that she had never had the occasion to stand beside him. She noted that she had the advantage in height and spoke with new confidence. "Hezekiah, I have knives to be repaired."

The man was startled to see her out of the tavern—she looked eerily out of place. He cleared his throat to cover his surprise, but it was too late. She was quick to record his uneasiness. She carefully observed her prey with the stillness of a cat.

"Of course," he stammered. Leave the bag with me. I have other work to finish first. I will bring it when I visit the tavern tonight."

She considered agreeing, but then said, "No, I will wait for you to do the work. I have other errands in town and will return later in the day."

However, she had no plan beyond this moment. Did she think she was going to kill him in broad daylight in his own yard? The truth was, she hadn't thought out a plan. She allowed herself to be guided solely by instinct, and now she was not sure how she was going to finish this.

As she turned and walked out of the yard, she considered that she needed the time to herself and to let this thing unfold how it would. She would know when to act. If instinct brought her there, she would trust it to play itself out. While she was completely committed to what she was about to do, she had to remain calm, but seeing him up close with not a visible mark to indicate his deplorable behavior the day before renewed her anger. She was momentarily blinded by her fury and wanted to kill him on the spot, daylight or not. Instead she left Hezekiah there with his work and wandered down to the beach.

She sat on the shore, looked across at the island, and considered the long life she had spent there. She was old now—in her early sixties—to have lived this long had been a blessing when so many of her people had succumbed to the sickness brought by European colonization. Her life had been enriched by so much: the women she lived with, the work she enjoyed, the wonderful man who brought pure love to her life, Anawon. The beacon of her existence, his daughter. The daughter whose pain she would soon avenge.

In a panic, she wondered if in her advancing age she would be able to overpower this younger man. She told herself he was not so young, somewhere in middle age, and he was small—birdlike. His eyes darted anxiously from side to side. His frame was slight. His fingers were bony and claw-like. She was amazed that he had it in him to father so many children.

Then she stopped sifting the sand between her fingers and slammed her fist into the mound she had made. And felt another wave of rage as fierce as when she first discovered what he had done to her daughter. He had made considerable use of his prick. She would see that he never put it where it didn't belong again.

The afternoon passed, and she built her strength, physically resting on the beach—if her mind were not in such turmoil, this would be a holiday—and mentally preparing to be ready when the opportunity presented itself. She would need to be focused and quick. He must not suspect her. When she returned to Hezekiah's shop later in the day, he was just finishing the last knife and placing it back in the leather bag. He turned to her.

"There you are. Good timing. Since you are heading back over to the island, perhaps I can share the ride with you. I was planning to come over this night."

"Of course," she said. "I was going to suggest that we cross the harbor together. No use taking two boats over, is there?"

"Good, then. You can pay me for the work I did for you today by letting me eat and drink on the house."

"We have a deal. I'll wait for you on the beach."

After informing his wife, he took off down the road to meet Dark Ray. They spoke little on the short journey, but as they embarked on the island shore, and he was about to walk up the familiar worn path, she said, "Why not take the back path to the tavern? It is much quicker."

"I did not know there was one. Show me the way, then."

Although it was steeper and led up and over a tall dune, the path appeared closer than it really was to the lights that already illuminated the tavern windows. She had brought a taper with her and urged him to hold it. With the lit candle, he could follow the path easily. She would follow, she told him, as she walked more slowly and knew the way even in the dark of this new moon. The path produced unexpected twists and turns, and Hezekiah soon realized that this walk was one of the many cut by the hooves of the sheep that roamed the island freely. This was not a path cut by humans.

He turned to tell her so, and she was upon him, one of the freshly sharpened knives slashing at his neck, instantly bringing his blood gushing to the surface of his skin. He was astonished by her speed and stealth, so shocked he couldn't speak or cry out. When the knife found his heart, he gasped and choked on the bloody ooze that poured from his mouth. As he lay dying, she knelt at his side, breathing heavily and watching his life expire. Then in the seconds preceding his last breath, she scalped him the way the French taught her people long ago. She knelt in the complete darkness over her prey, the scalp dripping from her hand. She stared at the hairy piece of bloody skin in disbelief. Her body had acted viscerally; her mind was still catching up. Did she really sever the taut skin from this man's skull? Had she been planning to do this all along?

She had. Next, she dragged the dead Hezekiah off into the nearby bayberry bushes where she covered him with sand and the scant remains of last autumn's leaves and grasses. As she pawed at the sand to cover her cache, she was overcome by a sudden urge to urinate. She stood up, lifted her skirt, and peed as if to mark her territory.

Once the immediacy of emptying her water subsided, her mind caught up with her body again, and she could hardly believe what she had done. Physically relieved but mentally shocked, she resumed her work in a state of detachment, wrapping the scalp in her apron and putting it in the leather bag with the knives. She retraced her steps to the water and washed herself of his blood. She washed the knife. Her dress was of a dark red fabric, and so any blood that was on it could not be detected now that her apron was removed.

She straightened up and headed for the tavern, knowing her way clearly to the path that led to the front door. As she walked, she regained her focus, and the moment felt strangely familiar.

At last she recollected the cat and bird dream of a few years ago—now she knew that her dream soul had made this journey before. Like the large cat of the dream, she had no remorse for what she had done to the bird. She believed the day's work was a necessary act of survival even though she knew that cats did not kill out of vengeance. Yet, she felt no shame.

****

It was quiet and dark in the tavern except for a single candle. Rachel had attempted to keep vigil for her but was now fast asleep, her body slumped over a table illuminated by the taper. Yet, as Dark Ray stepped through the door, Rachel jumped up alarmed.

"Ray," she whispered. "Where have you been? We were planning to send a search party out for you, but I told Mariana that you were fully capable of taking care of yourself, so she and Terra went off to bed. However, Terra was unusually weepy. She cried herself to sleep. What is ailing her besides her mother being gone—which is uncommon enough?"

Dark Ray motioned for Rachel to move closer to her. Together they huddled on the heavy wooden settle by the front door.

"Rachel, I am telling you and only you what has happened these last two days. I trust you will keep this story to yourself. I don't mean to burden you, but in the days ahead, I will need your help. You are my dearest and most constant friend."

"Whatever is going on?"

"Nothing now. The worst is over. You accurately observed Terra's distress. It wasn't just because I left for the afternoon."

Dark Ray whispered as she disclosed her daughter's rape to her friend. Rachel began to weep silently, her hand over her mouth to stifle her sobs. It wouldn't help anything if she awakened Terra and Mariana.

"I couldn't let him live, Rachel. He hurt my baby. You should see how he tore her up. Well, I tore him up as well, but I feel no remorse for my actions. I just need to figure out what to do with the body is all."

"Is all? Where is it?" Rachel paused. "What is in that leather sack?"

Dark Ray looked down at the bag that she placed on the floor when she sat down.

"Mostly knives that he repaired for me today. Then there's my apron and this." She reached in and produced the bloody garment and unfolded the fabric to reveal Hezekiah's scalp.

Rachel's eyes widened in horror.

"Ray, you scalped him? Why?"

"I wanted to humiliate him. I didn't know of any other way. I wasn't about to handle his prick, but let me tell you, it crossed my mind to cut that off instead."

"What are we going to do with it?" Rachel's eyes scanned the rooms on either side of the fireplace. "I know. Come. Let us throw it in the fire right now."

She stood up immediately and then stopped. "Where is the body?" she repeated.

Together they moved to the side of the hearth that was used for cooking. Dark Ray took the bloody scalp and placed it in the fire. It smoldered for a few minutes and slowly became consumed by the flames that Rachel created with some kindling. As it burned, it gave off the familiar scent of roasting flesh along with the acrid smell of scorched hair.

She stared dazedly at the fire. The scalp no longer resembled the top of a man's head. Now it looked like a piece of charred whale meat. Finally Dark Ray spoke. Not looking at Rachel, she whispered, "The body is on the other side of the island behind the tavern and over by one of the sheep paths. I dragged it into some bushes for now. I don't think anyone will find it tonight."

Rachel saw how exhausted the older woman was. Dark circles of fatigue framed her eyes. "Come, Ray," she said. "We will decide what to do with the body tomorrow." She took Dark Ray's elbow and steered her up the stairs where they both fell into a restless sleep until dawn.

The next morning Dark Ray was awake before the others and began the bread making for the day. To her surprise, Rachel joined her within minutes. Alone in the back kitchen, they drank warm ale to clear their heads and to discuss a plan. Dark Ray continued to knead the dough as they talked.

"I have been thinking about this, Ray," Rachel said. "We have to get back to the body tonight. Wild animals will surely begin to smell it and expose the hiding place. Oh! I do not want to think about what we might find. We cannot delay, so when everyone is asleep—we still have the new moon; it will be dark—we can go and retrieve the body. We have to bury it tonight."

"I had the same thoughts, Rachel, but we have to prepare a burial place before then. Finish making the bread, and I'll go down to the storage cellar right now under the pretense of making room for this winter's storage. While I'm down there, I'll dig a hole large enough to bury him.

"Don't look so horrified. Yes, we'll know he's down there, but we'll also know that someone won't discover a fresh grave on the island without our knowing it. We are usually the only ones who go into the cellars. We'll have a better chance of his never being found if he's buried under the tavern."

"Well, all right. I suppose it would seem strange if one of us went off into the dunes with a shovel today. At least down there, no one will see what you are doing because I can keep watch up here. But the thought of him rotting beneath us…."

"Rachel, this is no time to become delicate. Or are you afraid of ghosts?"

"Of course not!"

"Well," declared Dark Ray, "I am at least respectful of them, and that's another reason I'm choosing the cellar. There I will have a better chance of keeping an eye on that evil one's spirit should it decide to cause us further harm."

With that last remark, Dark Ray waved her hand to end the conversation.

As Rachel began to shape the dough into loaves, Dark Ray wiped her hands of flour and went outside to the garden to retrieve the shovel. The tavern was still quiet when she lifted the trapdoor in the sitting room and descended down the stairs to begin her task. At least in this summer heat, she would be cool as she dug the hole. The consolation of the day.

Later that night, after the last of the men left the lookout towers in search of summer whales and returned to the mainland, the two Rays, the Dark and the Light, treaded down the sheep path. The Dark one led the way. The Light one followed because she could be persuaded to do anything for this woman even if it involved complicity in murder.

Fortunately for Rachel's sensibilities, predators had not discovered the corpse although the flies had certainly located the feast. Because of the summer heat, they swarmed the carcass, inching their way to the dried blood that caked the raw spots of his chest and head.

The smell caused Rachel to step back momentarily from removing the sand and debris to strengthen her resolve. She straightened up and helped Dark Ray with the old blanket they brought. With some rope they tied the blanket securely around Cobb to keep him from falling out one of the ends. Then they tried to hoist the bundle onto their left shoulders, but Rachel was too small to handle the weight and her end fell, causing her to slide with it. Trapped, she lay under the dead man. She wanted to scream, but she suppressed the urge. Dark Ray swiftly removed the bundle off Rachel and lifted it onto her own shoulder in one movement. Rachel stood up, brushed off her dress, and patted Dark Ray's other shoulder.

Slowly Rachel walked behind Dark Ray to the tavern. Once there, Rachel stepped around Dark Ray and her burden and went inside to be sure no one was awake. She lifted the trapdoor, lit a lantern, and placed it in the cellar, and then scrambled up the ladder to assist Ray who was already waiting above her. Together they lifted the body off Ray's shoulder and slid it down the rungs of the ladder. Then they went into the cellar themselves and dumped the body into the shallow grave.

After they buried the blanket and its contents in sand so it was no longer visible, they took a wide barrel used for storing flour and rolled it over Hezekiah Cobb's final resting place. Then they gently stamped the sandy earth around the barrel so it looked like the rest of the hard packed ground. Nothing was out of place to cause suspicion should anyone search this cellar.

The complicity of their activity and its successful completion made them perversely giddy. When they returned upstairs, they both suppressed the desire to giggle like young girls who had just engaged in something for which their elders would not approve. With the trapdoor back in place, they went over to the bar for a stiff shot of the best rum in the house. No words between them. A nod of understanding. Justice served. Innocence gone.

****

It didn't take more than a week before two helmeted militiamen appointed by the Billingsgate magistrate visited the island to question the whereabouts of Hezekiah Cobb. They disembarked from their boat with an air of pomp and superiority. At this hour of the day, the whalers were on the beach trying out an unexpected late stranding of whales in the harbor. They looked curiously at the two. Some waved for they were neighbors of these men over on the mainland. When the officials asked if Cobb had been on the island, the general consensus was that he had not visited in about a week. One whaler snickered and suggested maybe Dark Ray might have a better estimate of when he drank his last pint. They all laughed and returned to their work.

The two militiamen headed up to the tavern, wishing they were not here on official business at all, but neither admitting the desire to each other. When they approached the yard of the tavern, they saw Dark Ray tanning a deer hide, her arms deep in a bucket of some kind of disgustingly slimy substance. Her sleeves were rolled above her elbows, and to protect her dress, she wore a thick canvas apron that was discolored from previous tanning jobs.

A stunningly beautiful young girl of about ten sat nearby as Dark Ray explained the technique to her. From time to time, she looked lovingly at the older woman. Her dark eyes were shaped like almonds. Her skin was an exquisite tawny brown. Her hair fell straight and black down her back. The men had trouble looking away from her. She was completely unaware of their admiration. Her attention instead was distracted by an army of ants that were carrying food crumbs larger than themselves across the grass. She wondered where they were going.

"Watch what I'm doing, Terra."

The men and the young girl looked up at Dark Ray.

"This is not a task for the squeamish. Now that I've stretched the hide on this wooden frame, I must treat it quickly so it is well preserved. In the bucket here are the deer's brains. First I have to squish them like this with my hands. If you don't think about what it is you're squeezing, you won't mind doing it. Then I take a handful and rub them into the hide like this. The rubbing makes the leather soft."

Dark Ray was aware of the two men as they approached, but she ignored them and continued to address Terra. "And now here's an interesting fact. I've heard that every animal has just enough brains to preserve its hide. What do you think of that?" She delivered this last question at the very moment she decided to recognize the two men. She stopped her rubbing, threw what was left of the brains back into the bucket and faced the men.

"May I help you?"

They appeared uneasy, as they quickly directed their eyes away from the drawn hide that was attracting flies frantically consuming the oozing brains that slid to the ground.

"Are you Dark Ray? We were told you might be able to tell us when you last saw Hezekiah Cobb at your tavern."

At the mention of this name, Terra stiffened and went to stand behind her mother. Dark Ray ignored her daughter's reaction so as not to draw further attention to it.

"Well, I can't keep track of the comings and goings of all the folks who visit this place, that's for sure, but I suppose the last time I saw Hezekiah Cobb was about a week ago. Why are you looking for him?"

"His wife has reported him missing. Says you came over to see him about a week ago. Says he told her he was coming to the tavern that same night."

"Yes, I did visit his shop. I had some work for him. Then I came back. I don't recall seeing him here that night though. Is his wife really looking for him? I would think the poor woman would consider herself lucky he's gone."

Dark Ray looked down at the ground. Stop it, she told herself. Hold your tongue.

"Now I do not know how you *Nausets* feel about losing a neighbor, but I will tell you this, good woman. We English are responsible for our Christian brethren, and we have been appointed to locate Goodman Cobb. We have a warrant signed by the local owner of this place, Samuel Hawes' son, allowing us to search the premises. He said you would assist us."

"Go right ahead, good men," she mimicked. "I'm not about to stop you, but if I don't get back to this tanning job, I will have a spoiled hide on my hands, and we *Nausets* can't abide wasting a perfectly good animal. You see, we believe we are responsible for ALL our brethren."

With that she nodded to Terra to return to her seat on the ground and returned to her task. Just as they brushed past her, she made a point of squishing some brains from the bucket and splashing their shoes as she lifted her arm in a wide arc to the hide and began to rub in earnest.

"Momma," whispered Terra once the men were out of earshot.

"Say nothing, Dear One."

Terra lowered her eyes and picked at the grass growing in sparse clumps around her. She was reliving Cobb's attack. She could not erase the horror from her mind. She had nightmares about it. Her young body still ached from Cobb's thrusts.

Dark Ray too was troubled by images that she would have liked to forget, but there was no forgetting the events of last week. Not ever.

After a few minutes, the militiamen returned followed by Rachel who was still holding a jug of flip in her hand. She placed the jug on the settle by the door. They were less serious now than when they entered the tavern.

"Now, I hope you two will come back and visit us when you do not have official business. We can make it worth your trouble," Rachel singsonged as she lifted her skirt to expose a leg in the pretense of tying her shoe.

Dark Ray looked up from her work. "So. Find him?"

"No, clearly we did not. And I would thank you to be more cordial," retorted the more talkative one. "You have acted ornery since we arrived. If we had not searched every corner of the place with the assistance of Mistress Sloane and found nothing to implicate you, we would be taking you in for further questioning. Now it looks like we will have to widen the search to other townships. Sorry to trouble you all," he declared. But he was clearly smitten with Rachel who continued to reveal more of her leg for his viewing pleasure.

"No trouble at all," said Dark Ray as she glanced over at Rachel who raised her eyebrows in mischief.

Chapter 29

1730

Witness

(Terra)

Momma and Rachel thought no one had seen them, but I knew what they did that night because I followed them. When my mother left for the mainland the day after Hezekiah hurt me, I sensed she would harm him. I feared for her, not for that man, for he had shown me his true nature, and I was never going to allow him near me again. I believed Momma was strong and capable of defending herself, but I was not sure she could survive the assault of that cruel person. I shuddered to think of her caught in the grip of his monstrous hands. Yet, from the time I could understand her words and maybe even before, I believed her promise that if anyone hurt me, she would hurt them worse.

I was useless and fretted the whole day unable to complete any task Rachel or Mariana asked of me. Not only was my body still hurting, but I was afraid that my mother, in her fierce protection of me, would get herself in trouble. I could not bear the thought of losing her the way Mariana had lost her mother.

There was no sleeping for me when Momma did not return by nightfall. Rachel told me not to worry. Ray, as she called her, was the bravest and strongest woman she ever knew. There was nothing to fear. To ease Rachel's mind, I went up to bed as she urged me. Rachel said she would wait up for my mother, and when she returned, they would come up to wake me to let me know she was home safe.

A light sleeper, I heard the whispering and knew Momma had returned long before she and Rachel informed me. In my impatience, I crept to the top of the stairs as they talked quietly on the settle, but I caught enough words to suspect what my mother had done, and though I was horrified anew, I kept my body from making noise and betraying me. From where I was hiding, I could not see what they did once they left the settle and stepped over to the fireplace, but then, the smell of charred meat traveled up the stairs. I became very confused. Were they cooking at this hour? Was Momma so hungry from her journey that she could not wait for breakfast? How Mariana slept through it all, I will never understand.

It was clear to me that neither Mariana nor I was meant to be part of whatever Momma and Rachel were doing, so I did not reveal myself. By the time they came up to the bedchamber, however, I had already returned to the bedstead and feigned sleep when they tried to wake me.

The next morning, Momma and Rachel awakened earlier than usual. The new day's light had just barely begun to brighten the room. The birds had just started their morning song. I awoke early as well after a restless sleep caused by my mind racing with questions I could not ask.

Once I knew they were both in the back kitchen, I tiptoed down the steps, avoiding all the creaky places that I had learned over the years and listened behind the door. Once more I could not hear everything, but I did catch these words: *cellar, body, tonight, ghost, evil one's spirit*, and I stood frozen with fear. I almost did not make it back upstairs before Momma came bounding out of the kitchen. I thought she had caught me listening. But she had not because she dashed right past the stairway, never seeing me at all, and spent a good deal of the morning in the cellar under the sitting room.

When I asked Rachel at breakfast if I could join Momma, she said I was not needed in the cellar. Instead Ray had instructed her to keep me busy spinning wool for next winter's shawls. Rachel was not offering any more information. If I asked the questions that plagued me, they would have remained unanswered, so I attempted to do what I was told and decided if I was to learn anything more, I would have to discover it for myself.

Mariana did not seem to have any awareness of the goings on. She had slept through my mother's return, and after her chores that morning, she walked, as she always did when she had free time, to her Mary shrine. More and more as she aged, Mariana chose to keep a friendly but isolated distance between herself and the others. Her attention to her prayers consumed the time she used to spend with Momma, Rachel, and me. Mariana never acted unkindly towards us. She increasingly seemed to prefer solitude to our company.

That night I waited in the bedchamber and listened to the movements downstairs. When Rachel and Momma did not come up to bed, I left Mariana sleeping soundly with the room to herself and crept down the stairs just as the front door quietly closed. At the settle, I grabbed my boots and did not even bother to fasten them because I did not want to lose their track. I heard rustling to the right of the tavern building and followed the sound at a distance, sure that they did not detect me—I was very capable of walking silently—that was how I was able to catch my favorite lamb Friendly. The night was nearly moonless, but I knew the sheep trail well, and my eyes gradually became accustomed to the black night.

When I reached a safe distance from where they stopped, I hid behind a scrub pine to watch them. They began to brush away sand and old leaves to expose Hezekiah, now a lifeless mass of bloody flesh. With horror, I saw the extent of the harm of my mother's actions, and I remembered when I told her what Hezekiah had done to me and asked if I was going to die, and Momma had said very clearly—no, I was not. What she meant was that Hezekiah would die.

I was used to seeing blood and innards from watching the men cut up the whales and helping my mother butcher the lambs and chickens. After the shock passed of seeing his dead body and scalped head, seeing Hezekiah Cobb in such a bad way brought me great relief. I wondered what the ants would have done with him if they had gotten the chance. Would a large army carry off his body? For a moment, I allowed that image to distract me—scores of ants heaving this human mass and parading it off. It might have been a humorous image, but what I saw was not funny at all.

When my mind focused on what was really happening, it was even stranger than my ant vision. I was grateful not to be able to see the features of his face clearly in death. I would forever see his living, flushed face inches from mine after what he had done to me, and that was more than enough. I still felt unclean from his foul breath on my neck, in my hair and wondered if I would ever be free of the memory.

But even in the dark, I saw Rachel, who was not much bigger than I, stumble under the strain of holding her end of the bundle. Now Rachel experienced what I had felt under his terrible weight. I wanted to scream at the renewed thought of it, and I wanted to run to Rachel's aid, but I did not want to be discovered even by those two who loved me dearly. Their mission was dreadful enough, and they would be very upset if they discovered I was witnessing their every move. I was completely aware that my mother and Rachel were risking their lives for me.

When I saw Momma lift Hezekiah wrapped in that old blanket and sling him over her shoulder like he was nothing more than a sack of potatoes, I knew there would be no interrupting what she'd started. Awed by her strength, I resolved right then to do whatever I could to bring joy to her life. What I did not realize as a child of ten was that I was already fulfilling that task simply by breathing.

Momma and Rachel would soon begin their return and discover me if I did not leave my hiding place immediately, so I retraced my steps as they were adjusting Hezekiah on my mother's shoulder. I managed to return to the tavern in plenty of time and waited at the top of the stairs as they went directly to the trapdoor in the sitting room.

I heard a sliding sound, and when I was sure they were in the cellar, I boldly ventured close to the opening. On the way there, my foot landed on a creaky floorboard, but they must have been too engrossed in what they were doing to hear me. The light from their lantern cast an eerie glow, and all I could see were their distorted shadows dancing along one wall of the cellar as they filled the hole with Hezekiah Cobb and then dirt. As soon as the shadows began to advance to the ladder, I tiptoed back up the stairs and slipped under the covers. In the other bedstead, Mariana never stirred. Momma and Rachel did not come up immediately. I assumed they were thirsty and went to the bar for a drink, but I had witnessed all I needed. I slept. I slept so soundly. I felt safe again.

****

The following week when the two militiamen arrived to search the island for Hezekiah, I once more felt suffocating panic at the thought of my mother being taken away from me. She was teaching me how to tan a hide when they walked up the path. At first, I wanted to laugh aloud when I saw them standing there in their funny metal helmets looking official and serious as Momma greeted them with deer brains cupped in her hands. The men did not seem to know what to make of her—she had that effect on strangers—and I merrily watched the exchange forgetting their reason for coming until they mentioned Hezekiah Cobb's disappearance. Then I began to tremble, and in order to conceal my shaking limbs, I hid behind my mother's skirts like a bashful child. She never let them see any fear, if she had any, and I felt ashamed of my own weakness.

When the men went inside the tavern to search, I was convinced they would find his rotting corpse in the cellar, but Momma spoke quietly for me to say nothing of what I had seen. It was then that I realized that she and Rachel knew I had witnessed the activities of that moonless night. Since the death of the one whose name they never use, nothing goes unnoticed by my mother. I have heard accounts my entire life from the other women that Momma blamed herself for that one's passing. As a result, she became fiercely vigilant in her protection of those she loved, her actions of the week demonstrating the depth to which she would protect them.

When Rachel at last escorted the two officials back outside, I knew we were safe although Momma had not been very kind to them when they arrived. Her unfriendly manner had irritated the men before they entered the building. However, Little Light Ray, as she was so affectionately known, had clearly dazzled them with her beauty and charm even though she was well past fifty years of age. The men walked out of the tavern momentarily forgetting their mission and openly fascinated by Mistress Sloane as they called her. The playfulness in her voice removed any doubt that anyone at the tavern would ever have had a role in Hezekiah's disappearance. They bid us farewell and stumbled away in merriment. About a week later, one of them returned to the tavern to visit Rachel. He left the next day a smiling man.

And so the suspicion faded, and we went back to living our simple lives at the tavern. But something terrible had happened, and Momma, Rachel, and I had to live with it daily. Plenty had happened. To me. To Hezekiah. To my mother. Life, though still simple, changed.

Part III

1730-1740

The Passing On

"Life here on earth is an intensely reciprocal arrangement." ---

from <u>Celebrate the Earth </u>by Laurie Cabot with Jean Mills, 1994.

Chapter 30

1730-40

And So It Went

The years of women's lives are indistinguishable when what they do on a day-to-day basis is uneventful and mundane. While they are the backbone and life of any civilization, apart from exceptional cases, their work and their influence become overshadowed by the doings of men. Certainly the lives of the Great Island women are not recorded in any history book.

It seemed to Terra that the women were aging fast, and perhaps it was better that the whaling had all but ceased from this location, and the bulk of their days was spent living at the slower pace that now suited them. They were content finally to attend only to their needs and not those of the men who used to work and spend time at the tavern.

Even though Terra was younger than the others, she welcomed the increasingly quiet days. Hers had been an isolated, sheltered childhood, and except for her violent encounter with Hezekiah Cobb and the subsequent nightmares that haunted her sleep, she spent her time enjoying the simple pleasures of female camaraderie, completing domestic chores, and tending the unnamed one's garden.

Terra often wondered about that young woman who took her life on the day that she was born. What a strange coincidence that their lives brushed each other in the parallel throes of birth and death. That day was a beginning and an ending for each of them. Would they have become friends? Would her presence have caused the other to embrace life instead of death? It was not Terra's fate to meet the sad-eyed one that she felt she knew anyway from the stories her mother told her. She continued to wonder if their *Nauset* blood would have kindled a bond that was stronger than the one she shared with Rachel, Charlotte, or Mariana. Yet, she couldn't imagine being closer to anyone more than her mother and these women. However, she would always wonder about Cessie—that was her name—Charlotte had told her once and made her swear never to speak it if Terra didn't want her mother to slip into one of her moods.

The ten years of Terra's life after her rape produced other changes that the women were forced to weather and survive like the mighty nor'easter storms that rack the land from time to time. While humans prefer their lives and relationships with loved ones to remain true and intact for all eternity, time creeps in much like the sand that slowly made a peninsula of the island and forever connected it to the rest of humanity. Although Terra might have favored the isolation that an island assures, she knew humans couldn't change the natural course of water and its ability to shape the land at will. The people were mere visitors on this land that had undergone numerous changes before they arrived and would continue to morph in form long after they were gone.

Dark Ray died in her sleep two years after she murdered Hezekiah Cobb. Once Terra became a woman, she and Rachel spoke freely about that time. Terra confessed that she had overheard her mother's and Rachel's plans and followed them the night that they delivered Hezekiah to his resting place. Rachel said they were aware Terra had followed them, but because they hadn't wanted her to participate, they let her believe she had succeeded in being unnoticed. Rachel was convinced Dark Ray never quite got over what Hezekiah did to her daughter and what Dark Ray did to him in return. She confessed that Dark Ray admitted to having seen Cobb's ghost on more than one occasion when she entered the cellar in which he was buried.

That her mother had encountered Hezekiah's spirit was believable to Terra. There were times when she would come upon Dark Ray stopped at whatever task she was performing. Her mother would stand rigid and look at the trapdoor to the cellar. Terra would ask her mother a question, but she never received a response—as if her mother had not heard her. Then Dark Ray would shiver, pull herself together, and say, "Did you ask me something, Terra?" And Terra would say, "No, Momma, it's nothing."

Dark Ray became obsessed with that cellar after she and Rachel buried the body, not allowing anyone other than herself to descend the ladder steps to procure or store supplies. On dark, overcast days, she would burn sage throughout the rooms in her attempts to purify them all of Hezekiah's evil spirit although she never stated her reason for doing so. Rachel and Terra assumed this was the reason. Mariana just assumed Dark Ray was returning to her *Nauset* ways and prayed more fervently for her. When Terra asked why—she always had questions for her mother—Dark Ray would say she was just doing a good house cleaning.

In the days before she died, Dark Ray became increasingly distracted as if a part of her consciousness was already living in some other reality. Once she was on her knees and weeding in the garden. Unexpectedly, she stopped her work and sat down on the ground swaying her shoulders as if she was listening to music. When Mariana asked her what she was doing, she said, "I'm listening to Anawon's flute." After a few moments, she pushed herself back up on her knees and went back to weeding without another word.

Another time Dark Ray seemed to be talking to herself as Rachel came upon her in the kitchen. When she asked her to repeat what she had said, Dark Ray declared she wasn't talking to Rachel. She had been conversing with Anawon. The exchange shocked Rachel into recognizing that Dark Ray's end was near. She made an excuse to leave the kitchen and went off to grieve in private.

The very day of the night she fell off blissfully into the sleep from which she never awoke, Terra had been sitting outside with Dark Ray, working on winter shawls. All of a sudden, Terra looked up from the wool in her lap to witness the broadest smile she had ever seen cross her mother's face. When Dark Ray raised her arm to wave towards the footpath, Terra asked her who was approaching. "Terra, dear," she said, "It's your father. My beloved. He's coming to take me with him." As much as she longed to see the man who fathered her, Terra experienced anger, even jealousy. Her mother was hers and hers alone. She did not know a world without her, and she wasn't prepared to have her leave it.

These incidents disturbed Mariana, Rachel, and Terra greatly. They wept and attempted to console each other in private, but around Dark Ray, they acted strong, resolved to let her go freely, unhampered by their need to keep her with them longer. But when she finally passed, all the mental preparation had been useless. Terra missed her mother terribly. They all did. She was the mortar that held them together. She was the center of Terra's life. She had given her life. But for Rachel and Mariana, she was also a mother. Despite her outwardly brusque manner, she took them in at their worst hour and nurtured them. For women, losing a mother meant losing something of themselves.

Rachel and Mariana both confided to Terra that when they first met her mother, they were terrified. Not only did her great size intimidate them; her sharp, clipped style of speaking simply leveled their confidence. Through their tears they explained that it took approximately forty-eight hours to discover she was "all bark and no bite," as Mariana put it. Dark Ray even tempered her feelings about Charlotte, Rachel said, once she saw how smitten Charlotte was with Terra at her birth.

The men, however, with the exception of Anawon, never saw that tender, loving side of Dark Ray. She knew that most men didn't respect a businesswoman who appeared soft, so she ran the tavern sternly. And as a result, not one man ever disrespected her, even the ship-wrecked pirates who had visited years ago.

Once the tears and wailing subsided the morning they found her, the women buried Dark Ray at the center of the island. There her energy would radiate outward in all directions to nourish the land she so loved. As they dug her grave, two red-tailed hawks watched from a distant pine branch. After they placed her in the ground, the birds flew off together towards the southwest.

The women didn't bury Dark Ray's work tools with her as was customary for a *Nauset* because they wanted her to rest at long last. Instead they placed Anawon's flute beside her. None of them had ever had the heart to learn to play it. They believed the hauntingly airy sounds would make Dark Ray too lonely for her beloved. On her journey to meet *Kiehtan*, however, they wanted her to be accompanied by Anawon's music.

Rachel took charge of the tavern after the grieving period ended. When she was cleaning out Dark Ray's belongings to burn or re-use, she came across a tin with a note and some currency. The writing was in her father's hand, and Rachel shook as she read its contents:

Dark Ray,

Please see to it that my cherished daughter, Rachel Sloane, receives this money at the appropriate time you deem her needing it. It is the least I can do. Tell her it comes with remorse thickly laced with undying devotion.

Elijah Sloane

Rachel had no idea when Dark Ray received the contents of the tin or even, if she read the message. However, she was gratified to have found the contents on her own, and perhaps Dark Ray had intended it that way. Rachel was sure she would have destroyed the note and currency had Dark Ray given them to her when they arrived. As it turned out, this money would allow Terra and her to live on the island and have the means with which to secure provisions from the mainland now that the business of the tavern was over. So in the end, her father's money supported Rachel, and his note served to soften her resolve and forgive him in her heart at long last.

Although the blackfish had seriously declined in numbers and the whalers were engaged in the growing offshore industry, the tavern remained open for the occasional guest. Visitors became so infrequent that Rachel and Terra would often spend several weeks alone before someone dropped anchor on their shores for a brief rest.

That was the way Terra liked her days. The tavern was after all her home, and she enjoyed the increasing quiet of the place. While the pace of Billingsgate was picking up with more and more new colonists, Terra was happy to live in tranquility on her island. Rachel was not much younger than Dark Ray, and she too was thankful for the slower pace of life. In this quiet time, Rachel declared her greatest enjoyment was teaching Terra how to read. Often they would spend whole evenings alone, reading one or another of the English books Rachel had managed to persuade visitors and fishermen to bring her in days gone by.

Within a year of Dark Ray's passing, Mariana announced to Rachel and Terra that she was leaving. Over time, her devotion to her Mary had increased in intensity. Like Rachel, she was growing old. Quite often, Mariana spoke of spending her remaining days in meditation and prayer. On her last trip to visit a dying Charlotte in Boston, Mariana became acquainted with a Catholic priest. He informed her of a place for women who denounced their worldly ways and sought salvation through Jesus Christ. There she could relinquish all human communication and spend her hours in constant prayer to the Lord's Mother.

Mariana returned from Charlotte's deathbed terribly saddened at the loss of that brash woman she had come to love, but the priest's words comforted her, and she resolved to live the rest of her earthly life among another group of women. Not better women, she joked, but certainly ones with different habits!

When she left, Mariana vowed to pray for the souls of her island women as she had the entire time she had lived with them. She insisted Rachel and Terra keep her plaster statue of Mary in its shrine to protect them, and she made them promise that they would adorn Mary's altar with flowers, especially the little blue ones that were her favorites. She lovingly confessed that her life on the island had taught her that besides the Virgin Mary, there were other Marys to honor, and here she had lived among them all.

Mariana's leaving left Rachel and Terra to depend solely on each other. Although she had distanced herself from them as the years progressed, she was still a presence. She slept beside them, her breathing filling the bedchamber and mingling with theirs. They loved her despite her obsessive belief in her Mary. Instinctively they knew she only wished for a better world for all of them.

****

Rachel remained with Terra as her second mother until 1738 when all the world beyond the island was aglow with the fever of a great awakening. God-fearing Christians encouraged individuals to take complete responsibility for their own moral actions. Some of the more fanatical women from town marched over the ever-growing sand spit when the tide was low. They proceeded to sing Christian hymns and exhort their God to destroy the tavern, even though there had not been any activity there to scorn as in years past.

Fortunately, they weren't zealous enough to set fire to the building themselves, for Rachel and Terra would have perished.

Whenever they heard the women coming up the worn path, Rachel and Terra bolted the door and hid in the other storage cellar—not the one that contained Hezekiah's remains. There they waited until the sound of the women's voices faded before they climbed the ladder steps to the dining room. One time the women visited, Rachel and Terra decided not to hide, as Rachel was getting too old to scurry down the cellar ladder. Instead, they watched the women march up the path as they huddled behind a shutter. Rachel recognized some of them as her childhood friends. This made her sad for days, but eventually she declared that she would never have traded her island life for their self-righteous existence.

The last time the women stormed the island, one of them found Mariana's shrine. She shrieked that not only were the women who lived there harlots and heathens, but they were papist worshipping idolaters as well. With fury, she lifted the plaster statue of the Virgin and threw it against an adjacent rock. It smashed into unrecognizable shards, but the women seemed vanquished and left, never to return. When Terra and Rachel examined the destruction later that day, they agreed that Mariana's prayers must have had something to do with the women's retreat.

She had loved them that much and would have chosen a destroyed statue to any harm befalling her dear friends.

Rachel died that year from heart failure at the age of sixty-two. Terra mourned her greatly, for now she was alone. The tavern and its function as a whale station had been a necessity of the past, but no one had visited it for months once the townswomen stopped coming to protest its existence. Terra was reluctant to put Rachel's body in the ground, so she left her lying in their bed for two days until the smell of her rotting frame became intolerable. Since she couldn't be responsible for any indignity towards that good, sweet creature, Terra garnered the courage to lift Rachel's body and carry it to the center of the island so the two Rays, the Dark and the Light, could rest side by side.

The feathery lightness of Rachel's weight astounded Terra, who at eighteen, was far taller and more robust than Rachel had been at any age. Terra placed her on the ground and began to dig a hole in the sand, weeping so hard, she could barely see what she was doing. It didn't take her long to make a hole large enough for Rachel's body to fill. She gathered Rachel's favorite woven blanket and tenderly wrapped her body in it before she placed

Rachel in her resting place. Once the job was complete, she erected a marker of stones, much like the one on Dark Ray's burial mound. Then she sat down beside the two women she had loved the most and wept for her losses.

Eventually, an impulse emerged out of the tears, and she dried her eyes with her apron and smiled over at Rachel's gravesite. She stood up, brushed the sand from her clothes, and began to hum a melody. She danced.

Chapter 31

1740

Human Kindness

Autumn was fast approaching, and Terra had buried Rachel in early summer. The days were no longer filled with their companionship, the endless rustling of their skirts, the giggles in the dark, the evening music and songs. Terra's home had been abandoned by the original owners when they opted to pursue the offshore whaling industry, and the building would have fallen into disrepair quickly had the women not stayed on to live there. To keep herself busy, Terra tended the few sheep and chickens left on the island, brewed ale and her mother's prized flip recipe with what supplies remained, and cultivated that space that was now her garden—some of the plants initially started with her father's help before her birth.

As she worked, she talked aloud just so she could hear a human voice. She was happy to listen to the tides rolling in and out. She enjoyed the various birdcalls that permeated her silence—the rooster's crow and the sheep's bleats. But how she missed human company.

Had the local men realized how extraordinarily beautiful she had become, she would have had more company than she wanted. However, it would not be the kind of company she craved. In truth, she would not have welcomed it. Since her experience with Hezekiah Cobb ten years ago, she had not sought intimate relations. Even when those stray sailors visited from time to time over the last years she and Rachel managed the place, she steered clear of their ardent attention. The memory of Hezekiah's violent thrust into her body destroyed any desire she would ever have in coupling. But companionship? A friend? How she longed for that.

Over the summer, as she spun the season's wool to make new blankets and wraps for the coming winter, she considered taking the small island boat across the harbor to make new friends. Now that the sand bar connecting the island to the mainland had formed, she could walk over, but the boat trip would actually be quicker and less tiresome. Like her father, her creations possessed fine workmanship and design. Surely, she could trade her woolen shawls and her beaded moccasins, and perhaps make a friend in the transaction. She could even purchase sugar and other foodstuffs no longer delivered here since the whales left.

Rachel's father's money was gone. She ran so low on these basics, she would not be able much longer to prepare her food and drink. But always, when she thought she was ready to venture out, her legs refused to move her body forward. She remained riveted to the spot where she was standing and looking out at the harbor because she remembered all too well the feverish marching of the women who shouted admonition outside the tavern door. How would she ever hold a conversation with them? Solitude saturated her bones, caused her to choose it over society, wrapped her in the safety of complacence.

Terra stayed the entire summer alone on the island, the remaining member of a lively community of whalers, women, and traveling sailors that bustled for fifty years when the whaling industry thrived in the harbor and on these shores. Now the fishermen traveled many miles offshore to harpoon even larger whales in distant and dangerous waters. Now the women were dead and gone. Terra was what was left over from that earlier time, a stray blackfish separated from her pod.

Then on a crisp early autumn day, she awakened with new resolution. Maybe something in the morning light signaled the changing season and renewed her conviction to seek society. She threw off the bedcovers and dressed with determination. "I WILL row over to the mainland today," she proclaimed aloud to no one. She could not imagine surviving the winter alone. The unrelenting rain of the last four days had nearly driven her crazy. The only time she went outdoors was to collect eggs. She found herself dwelling on Hezekiah Cobb. She imagined she saw his form looming over her one early morning recently.

She stowed her boat in the same quiet cove that her mother had used ten years earlier. Gathering her bag of goods to trade, she scanned the land beyond the beach and the road that would bring her into the town. Fishermen were on the beach preparing their nets. They looked up when she walked by and stopped dead in their activity. Her beauty and grace startled them. Who was she? Her skin tone, sleek black hair, and clothing marked her as a *Nauset*. Could this be Dark Ray's young daughter? Was she a woman already? The word had gotten around that Dark Ray and the other women had died or left the island. Where had this one been living?

In her resolve to remain on course and not turn back to her boat and retreat, Terra did not even notice the effect she had on the men she passed. As she approached the main street of Billingsgate, she saw the town's women setting out their goods on sturdy wooden tables in the marketplace. They boisterously called to one another and seemed to exude the companionship of womanhood she so missed. She was encouraged to approach them, sure they would welcome her. It seemed all that talk of hellfire and damnation had left them. They were cheerful, joking with each other as they worked. Terra even saw some old *Nauset* women at their tables across the road from the Englishwomen's.

Perhaps she should go directly to the *Nauset* tables. No. She would be strong. She would not judge the English. She certainly knew plenty of them in her lifetime. Her beloved Rachel and Charlotte were English.

A beautiful young woman whose sensuous body curves were accentuated by her soft deerskin dress was not a common sight in the middle of town anymore. Now that Terra was in their midst, the Englishwomen ceased their gossiping and stared at her. She began to feel an icy chill even on this bright sunny morning. This girl was so incredibly striking and self-assured in her movements that the women got suspicious. And jealous. And then angry. Territorial.

"Who are you?" inquired the loudest of the group, a middle-aged woman whose own beauty was scarce even in her best years.

Terra disguised her growing discomfort and answered in a matter of fact tone. "My name is Terra. I have lived all my life over on Great Island. My mother ran the tavern until her death a few years' ago. Everyone else is gone as well. I thought to make friends across the harbor, so I have come to see if you would like to trade with me." She was as amazed as the women she addressed. How was she ever able to issue so many words at once? And so confidently?

Collecting her wits again, she began to bring out her goods to show them, as the women whispered among themselves. The apparent leader—who Terra now recognized as one of the religious zealots who marched on the island a few years back but who she did not recognize as Hezekiah Cobb's widow—provided the voice that spoke their whispers. "Trade, you say? What would a woman the likes of you have to trade besides her whoring ways? And THAT is not for sale on this side of the harbor. Just because that business was done on that evil snake pit of an island, do not think you are welcome to show up here and ply your wares. Am I right, good women?" This last she addressed to the other English women.

"Yes! Be gone, whore! Repent! The flames of hell are upon you!" They screamed.

Horrified and frightened by the same censuring cries that had caused her and Rachel to hide in the cellar, Terra feebly protested, "But I am not a whore. I am...."

Their shouts muffled her words, and she looked around for an escape route, ready to flee. From across the road, the elder *Nauset* women signaled for her to join them. She backed away from the angry women who were advancing towards her and ran over to the *Nausets*.

One elder in particular stepped forward and took Terra, wrapping her in her own shawl. They slowly walked away from the main road and onto a side path. By now, Terra was sobbing and regretting that she left her home in the first place.

"Do not waste your tears on these women, young one," the elder whispered in the old language. Although Dark Ray had taught her daughter the native tongue along with English, she wasn't accustomed to speaking it, and she appeared to have difficulty understanding every word. The old woman saw Terra's confusion and continued in English.

"I am Solosana. I grew up with your mother. The English know her as Dark Ray, yes?" She stopped walking and brushed the tears from Terra's cheeks. "Has she gone to *Kiehtan*? We chose different life paths, your mother and I, but we both have lived among the Europeans. We were tough and did not succumb to their diseases or their ways."

"Yes, I have heard of you. My mother spoke of you with affection. She told me you were there at the *powwaw* gathering when she met my father."

"That is correct. What a joy to see two people in their advancing age behave as passionately as young folk. You are a fortunate woman to have both of their spirits living within you. But tell me."

They came to a grassy spot, and the old woman sat down with a deep sigh and patted the earth next to her for Terra to sit. "What are your conditions? Are you truly alone? There are few of us full-blooded *Nausets* left and we are old, but we would welcome you into our part of the village if you chose to live among us."

Terra's eyes sparkled with tears. "You are so kind, and you have just met me. It is good to talk with you."

She shared stories of her life on the island—of the special relationships she had with each of the women. Solosana remarked that she was without doubt Dark Ray's daughter. Terra had lived and learned among the Europeans, and yet, she had not forsaken her *Nauset* way of storytelling.

Terra fell silent, wondering if she had the courage to utter the story that irrevocably changed her life and her mother's. She wanted to tell this dear woman, her mother's girlhood friend, but the knowledge of her rape and Hezekiah's murder were ghosts that haunted her memory. She believed she could resist their control if she did not say the words that would give them life. So she decided to keep that story to herself, and concluded with, "And so you see, the island is my home. I cannot imagine living here so close to these people who despise me for something I am not. And yet, I do not know how I will survive without company. I cannot bear the thought of the long winter ahead."

"Well, dear one. Is it simple company that you want? I may be able to help you, after all. Let us go to my home. The other women can work the trading table for a while. I have someone I would like you to meet."

Together they walked to the outskirts of town, and as they did, Terra saw scattered beyond the English style houses the cruder but just as efficient bark wigwams of the *Nausets*. Solosana directed Terra to the back of one of them, and there they found three puppies nestled comfortably around their mother in the tall grass. When they saw Solosana, the puppies scurried over to her on their stubby little legs and started crying and fussing.

"This is what I get for spoiling these three," she declared, 'but they are too attached to their mother. I must help her wean them. So I give them scraps of dried meat, and now they will not leave me alone." She reached down to pet them with her stiff arthritic hands.

Terra picked up the most talkative one, a round black male. She cradled him in her arms, and he produced sounds that resembled the cadence of talking. Then he let out a great sigh of contentment and gazed adoringly at Terra.

"These pups are ready to leave their mother. Would you like that one in your arms? He will be loyal and affectionate company for you. His mother is very gentle and smart. His father is a wolf, a sly one that the bounty hunters missed. I watched the father as he came around smelling my bitch, and I saw them coupling right here in my yard."

She paused to watch the growing affection between Terra and her chosen pup. "Because he is part wolf, he will be independent, but he will also adopt you as one of his kin. That 'talking' you heard is also from his wolf side. Wait until the next full moon. These pups have already begun to howl. I do not offer you human companionship other than my request that you visit me often, but this little one is the next best thing at your island home."

"Yes! I will take him. How can I thank you? Will you take this shawl in trade?" This exchange Terra spoke in the native tongue as proof of her deep respect for the elder. She put the puppy down at her feet and dug through her bag, withdrawing a multi-colored shawl.

"You made this fine piece? Such a tight weave. And the colors. I will gladly take it in trade, but you must promise me one more thing. You must not be afraid to visit from time to time. Come directly here along the path that I will show you, and you will avoid the English women. Bring your handiwork. The elder women will trade it at the market for you." Solosana reached over and hugged Terra. "Be strong like your mother. She would have been proud of you for coming here in the first place."

Terra left the remaining articles from her bag with Solosana and placed the puppy inside. Its head twisted every which way as he watched the scenery from Terra's back. He was already in love with her smell and the warmth of her body. She moved briskly, avoiding the main road, and soon reached her boat using the short cut.

The first thing Terra learned about her new companion was that he was terrified of water. She struggled to get him in the boat, and when she finally did, he hid under her skirt for the entire trip across the harbor. When they arrived on dry land, however, he pranced up the path to the house as if he had lived there his whole life.

Chapter 32

Reciprocity

1740

The tranquility of the year Terra lived with her Tamar and her visits with the last pure bloods of her mother's people sustained her spirits. What she continued to miss, however, were the tavern women. While she made up for their absence on the days and nights she spent with the *Nauset* elders, it was never the same as Charlotte's doting, Mariana's words of wisdom, Rachel's ready laugh and radiance, or her mother's strength and bottomless love. Terra was grateful, nonetheless, to the old women for taking her in as their daughter.

On one visit to town, Terra confessed that she had always wondered about Cessie, so Solosana told her of the one who was deposited on the island's shores long ago and placed in Dark Ray's care. How she had always been a sad, serious child. How she seemed on the brink of quiet madness at the age of six as she watched first her mother and then her grandmother succumb to the spotted fevers. She explained Cessie had been especially close to the older woman, and her death threatened to rob the young girl of all traces of sanity. To save her, her father returned her to the old island their people had once inhabited in earlier years of contentment and plenty. He believed Terra's mother would know how to raise her, just as he hoped the island would nourish her soul. Solosana and the other elder women were saddened, however, when they learned from Terra what the unnamed one did to herself on the day Terra was born.

On another visit, Solosana told her about Maria Hallett, the Englishwoman who had the misfortune of falling in love with Black Sam, the pirate whose vessel was wrecked in a nor'easter as he tried to visit her in 1717. Terra said she knew of this pirate and his band of sailors. Her mother once told her the story of how some of the survivors of the wreck visited the tavern and how Dark Ray was prepared to sedate them into submission if they became too ornery.

Solosana laughed and said Terra's mother knew how to handle unruly men. Then she returned to the story of Maria. It was Solosana who helped Maria deliver Black Sam's child, who helped Maria to go on when she lost the child, and it was she who'd taught Maria how to gather the herbs to make the medicine and assist Solosana in healing English clients. Solosana explained that Maria sounded very similar to Terra's Rachel—a loving, sincere Englishwoman. And yet, Maria was scorned and labeled a witch after she delivered a bastard child. Her last days were spent in exile living in a small dwelling in the dunes that overlooked the place where Black Sam's ship sank. Solosana alone visited her, and she alone buried Maria after she died of a broken heart.

Now Terra was in Solosana's care. It was a matter of reciprocity, the old woman explained. The fine balance between the giving and the taking. Terra asked about love. How did one know to give it? Or to take it? Solosana said love was not something that could be measured out at will. It came from deep within each person. If we opened ourselves to it, we would know instinctively when love was offered. We knew in the same way when to withhold it.

After that visit, Terra spent days contemplating the nature of love. Clearly, her mother and father had sensed a bond between them from first sight. It had sustained them in the years they were together. Yet, Charlotte had fought that urge to give herself over to Jack most of her life. Had something in her past caused Charlotte to remain so headstrong? And what had blinded Mariana into thinking Manuel's love was as strong as hers for him? Rachel too had been sincere in her devotion to Matthew Sweet. Yet, he had used and then abandoned her when she needed him most. Had the lack of love caused the hanged one's demise? It seemed to Terra the inability to know the difference between real love and its imposter was the problem. In her quest to find an answer, Terra only uncovered more questions, but she was sure of one fact: she was the product of a union laced with love throughout its existence.

Yet, Terra wondered, where did she herself fit into the scheme of love? Certainly she knew how to love women with her head and heart, but she had never felt any physical yearnings towards them. Nor had she ever felt any physical yearnings towards men. But then, Hezekiah destroyed any desire to pursue physical intimacy in her when she was a child. Could one live without this kind of love her whole life and still find contentment? A purpose for living?

On her next visit to Solosana, Terra shared these thoughts. She was bashful at first, but the older woman assured her that they could talk freely about anything. Never would Solosana judge Terra, nor ever betray her trust. It was then that Terra exposed the secret she promised herself she would not tell another soul. Upon hearing Terra's recollection of Cobb's assault, Solosana wrapped Terra tightly in her arms, and the two wept.

Afterwards, she said that *Kiehtan* had made Terra strong enough to bear this memory, and she had not missed out on love despite her unthinkable experience. Terra had given her love freely to the women she lived with, and they had loved her back with equal intensity. She was sharing love again with her dog

Tamar and the elder women. Not every woman grew up feeling the need to be a man's partner. Solosana had never sought male companionship, and here she was at the end of her life, and it had been satisfying. She assured Terra that the kind of love she gave out would always return to her.

****

Terra tried to live her life that way. She gave love. She took love freely. Her life had been good. Hardly had she ever been sick—her mother's care and the herbs of the one who died on the day she was born saw to that. Yet, since the morning, she had not been able to keep anything in her stomach. When she was not heaving its bilious contents, she was shitting a foul substance. Both made her so weak she could barely walk. The fog that shielded her was her only comfort. It lovingly isolated her, caressed her, hid the island from view, and cloaked her with obscurity. A seductive silence.

She was dying from carelessness. Although the noonday sun was passing over the island, the fog obscured its presence. In the haze of the day as she felt her strength dissipate with the light, she finally realized what made her so ill. It was the oysters she ate the night before. She had gathered them just as the sun was setting, and although she saw the carcasses rotting on the edge of the water from the unusual number of blackfish that beached themselves the week before, she paid them no mind and harvested the oysters nevertheless. It had been years since this harbor had seen so many of these small whales at once. She thought, here were all these blackfish trapped for the taking just like the old days, and the whalers were thousands of miles offshore hunting a bigger fish. What waste. What imbalance.

Death was at her doorstep, but she did not fear it any more than she had feared life. She learned early how to be strong—not turn away from anyone or anything. How to survive. She had a powerful mother whose student of life she was. She followed Dark Ray everywhere, her shadow, discovering things even when her mother thought she wasn't paying attention. She was always paying attention. And she learned. Learned the *Nauset* ways. Learned the English. Learned other European ways as well.

But that was long ago, and while her mind was still her best companion, except for Tamar, her trusting dog, her body weakened. It was about to expire and join the others who passed

on before her. Was she ready, she wondered? Was the fog, which

clothed her like a dense feathered blanket, preparing her for the

long sleep? *Maushop* was her protector, and in him she placed her

destiny.

As these thoughts raced through her mind, she looked over

at her dog and was saddened. She hated to leave Tamar behind—

his constant presence at her side, a blessing; his loving devotion,

her sustenance. Who would care for him? Maybe Solosana

would, but she was so old and feeble, she would not be able to

travel to the island. Terra spoke soothingly to the animal,

expressing every thought and concern aloud to avoid focusing on

her pain. "If you weren't so afraid of water, you might swim over

to Solosana. Yes! You can swim, my friend. You would be

amazed. Oh, your nose is cold as it nuzzles my neck. Easy. You

will knock me over with your enthusiastic affection. Are you

lonely already? Do you sense Death's presence? Come. Let us

lay here together. That is right. Here, on my bedstead. Better."

She placed her two hands just under his ears and cupped his

jaw. "Be sure to catch your share of mice and rats and thus keep yourself well fed because there will be no one here to love you, to sleep alongside, to see you safely to your own end. Maybe I will become your food as my decaying body resembles less the last human presence on this island and more the object of your hunger. I will understand, sweet dog, but do not eat me too fast, or you will not have physical company for very long. Spend your time fighting the crows and other predators away from my bones. Do me that favor. That task will keep you busy until those who maintain a curious vigil, watching for island lights and seeing none at last, come over when the tide is very low and find you. Alone with my remains." She eased back on her pillow.

Tamar kept licking her face. He was nervous. Such a smart animal. He was worried because he must smell death on her, she thought. She lay on her back stroking his head until another cramp sent her tearing at the fabric around her stomach. She had attempted to comfort herself by lying with her legs tucked up on her left side. It was no use. There was no relief. Her beautiful face was contorted by pain. She cried out for help, but of course, only Tamar heard her. He started talking to her as he circled the room. Just as suddenly as she once burst forth into life, the effort to live eluded her, and she became still. The force of energy that once defined her slowly ebbed out of her body, and as time passed, drool coated her lips, mucus caked her half-closed bloodshot eyes. Her unattended hair spilled over her face, hiding the almond-shaped eyes that no longer saw.

In his frenzy, Tamar ran down the stairs and out the door, but not before his bushy tail knocked into the lantern on the table next to Terra. As he raced down the beach, the bedstead ignited, and it wasn't long before the bedchamber was engulfed in flames. The dog didn't see this. He was desperate to get help, but he was pacing frantically along the beach, terrified to enter the water. Finally, he let out a whine and plunged in. His paws performed the uncanny motion of paddling and thereby carrying his body across the surface. He hated being immersed in the water, but his body reacted to it by doing what it knew: how to swim.

When he got to the other side, he shook out the excess moisture from his thick coat of fur and dashed along the short cut to Solosana's. She calmly awaited him. She already had known there was death coming from the island. She smelled the smoke from the flames that the lantern ignited, but because of the foggy dampness, she knew the fire would not totally destroy the tavern. It would smolder instead for days even after the fog lifted.

Solosana let out a wail to signal the mourning process to the others, and when Tamar finally reached her, she encircled his wet head in her arms, and she wept for the sweet woman who had brought joy to Solosana's last days. She thought about something they spoke about on one of Terra's last visits. Solosana enjoyed the stories of her youth more than any of the others they shared, and they had been reflecting about the past—of Terra's mother as a young girl. She was saying that she and Dark Ray were constant companions. They lived part of the time on the island and part of the time on the mainland, the rhythm of their lives dependent on the seasons as it had been for countless years before the Europeans arrived. Before the new rhythm of life changed forever the ways of Terra's ancestors.

"So, what is to become of us now, Solosana?"

"What do you mean, Child? You are very serious today."

"The world is changing. You and I and the other old ones are like the blackfish. There is no place for us anymore. Our usefulness is over. Soon enough, we will die, and no one will ever know we existed."

"Is that it? You want to be remembered? How could we ever be forgotten? Do you not know that we human beings are simply part of the great life story? We are not the center. When we die, our bodies will return to the earth from which we came. But our spirits? Our spirits live on. You still feel the presence of your mother and the other women you so loved in life, do you not? The same will be true of you. When it is your turn to join *Kiehtan*, your spirit will not leave this place but remain every bit a part of its fabric, its earthly design. Many years from now, people who walk where you walked will sense your presence, and it will do them good to remember they are just like you. Simply a part."

The young woman had nodded her head, seeming to agree with Solosana's words, but the old woman looked deeply into her eyes and saw that Terra wasn't so sure.

Epilogue

On a gray day that promised no glimpse of sun, Terra felt the beginning wave of her sickness, as the fog ceaselessly enveloped the island, leaving the houses and people across the harbor invisible. While the fog was in the harbor, they could forget about this place for a while, pretend it never existed.

But it did, and for fifty years, it thrived despite their refusal to admit even in their most solitary moments that a place like this tavern satisfied their basic needs and desires. Those who came here to work or to escape were reputable town leaders and not so reputable citizens alike. The island environment with its stark, punishing beauty dissolved these social distinctions. As the fishermen waited for the schools of pilot whales to enter the harbor, the island and this tavern provided what the local mainland would not. But this tavern was also Terra's beloved home, no matter what uses others made of it.

She was of this place—born here where no other babies survived long enough to be born. Her mother refused to reject her even though she was well into middle age when she discovered she was with child. She had a *Nauset* name that no one but Dark Ray and she knew. To everyone else, she was Terra. She was of the land she lived upon, and she had protected it. And after? Well, after, she left the safeguarding of this place to the spirits who inhabited it, to the birds, the wind, the harsh sun, *Maushop's* smoke.

In the tavern's prime, the women worked here to satisfy the needs of the men, but to think they only served the men would be false. The women worked for themselves and were responsible for most of the decision-making of the establishment—for its very life. This was a place where men toiled to provide the community with whale oil and other byproducts of that noble but doomed creature.

This place was built for them, and not surprisingly, the men who spent time here believed they controlled its environs.

But the sea that created this island—the sea where they made their livelihoods—they called by endearing feminine names. This very island, where they drank, ate, smoked, played, danced, sang, consorted, waiting for the whales to return, was largely composed of the female. The feminine surrounded them, those outwardly, masculine men, and they never imagined the real source of their strength—their inspiration—their reason for being.

Terra had embraced the stories of the women who lived and worked here. The events that happened before her time were repeated to her over and over throughout her life. All but one woman she knew, and she loved them almost as dearly as she loved her mother. They were all her mothers. She heard their voices whispering to her the day she approached death. They called to her. She heard them as the fog encircled the places where they used to be, not allowing their spirits to disperse, but to remain intact and eternally present. Rachel's merry humming. Mariana's solemn prayers. Charlotte's brazen laughter. Her mother's wise counsel. She remembered their stories as she prepared to join them. She felt their presence in the bedroom as she lay dying. She saw the shadowy outline of their forms hovering over her. Their arms opened wide to accept her. The women of Great Island.

Postscript: A gravestone, placed at the entrance to the Great Island Trail, is adorned with shells, rocks, driftwood, and human artifacts. On the stone, the following is engraved:

" HERE LIES

AN

INDIAN WOMAN

A

WAMPANOAG

WHOSE FAMILY AND TRIBE

GAVE OF THEMSELVES

AND THEIR LAND

THAT THIS GREAT NATION

MIGHT BE BORN AND GROW"

REINTERRED HERE MAY 30, 1976

WAMPANOAG TRIBAL COUNCIL

WELLFLEET HISTORICAL SOCIETY

Afterword

On the western side of Wellfleet Harbor in Cape Cod Bay, lies Great Island, now a peninsula which decades of deposited sand have connected to the Cape Cod mainland. Approximately 50-60 feet above sea level at its highest point, the six hundred acre island was once the site of a colonial English tavern that flourished between 1690-1740, according to an archaelogical dig sponsored by the National Park Service and Plimoth Plantation in 1970. The 50 feet by 30 feet saltbox construction seems to have functioned primarily as a refuge for early colonial whalers who had learned from the local Indians the on-shore whaling technique of herding the blackfish (or pilot whale) in small boats to shore and then killing them. Information regarding this early whaling enterprise is readily obtainable from a variety of historical sources: texts by James Deetz, Erik Ekholm, Nathaniel Philbrick, Paul Schneider, Kathleen J. Bragdon, Henry C. Kittredge, and Enoch Pratt among others. The demise of this whaling practice and the tavern itself coincides with the diminishing numbers of blackfish in that area and the growing popularity of off-shore whaling by the middle of the 18th century.

Local legend suggests that the tavern was once THE place for whalers to eat, drink, and be merry while waiting for the schools of blackfish to appear. Some have argued that the building was simply a residence and not a tavern at all. Yet given the vast amounts of drinking utensils and chamber pots said to have been located at the site, I would agree with the archaelogists and the local storytellers who identified the structure as a tavern. Sometimes I think we like to sugarcoat history to suit our idyllic fantasies of the good old wholesome days of our ancestors. Personally, I don't suspect the good old days were ever "wholesome." One wonders how "good" they were as well.

The archaelogical site itself is unimpressive—what remains of the dig is a recessed hole, some scattered rocks, and a sign that the National Park Service erected, identifying the Great Island Tavern Site and asking visitors not to disturb the area. On the direct path to the site are waysides with photographs of the excavation, retrieved artifacts, and speculative renderings of the tavern and lookout towers. The land itself is stark and beautiful. At the time of inhabitance, it was little more than a huge sand dune; most of the land like the rest of the Cape had been deforested for building and heating needs. The scrub pines and oaks that cover the site now are the result of an 1830's effort to stop erosion. But the place itself is magical with wonderful water views all around. The visiting public is indebted to the Henderson family for donating the land to the National Seashore in the 1960's.

I first became acquainted with Great Island during a spring break from teaching at Roger Williams University in Bristol, RI. My husband and I, frequent visitors to the Cape, were spending a few March days in Wellfleet; on one of them, we hiked the Great Island trail, a good, hearty walk on such a cold day. An informational wayside at the entrance to the trail completely piqued our curiosity. Along with photographs of found pottery shards and a pipe, a map of the island, and a legendary sign of the assumed owner, the text of the wayside reported that at this tavern, whalers "could recount their adventures, fortify themselves with toddy, and consort with sympathetic ladies, while whalewatchers kept vigil nearby." Hmm. Sympathetic ladies. Who were they?

How did they live their lives? What roles did they play at this tavern across the harbor? Researchers claim to have found pieces of carved ivory fans on the site. Historically, fans have been associated with ladies of the night—prostitutes. As we hiked that day, I thought about the women, especially women like these, whose stories so rarely get told, whose voices were not necessarily heard even when they lived. I thought about life on this island, about the turbulent time period in which they existed—the impact of different cultures co-existing despite the vastly different worldviews of those societies—and where women fit in the scheme of the day to day.

Thoughts of the women have resonated with me throughout that hike and on all subsequent visits to that area of the Cape. Theirs is but a shadowy account of lives deeply shrouded by their circumstances and places in society. I decided to write a fictional account of the times from their perspective simply because I could hear their voices so clearly, even though what little we can know about them now is what we can hear of their voices in the fog. I wanted others to hear them as well.

Please note: Wellfleet was known as Billingsgate until 1763;

therefore, I used the earlier town name in this story. Other place

names that might confuse the reader: *Noepe* is the *Wampanoag*

name for Martha's Vineyard; *Aquinnah* may be known to some as

the Gay Head region of the Vineyard. All Cape and Island Indians

were identified in general as *Wampanoag* as a result, some believe,

of King Philip's (*Metacomet*) confederation of Indians. However,

there were many small bands of native people in the region of

southeastern Massachusetts, and the *Nausets* in particular dwelled

in the Eastham/Billingsgate area of the Cape. All historical

misinterpretations and flights of imagination about this time and

place are mine.

Acknowledgments

Thank you to my family and friends who read the first draft of this novel to the last. A special thanks to Glenna Andrade for guiding me through the final draft. To my husband, Bob, and my daughter, Breana, my gratitude for reading many more drafts than you might have liked. I am humbled by your patience with me throughout the many years of this project. Liz Peirce: if you hadn't urged me, this manuscript would still be collecting dust on a forgotten shelf.

07. 20 - 14
3 5999 00095 3515

Made in the USA
Charleston, SC
19 June 2014